A Gentleman's Gentleman

"*A Gentleman's Gentleman* is an endearing and tender romance that delivers the unique joy of finding that person who can love you for exactly who you are. This book was a delight and TJ Alexander a welcome and exciting voice in historical fiction."

—Adriana Herrera, *USA Today* bestselling author of *An Island Princess Starts a Scandal*

"A delicious romp through Regency England and exactly the romance we need right now. TJ Alexander builds the heat between their unforgettable heroes with an achingly slow sweetness while giving tropey historical hijinks the most sumptuous queer flair."

—Joanna Lowell, author of *A Shore Thing*

"*A Gentleman's Gentleman* is exactly the sort of historical romance I love, featuring two deeply lovable characters, a seemingly insurmountable obstacle, wonderful period detail, and a happy ending that feels so perfectly, wonderfully right. This is a beautiful—and wonderfully queer—romance that reminds us of all the many sorts of love stories this genre can encompass, and reading it felt like a gift."

—Martha Waters, author of *To Love and to Loathe*

"TJ Alexander's first foray into historical romance blew me away. *A Gentleman's Gentleman* is Alexander at their best: witty, romantic, gorgeously queer, and frequently poignant."

—Rachel Runya Katz, author of *Whenever You're Ready*

"Witty, exhilarating, and achingly tender, *A Gentleman's Gentleman* lavishes its trans hero with the elegant waistcoats he desires and the love and acceptance he's resigned himself to living without. His reserved valet stole my heart. I adored this!"

—Felicia Davin, author of *The Scandalous Letters of V and J*

TJ Alexander

A Gentleman's Gentleman

TJ ALEXANDER is the author of *Chef's Kiss*, *Chef's Choice*, *Second Chances in New Port Stephen*, and *Triple Sec.* They received their MA in writing and publishing from Emerson College, and they live in New York City with their wife and various houseplants.

ALSO BY TJ ALEXANDER

Chef's Kiss

Chef's Choice

Second Chances in New Port Stephen

Triple Sec

A Gentleman's Gentleman

A Gentleman's Gentleman

TJ Alexander

Vintage Books
A Division of Penguin Random House LLC
New York

A VINTAGE BOOKS ORIGINAL 2025

Published by Vintage Books, a division of Penguin Random House LLC, 1745 Broadway, New York, NY 10019.

Vintage Books and colophon are registered trademarks of Penguin Random House LLC.

Library of Congress Cataloging-in-Publication Data
Names: Alexander, T. J., author.
Title: A gentleman's gentleman / by TJ Alexander.
Description: New York : Vintage Books, a division of Penguin Random House LLC, 2025.
Identifiers: LCCN 2023057500 (print) | LCCN 2023057501 (ebook)
Subjects: LCGFT: Queer fiction. | Romance fiction. | Novels.
Classification: LCC PS3601.L3559 E34 2025 (print) | LCC PS3601.L3559 (ebook) | DDC 813/.6—dc23/eng/20231218
LC record available at https://lccn.loc.gov/2023057500
LC ebook record available at https://lccn.loc.gov/2023057501

Vintage Books Trade Paperback ISBN: 978-0-593-68620-1
eBook ISBN: 978-0-593-68621-8

Book design by Steven Walker

penguinrandomhouse.com | vintagebooks.com

Printed in the United States of America
10 9 8 7 6 5 4 3 2 1

The authorized representative in the EU for product safety and compliance is Penguin Random House Ireland, Morrison Chambers, 32 Nassau Street, Dublin DO2 YH68, Ireland. http://eu-contact.penguin.ie.

For my forebears

A Gentleman's Gentleman

Chapter 1

May 11, 1819

For His Lordship Christopher William Fitzwilliams Winterthrope, the Right Honorable Earl of Eden, waking in sweat-soaked terror was a regular occurrence. Therefore he was hardly bothered when it happened on this particular morning—that is, until he remembered the date. He blinked at the luxurious lacework canopy that draped over his bed and groaned. It was a Tuesday, which in itself was not so awful, but it was the Tuesday he had been dreading.

He ignored his racing heart and slipped out of bed, shoving his feet into slippers to save them from the chilly floor. A pitcher of cool water awaited him at the washbasin, and he employed it liberally. As he dabbed himself dry, he glanced at his bedside table, where a letter addressed to His Lordship sat mockingly. Just the sight of it was enough to set his teeth on edge. He didn't wish to dwell on disagreeable thoughts, so he focused on how he would dress for the day instead.

Unlike most gentlemen of his age and status, Christopher always dressed himself before taking breakfast. It was one of the young master's many quirks, this tendency to do things for himself instead of employing a valet or footmen or chambermaids or a dozen other unnecessary servants. There were a handful of day workers who could be called from the village to assist the skeleton staff, but Christopher didn't concern himself with the details, so long as his home was kept as empty as possible.

He opened the door to his dressing room, which had always served to calm his nerves in the face of tumult and strife. There was nothing like it. He inhaled the scent of clean linen and wool and smiled.

"What shall we do today, lads?" he murmured to the assembled wardrobe. As the day was to be a wearisome one, he felt only his best armor would do.

He ran a hand over the rack where the riding breeches hung in a neat line. Supple fabrics and straight stitching met his palm, the feel of well-made pieces pleasing him greatly. There were leathers, too, both in soft buckskin and sturdier specimens for more vigorous journeys on horseback. Tall riding boots lined the perimeter of the floor in shades of tan. Stacks upon stacks of crisp white muslin shirts waited patiently in their dresser drawers.

The eggshell breeches, he decided, with the coat of fawn. A waistcoat of exquisite pale silk, embroidered in gold vines. A pristine shirt paired with his everyday cravat: they were all placed meticulously on the small upholstered bench that stood in the center of the dressing room, lined up like soldiers ready for battle. Christopher surveyed his troops with a keen eye and found no loose threads or stray scuff marks. As it should be, he thought before donning the ensemble. He took great pleasure in maintaining his clothing and always sent anything less than perfectly presentable to the village seamstress for mending, as he was quite useless with a needle.

Of course, a valet should have been the one wielding that needle and overseeing the mending, as Cook so often reminded him. And yet.

Without a valet present to temper Christopher's strange habits, he had taken to wearing almost exclusively light colors throughout the year, which matched his head of white-blond curls. Even in the darkest months of winter, he donned only pale buckskin breeches, cloud-colored coats, and boots reminiscent of milky tea. His middle would sometimes sport a waistcoat of dove grey or a fine tan, or, if he was feeling very saucy indeed, a hint of pastel blue, but never anything darker. During one rare occasion when Christopher had accepted an invitation to dine at a neighboring estate, a fellow guest had wondered aloud what Lord Eden might wear to a funeral, if indeed His Lordship owned something suitable for such a thing at all. Christopher had replied that he avoided the issue entirely by making it a point never to attend funerals.

The other dinner guests had laughed at this display of ready wit. Christopher, meanwhile, had proceeded to drink far too much wine and kept silent for the rest of the interminable evening. The next morning, he'd found himself afflicted with the worst headache he'd ever endured, not to mention the memory of the especially awful terrors that had plagued his sleep.

He hadn't been foolish enough to accept another dinner invitation since.

Christopher gave his cravat one final twist and tuck, then

raised his chin to look at himself in the mirror. *Gentlemanly perfection,* he thought with a pleased nod. He was on the shorter side and fairly stout, but that was fine. His face was perhaps a bit more delicate than he would prefer, but if the men's fashion periodicals out of London were to be believed (and those were the only sort of periodicals Christopher read), it was rather desirable for a dandy to have rosebud lips and a button nose. He turned his head as he considered the mirror's reflection. His side whiskers, of course, would never be as long and lush as some of his peers', but with his fair coloring, this could be chalked up to the curse that plagued many blond men in their quest for facial hair.

All things being equal—though they were most certainly not—Christopher made a fine picture of a young Lord Eden.

As he left the dressing room, he pocketed the letter on the bedside table in case he needed to refer to it later, then unlocked his bedroom door and went clattering down the stairs.

Each footfall echoed terribly, as did every sound in Eden Abbey. The old manor house might have been the jewel of the surrounding countryside once upon a time, but those times had long since ended. Christopher passed many a shut door on his way through the hall. If he bothered to open them, he would have been greeted with the sight of white sheets draped over disused furniture like frozen ghosts. The majority of the Abbey's twenty-six bedrooms were closed up and left to gather dust. The ballroom, which had seen no dancing since the time of Christopher's grandfather, was filled only with silence. The rooms meant for dining and music were wholly unnecessary, and Plinkton, the ancient butler, had long since given up on keeping them in good repair on the outside chance that they would receive guests.

No guests ever came to Eden. Not any longer. Not since Christopher had become earl—the mechanics of which he did not like to contemplate.

Two portraits loomed large in the main hall, and Christopher gave these not a glance as he passed them by. The figures in those paintings depicted only what was dead and gone.

Yet there were signs of life still—the scent of breakfast was already permeating the halls, making Christopher's stomach growl in anticipation. Normally an earl, even a lone earl with no wife or family, would break his fast in the morning room. A handful of footmen would line the walls, ready to pour more tea or deploy another slice of toast to His Lordship's plate. Letters and such would be delivered on a silver salver as he ate. But Christopher did not conduct himself as other earls did, and it was his normal practice to take his breakfast belowstairs in the kitchens, in the company of his bare-bones staff.

"Good morning, Cook," he called out in greeting as he pushed through the door that separated the servants' domain from the rest of the house. His booted feet tramped down the steps in iambic pentameter. "How is my best girl today?"

"She's right tired of seeing your face," Cook said. She came into view as Christopher reached the bottom of the steps and turned into the kitchens. "When do you leave, again?"

"You won't be rid of me until next week, sadly," Christopher replied with a winning smile, in response to which she snorted.

Cook was a tall, broad, imposing woman of indeterminate age. She had been employed in Eden Abbey's kitchens since before Christopher was born, and even in his earliest memories of her, she looked exactly the same as she did that morning. Her hair was a fiery red shot through with burnished silver, and her eyes were couched in a fierce squint. Her eyesight was famously poor, making it necessary for her to taste all her dishes instead of judging them by sight, so she was always dipping a spoon into this or tearing off a bite of that. She had a given name, Christopher was certain of it, but he had never been told what it was and he felt that now it was too late to politely ask. Cook she was, and Cook she would forever be.

She placed a steaming cup of tea and a tray of fresh-baked buns on the long counter just in front of a wooden stool, Christopher's customary spot. He slid onto the seat and obediently sipped at the brew, which was just as he liked it: black with far too much sugar.

"Today's the day, isn't it?" she asked. "For the new valet to arrive?"

Christopher did not quite suppress his sigh. He couldn't ignore the fact any longer, it seemed. "Yes," he said. "Today your ranks swell with the addition of exactly one manservant." Another sip of tea. "Or they *might,* I should say; I told the solicitors I would send him right back if I didn't like the look of him."

"That's a neat piece of work." She glanced up whilst chopping carrots into smaller and smaller bits, no doubt in preparation for the evening meal. Christopher worried for her fingers, but Cook was naturally gifted at knife work and never seemed to slip. "If this chap works out, you can take him with you to London, eh?"

Christopher snagged a bun, still warm and steaming, from its tray. "Yes. London," he agreed miserably. To comfort himself, he licked the dusting of sugar off the top of his bun, the way he always had since he was a tiny child, before taking a bite. The flavors of currants and rosewater filled his mouth as he chewed. Cook had a deft hand with cakes and breads of all sorts, but these little morning buns, as she called them, were Christopher's favorite. He wondered if she had baked them specifically to be a balm to him on this harrowing day.

A country mouse through and through, Christopher was loath to leave Eden under any circumstances, but his impending sojourn would be especially horrid, for London would be in the throes of the Season when he arrived. Balls. Fêtes. Picnics. Outings. He shivered as he took another mouthful of bun. He detested social occasions. They so often required him to be sociable.

And yet, so much depended upon his success there. The letter from the solicitors weighed heavily in his pocket.

"It's a good thing you took my advice," Cook said as she dumped her carrots into a pot. "Getting yourself a valet to attend to you this summer, I mean."

Christopher grimaced, recalling the conversation they'd had in this very kitchen not one month ago.

You'll need to bring a man with you, Cook had said.

Why should I need a man? Christopher had replied in alarm.

Cook had merely rolled her eyes and continued kneading her bread dough. *To look after you, m'lord. London society's got expectations, don't they? You might get away with doing as you please out here in Eden, but in London they'll tear you apart for stepping out of line, pardon my saying so. All the lords and ladies have personal servants, and so should you. It's not as if old Plinkton is up to the task, is he?*

Cook had been right, damn it all. Poor Plinkton would wilt

in London. The aged butler wasn't as spry as he used to be, and there were so many carriages to dodge on city streets these days. Even going up the grand staircase at the Abbey was a chore for him, what with his bad knees. No, best to keep the loyal retainer at home where it was safe. After serving the last three Lord Edens, it was only fair for the man to be given a bit of a respite.

Yet as Cook had pointed out, a man of Christopher's station would be expected to live in a certain amount of comfort. He could hire a temporary staff of maids and footmen to keep the townhouse in order during his visit—a common enough arrangement—but a valet was another matter. If he did not appear in London with the requisite valet already at his side, there would surely be rumors that his eccentricity had given way to madness, or worse, tight-fisted frugality. For a man like Christopher, rumors were to be quelled at any cost, even at the price of his independence.

In the end, Christopher had swallowed his pride and written to his solicitors: *I am in want of a valet, and if you would be so kind as to find a suitable one, I would be most obliged.* He instructed that the man, when found, should be sent to Eden Abbey ahead of his London sojourn. *I understand this does not give you gentlemen much time to produce a candidate,* he scribbled in apology, *but I have no doubt you will find a decent enough man for me. My only stipulation is that my valet be on the younger side. I would prefer youthful vigor to experience in this case, as I have a notion that an older man might be quite set in his ways and unable to conform to my particular mode of living.*

He had also included in the letter a query as to how they were progressing on the matter of his late father's will, then sent it off to Cloy & Bellow, Mayfair, London. Their reply was currently sitting in his coat pocket.

We will begin making inquiries immediately, my lord, they had written, *and if it is convenient to you, we will send you a new man in a fortnight's time. Should you find him unsuitable, another can be procured.* No mention of who this man might be, which was fair, considering the solicitors had only just started the search when the letter was sent. Still, it filled Christopher with no little anxiety to know a stranger was to be expected shortly.

His brooding thoughts were interrupted as Plinkton shuffled into the kitchen with a mumbled, "Good morning, my lord."

Christopher greeted him heartily and pulled out the stool next to his own for the man. It was the least he could do, considering all Plinkton did for him. While other butlers might have left when it became clear that the new master was allowing the estate to become a shadow of its former self, Plinkton had stayed. Oh, he'd complained about Christopher's complete lack of division between himself and the help, but time had tempered his grumbles about propriety. It had taken quite a while for Plinkton to agree to sit down alongside the young master and breakfast together, but after years of Christopher wearing him down—and Cook withholding tea—the old curmudgeon had finally given in.

Now he sat next to Christopher and accepted his cup from Cook with only the lightest of sniffs. These abated as Cook offered him the tray of morning buns, which he sampled liberally. Cook kept busy with her work, having already eaten, and for a few moments, they all existed in companionable silence.

Then Plinkton's warbling voice ventured forth. "One week until you leave for London, is it not, my lord?"

Christopher groaned into his teacup. "You needn't keep reminding me, you know. I swear, it's as if you two can't wait to be rid of me."

"Certainly not, my lord," Plinkton said at the same time Cook cried, "Of course we can't wait!"

At Plinkton and Christopher's twin glares, Cook straightened from where she had been bent over her cooking fire, stoker in hand. "What? It will do you some good to leave the Abbey, see some real society instead of our wrinkly faces day in, day out."

"I am not going to London for pleasure," Christopher reminded her. "I am only going because I must." The letter from Cloy & Bellow burned in his pocket like a hot stone. He had not seen fit to share the entire contents of the letter with his two loyal staff; what good would it do to worry them needlessly?

"Yes, yes. Business with the solicitors. Don't see why they can't come here to you instead, but what do I know?" Cook shook her head and returned her attention to stirring the pot. "Bless my soul, m'lord, you really must find a way to enjoy the city. A man like yourself, in the prime of your life–you should be dancing and promenading and such, not spending every evening at home with a book."

Plinkton came to his defense, as he so often did. "Young Lord Eden's time is his own," he said. "It's his right to spend his evenings however he wishes."

Cook snorted and joined them at the counter. "Maybe the new valet will take my view and get him out and about. He should, if he's any good at the job." She pinned Christopher with a look. "What are you going to do if this man isn't up to scratch, m'lord? Waltz into London society with your cravat done up all wrong?"

Christopher tore off a chunk of the bun and ate it with more aggression than was strictly necessary. "I have never worn a cravat wrongly in my life," he said.

"Still." She poured herself a cup of tea and drank it while standing. "Every young gentleman of your station has a valet these days to show 'em what's what. I wager a good one will be fixing things for you that you didn't even know needed to be fixed."

"How is it that you're privy to what all the young men of my station are doing these days?" Christopher shot back with an amused raise of his brow. "Do you have some strapping young suitors hidden somewhere, Cook? Do they regale you with tales of their staffing situations?"

Plinkton gave an affronted wheeze that sounded much like an asthmatic sheep, but Cook just laughed. She had always been the more tolerant of Christopher's teasing.

"Never mind my suitors. You just concentrate on your business in London," she said. "And for god's sake, try to get along with this new man. You may even find you enjoy having a valet do for you, heaven forbid."

Chapter 2

Christopher took himself through to the study, one of the few rooms that saw any use. It contained his desk, where he was supposed to work, and his favorite armchair, where he read books when he was meant to be at work at the desk. The room had been his father's study before it was his, and the dark satin wallpaper and military oil paintings that made up the decor still reflected the last Lord Eden's tastes. Christopher didn't have the heart to change anything. He pushed open the French doors that led to the rose garden. The scent of blooms filled the air; birds chirped; damselflies buzzed. Far ahead in the distance, he could just make out the white lumps of sheep grazing on the hillside. He stood there for a long moment, surveying the rolling hills of his property with a sinking feeling in his stomach.

Eden Abbey was supposed to have been a Roman outpost, as evidenced by some ancient barracks that had been dug up twenty years prior when a farmer had tilled a mite too deep in a cabbage field. The manor house was a mile and a bit from the town of Market Eden, a small but beautiful collection of cottages and shops nestled in the green hills, and an hour's ride to the south, one would find the place where England meets the sea. On clear days, Christopher imagined he could smell salt on the air—a contributing factor, no doubt, to the derelict state of Eden Abbey. It had already begun tumbling when Christopher was born, and he had never known it to be fully upright. The turret in the western wing was nothing more than rubble, and the same fate was sure to meet the northern spire any day now.

Despite the decay, Eden Abbey still boasted a handful of delights within its sprawling grounds. The gardens that lined the rear of the Abbey were slightly overgrown, to be sure, but beautiful nonetheless. Though a man came by once every month to whack away at the worst of the primroses, it would take an army of gardeners to whip it back into shape—but the wild collection of walking paths still had its charms in Christopher's opinion. The wooded glens surrounding the grand lawn approached a fairytale in their perfection, all mossy hollows and charming brooks and a healthy population of deer—booming, now that no hunts were being held per Christopher's preference.

Three hundred and fifty-four years: that was how long his family had lived at the optimistically named Eden Abbey. Privately, he wondered if, in less than four months, he would no longer be permitted to stand at this door and gaze upon this grand view.

No, he reminded himself. He had a plan. It was a good plan,

a secret plan, and all he had to do was follow it to the letter to ensure his inheritance.

First, there was the matter of some little property to be handled, which was, as far as Cook and Plinkton were aware, the entire point of his journey to London. He was to sell the townhouse that he kept in the city center, along with most of its furnishings. In generations past, the Winterthrope family had been fashionable enough to necessitate owning such a house, but now there seemed little need for such extravagance. Christopher planned to use the proceeds to keep the Abbey from collapsing for a few more years. All this, he had already carefully outlined to Cook and Plinkton.

What Cook and Plinkton did not know, however, was the second, real reason urging Christopher to London.

His hand drifted to his coat pocket, where the solicitors' letter sat. Several lines haunted Christopher in particular.

> *We regret to inform His Lordship that we can find no legal loophole in the last will and testament of the previous Lord Eden. Your father (and his father, and his father's father, etc.) was unshakable in his belief that his heir should benefit from a solid helpmate as he himself did, and his will reflects this. It is uncompromising in its assertion that Your Lordship is required to marry before your twenty-fifth birthday in order to retain your inheritance, including the estate and the title of earl. As that date approaches this very September, we urge you to act with all due haste. Otherwise–as it is unlikely a distant relation will be discovered, given that we have already expended every effort–the Crown will assume ownership of the estate and the title will be dissolved.*

That settled it. This trip to London would serve a dual purpose: Christopher would sell a house he did not need and procure a wife he did not want.

He ruminated on this as he made his way to the stables, where he met a gleaming black stallion with a white blaze stamping in his stall. He led the beast out and set himself to readying the necessary tack.

"How is Orion this morning?" came Plinkton's voice after a few minutes of quiet saddle polishing. The old butler shuffled in and took up his usual position at Christopher's side, ready to hand him any brushes or rags he might need. It was a tradition of theirs, these mornings in the stable. Though Plinkton was not himself a horseman, he insisted on being present to assist the young master, as Eden lacked a stable boy. Not that he did much to assist; his contribution was mainly conversation, but Christopher didn't mind. Plinkton seemed to understand that Christopher had taken to riding to clear his head, and it was terribly sweet of the old man to ensure he stuck to it.

"In a fine temper," Christopher answered as the horse attempted to nip Plinkton's backside.

Plinkton stumbled out of reach just in time. "He's improving, then," he said, dry as sand.

Christopher patted the horse's strong neck, letting him huff and sniff at his waist. There was no reason for him to be concerned about his own well-being, as the beast no longer bit Christopher. They had an understanding; Christopher loved him more than anything. "Looking for apples in my pockets? For shame, Orion. You cannot be given treats after menacing poor Plinkton here."

Plinkton, it seemed, was not content to speak only of horses.

His eyes, not as sharp these days but plenty skillful, pierced Christopher with a look. "My lord, when this new man arrives today . . ."

Christopher slipped the bit neatly into Orion's mouth, feigning a need to concentrate on that and not Plinkton's words. "Hand me that polishing cloth, would you? There's a smudge on his browband."

Plinkton passed him the cloth but was not deterred from his little speech. "If you find him unsatisfactory, I can always come to London with you instead."

"We've discussed this, dear fellow. Your presence is sorely needed here at home while the young master is away." It was a lie and Plinkton knew it, but it didn't stop Christopher from repeating it. The truth, that Plinkton was much too frail for such a journey, would break the poor man's heart. And that, Christopher could not abide. Plinkton had been at his side when he'd come into his title; he'd seen Christopher successfully through university; he'd indulged in all his quirks and strange habits. He deserved all the consideration he had shown Christopher in his years of service, and so much more besides.

"Still, keep the option in mind, my lord." Plinkton braved Orion's reach to step closer and place a supportive hand on Christopher's arm. "I know this is quite the change for you, bringing a new man in."

Christopher dredged up a smile from somewhere in his depths. "I'm sure I'll survive, Plinkton. But thank you, as always, for being such a stalwart."

He made quick work of ensuring that the tack had been properly fastened before swinging himself into the saddle. "If the new man arrives while I'm out, see to him for me, will you?"

"Of course, my lord."

"Farewell, then!" he called as he rode out of the stable, allowing Orion to move at a brisk trot toward the riding path that led through the pastures and along the country lane.

Christopher inhaled deeply, filling his lungs with the scent of grass and horseflesh. The weather was fair and not too chill, but even if it had been miserable and pouring buckets, Christopher would not have missed his daily ride.

"What do you think, old boy?" he asked Orion, patting the side of his neck. "Fancy a gallop?"

Orion whinnied at the suggestion. It was likely that he'd learned the word "gallop" along with his own name. The horse was made for running full tilt, and Christopher indulged him at every opportunity.

"Come on, then." Christopher had only to touch his heels to Orion's flanks before the beast was off like a shot, eating up ground and streaking across the fields that surrounded Eden Abbey.

Christopher closed his eyes and felt the wind on his face. Beneath him, Orion was perfection, the powerful muscles and heaving sides a sensation unlike any other. This was bliss; whatever else he had to do, whatever discomforts he must endure in London, there would always be this to come home to. He wondered if perhaps it would be possible to find a wife who shared his love of riding. It would make the horrid chore of marriage a bit easier, he thought, if he could enjoy his morning rides with someone.

He opened his eyes in time to catch a strange sight. Normally, he would ride for hours in the morning without meeting a single soul; the people from the village had their work to see to, so there wasn't much chance of running into someone. Yet as Orion raced toward the spot where the riding path met the main road, Christopher spied the shape of a man dressed in black.

From a distance, he could have been some shade from a ghastly story, a funeral's lost mourner. He was standing there with a valise in hand and a sharp look in his eye, watching horse and rider with a thoughtful expression that spoke of more than a passing interest.

Christopher gave the reins a tug and slowed Orion to a walk as they approached the stranger. He could only be the new valet Christopher had been waiting for.

"You there!" he called, even though it seemed he already had the man's undivided attention. Then he got close enough to see the man's face clearly, and all rational thought left Christopher's head.

His new valet was quite handsome.

To an incredibly annoying degree.

The interloper wore an impeccable raven-black cutaway coat, tailored to his form with the aim, it seemed, of making him appear even more trim than he already was. The rest of his clothing followed suit, consisting of dark, somber colors and highly polished boots–an aesthetic befitting his station, Christopher supposed, but the palette also served to compliment his features. He possessed an ordinary hat, which he had removed in greeting, revealing sleek ebony hair worn in an unassuming close crop, not curled so much as slightly windblown. There was an unfairly attractive glint of intelligence to his eyes, which Christopher noticed were a deep, dark brown. He was not overly tall, but given Christopher's own diminutive stature, the man would tower over him by a few inches on even footing. He was possessed of a sizable nose, perhaps just a little crooked, that offset his otherwise delicate cheekbones (high) and mouth (small). There was a reserved air about him as he allowed Christopher's curious gaze, as if there were an invisible pane of glass between them that he did not wish to smudge.

He radiated the respectability and standoffishness that was so sought-after in the serving classes, and he seemed to effortlessly embody the kind of genteel masculinity that Christopher fought so desperately to achieve.

In short, the very sight of the new man was enough to put Christopher in a foul mood. What right did a valet have to look so handsome? For whom was this sharp jawline and lush, dark hair? Some people were too perfectly formed to be alive, and this man was one of them. Christopher could spit, he was so incensed, but he soldiered on. Even burning with envy, he had to be polite.

"Were you sent from London?" he asked from atop his high horse. Ordinarily he would dismount to continue a conversation, but in this case, he thought it best to stay above the man, if only in the equine sense.

"Yes. James Harding," said the man. He gave a polite bow right there at the side of the road. "At your service, my lord." His voice was surprisingly soft given his imposing figure. Christopher had half imagined he might open his mouth and let out a crow's screech instead of a melodious human voice. He tipped his head back to better see Christopher, and a lock of his hair fell over his brow.

Christopher thought this was all a bit much.

"So," Christopher said. "You're my new valet?" He nudged the horse closer so that Orion was no longer blocking the road.

"I am, my lord," Harding said. He was even more handsome up close, the bastard. There was a little beauty mark near the corner of his right eye just above the crest of one perfect cheekbone.

The absolute gall.

"Ah," Christopher offered. Not his most intelligent gambit, but the beauty mark was very distracting. Actually, the fellow was, in his entirety, maddeningly distracting.

Christopher was aware that valets these days tended to be good-looking; it was fashionable, he knew, to collect manservants who were as pleasing to the eye as they were efficient in their duties. Just last month he'd read an account of a pair of identical twin footmen with green eyes who were being paid an obscene amount of money to flank a baroness's carriage door. It was the same as any object in a household, went the theory. If you were going to have a man standing in the background of your life, he might as well be nice to look at.

Christopher, however, did not see the appeal.

He did not understand in the least how keeping a veritable Adonis around the house was supposed to please him. He already spent more time than he should comparing himself to the illustrated models in his men's fashion periodicals. He had once thrown an entire issue of *Tailor's Quarterly* into a roaring fireplace due to the unending pages of perfectly sculpted men displayed therein. Christopher was well aware, of course, that a flesh-and-blood man should no more compare himself to a fantastical drawing than he should to a myth, but it still rankled. Those men in the fashion illustrations all seemed to have exquisitely turned calves, jaws as strong as iron, tiny nipped waists, and damnably broad shoulders. He had spent many hours telling himself that such men did not exist in reality, and yet here was James Harding, wax wings strapped to his no-doubt exceptional back, flying very close to the ideal.

Or perhaps this James Harding was a very ordinary-looking man and Christopher was so shut away from the world at large that he was seeing extreme beauty where there was really nothing special. The thought buoyed him considerably.

Orion snuffed at the man's dark coat, no doubt searching for carrots. James Harding held out his empty hand, palm flat and facing skyward, and allowed the horse to huff and lip at his skin.

"Careful," Christopher said. "He does bite at times." Though he hated the man for his enviable looks, he did not necessarily want to begin their acquaintance with an injury. Valets needed all ten fingers, probably.

Harding gave him a flicker of a glance in reply but did not flinch away. And Orion, miraculously, allowed the stranger to scratch at the spot between his ears where he so loved being scratched. Christopher watched in wide-eyed wonderment as the horse dipped his massive head to better receive the attention. It was unprecedented for the temperamental animal to act in such a docile way with anyone, let alone a stranger.

"A beautiful mount," Harding commented. "He must be a pleasure to ride, if I may say so, my lord."

Orion, who knew a compliment when he heard one, preened

at the praise, strutting in place and puffing out his chest. Clearly, the beast had turned traitor.

Christopher adjusted his seat in the saddle. "He is, but only because he and I have an agreement: he does not try to kill me on a daily basis—at least, not anymore—and I spoil him rotten. He's thrown every other rider who's tried to bring him to heel, so I'd advise you not to get too cozy. He's a dangerous villain."

In an attempt to completely undermine his master at every turn, Orion nuzzled at the top of Harding's head. The man bore this with as much dignity as he could, allowing the horse his affectionate gesture before smoothing down his hair and replacing his hat.

"Indeed," he said, suffusing the word with more dryness than an utterance of agreement warranted.

Christopher hated being mocked, and this Harding fellow was just the type to make one continually feel the butt of some joke. He gave Orion's reins a little twitch meant to convey his displeasure at the horse's betrayal. Orion, of course, did not give a single damn and bent to nibble on some clover.

"Don't be fooled," Christopher said. "One wrong move around Orion and you may end up with a broken leg. Although I suppose you would have no way of knowing that, if you are not accustomed to horses." He paused, sensing in the subtle shift at the corner of Harding's lips that he was once again being silently laughed at. "*Are* you accustomed to horses?" he demanded.

Harding's answer was entirely proper. "Somewhat, my lord. In my youth, I was well acquainted with them."

"Oh?" Christopher could not hide his surprise. Owning a horse of one's own was not common among the serving class, nor was leisurely riding, as far as he was aware. Plinkton, even in his more sprightly days, couldn't stay in a saddle if you offered him a farthing. "And how did that come to be the case?"

Harding inclined his head. "As a lad, I worked as a stable boy and would often be tasked with taking the horses out for their daily exercises. It's been some years since I've ridden with any regularity, but I still possess some little skill in that arena, I should think."

Brilliant. Not only was he the finest specimen of manhood within fifty miles, he was practically a born horseman.

Christopher sniffed. "Well, that would not be among your tasks here at Eden Abbey. I am responsible for all of Orion's exercise." He ignored Orion's annoyed huff.

Harding stared up at him, squinting a little in the brightening morning sun. It glinted off the lock of hair on his brow, making it shine like black silk. "I would never expect to be allowed free rein of your horses, my lord," he said with more gravity than the comment merited.

"Oh, I like that!" Christopher grinned. "Free rein." He laughed, and at Harding's blank look, held the slack leather tack aloft in his fist. "Reins. As in—? Did you not make the joke on purpose?"

"I do not *joke,* my lord," Harding intoned.

Christopher let his hand drop. "Yes. I can see that."

Pretty though the man might be, this Harding was the dullest creature Christopher had ever had the displeasure of speaking to. He was cold and stiff and altogether stuffy. Christopher had heard valets tended to be a serious breed, but this was worse than he'd imagined.

Ah, well. The man was only here to fulfill a very specific role, and indulging in a sensible chuckle once a fortnight was not a prerequisite. As long as he was willing to make an appearance as Christopher's valet, his personality (or distinct lack thereof) did not matter.

Harding shifted on his feet, a strange flicker playing in his eyes, though the rest of him was solidly serious in every way. "Perhaps we should discuss the tasks I would be overseeing, my lord. The solicitors did caution me that the position was contingent on your approval." His mouth did that thing again that made Christopher feel very foolish. "Unless you have already decided to hire me without checking my references?"

Christopher's hands tightened on his reins. Beneath him, Orion shuffled on his feet with impatience and not a little secondhand (secondhoof?) embarrassment. Christopher had completely forgotten the terms surrounding his new valet: he had, indeed, told the solicitors the man would only be taken on if his references were in order and Christopher felt he was a proper fit, and only then on a short-term basis.

He glossed over all this with a smile. "Of course. Shall we discuss this further in my study like civilized people?"

"If His Lordship wishes it."

What a lobcock.

Christopher turned Orion back toward the stables with a roll of his eyes. Harding fell into step on the roadside. Christopher chanced a glance down at Harding and his heavy-looking valise. If it were any other person in the world, he would offer to share the saddle on the ride back, but he was not inclined to make such a suggestion to a man as dour and friendless as this greyhound in human shape.

Harding must have sensed the glance and thought it belied some sort of impatience, for he said, "You can ride ahead if you prefer, my lord, and I can meet you."

"Nonsense." Christopher was very good at pretending, and so he pretended to not be as flustered as he felt. "You don't know the way. We shall go together."

They walked on for several yards while Christopher considered the man. From his seat on Orion's back, he had an excellent view of James Harding's face, including the slope of his distinctive nose. Christopher's gaze drifted down to his lips for only a moment before he faced forward and admonished himself silently. It was impolite to stare. So what if this Harding was a well-formed man? Christopher was acquainted with several handsome men. He had gone to Cambridge with plenty of them.

The silence between them began to weigh on Christopher. It seemed so awkward to him to cover the short distance without exchanging anything further.

He tried the first conversational gambit that came to mind. "You aren't overly chatty, are you, Harding?"

"Would you like to chat, my lord?" he asked in the same bloodless tones that a doctor might use to pronounce your loved one deceased.

"God, no," Christopher said as they neared the stables. "It's only–I so rarely entertain guests here at Eden Abbey that I suppose I've no idea how to conduct a normal conversation. If you do remain here in my employ, you'll need to get used to these silences."

"I am not a guest, my lord," Harding pointed out. "You

needn't worry about keeping me entertained. I do not mind silence."

Well! A fine snub that was. Christopher steeled his jaw. If his possible valet never indulged in something as frivolous as light conversation, it was good to establish that now.

Christopher guided Orion through the stable doors and dismounted. The horse, seemingly confused about his morning exercise being cut short, lodged his complaint with a loud whinny, as there was no Plinkton around to bite. Christopher shushed him as he began removing his tack.

"I know, I know. Don't pout. Tomorrow we can go all the way down to the seaside, if you like."

One of Orion's huge black eyes fixed on something over Christopher's shoulder, and he turned to find Harding standing under the arch of the stable doors, staring at the scene as if it was a personal affront.

"My lord," he said, setting down his valise on the straw-strewn ground with a thunk, "allow me to do that for you." He strode forward and reached for Orion's bridle, but this familiarity was too much for the horse. He tossed his great head, shying away from the touch.

"Ah! Please don't," Christopher cried. He laid a soothing palm on the side of Orion's neck. "I can manage perfectly well on my own."

Harding looked around wildly. "But where is your stable hand? Should he not be the one to do this?"

"There is no stable hand." Christopher frowned and turned back to the work of releasing the tack. "A boy from the village comes every few days for a bit of cleaning, but for the most part, it's just myself and Plinkton in the mornings."

Harding stood by with his long arms dangling at his sides, watching the scene unfold with a slight furrow on his brow. "Your Lordship should not be expected to do such menial tasks. I can go fetch this Plinkton if you point me in the right direction."

Christopher shot him a look over Orion's back. "You would honestly pull that sweet old man away from his second cup of tea? Cook would skin you."

This made Harding even more confused, if his helpless blinking was any indication. "I was not aware flaying was one of the hazards of this post, my lord."

Christopher closed his eyes. He imagined a world in which he would not need to explain very basic things to a strange new valet, and he lived in that excellent world for the span of one breath. Then he opened his eyes and said, quite calmly, "Look. This position will likely be very different from the positions you've held in the past. I am not the sort of master who requires every little need to be managed by a servant. I am my own man. And Orion—" He patted the horse's bellowing sides. "He is my own horse. I do not mind brushing him down myself. There may even be an occasion where I am required to muck out the stalls." (Harding gave a choked-off gasp, which Christopher blithely ignored.) "If it offends you to see an earl doing *menial* tasks—though I would argue this task especially requires great skill—then perhaps you are not destined to serve at Eden Abbey."

Harding stood there, his mouth a thin, sour line, looking like the very picture of self-control. Clearly he had something to say, but his sense of propriety was not allowing him to contradict one of his betters.

Christopher sighed and reached for a currycomb. "All right, Harding, out with it. Speak your mind. Better we be completely honest with each other now before you throw in your lot with me."

Or as honest as possible, Christopher thought. He was still unsure whether he could trust a valet with choosing his cravat, let alone any of his secrets.

Harding seemed to pick his words carefully before laying them out before Christopher. "I take great pride in my work, my lord."

"Of course." Christopher stepped onto his handy mounting block and began brushing Orion down, thinking of how obvious it was that this cheerless creature cared only for his job. He'd only known Harding for a few minutes and that, at least, was perfectly clear.

Harding continued: "In my view, that work requires me to make my employer as comfortable as possible. While I respect your outlook on these matters, I–" He stopped and thought before speaking again. "There is an order to things, my lord."

"I see." Christopher sighed, patting Orion's great neck. "Perhaps this is a discussion better suited to sitting. Allow me to finish with Orion here," he nodded at the horseflesh beneath him, "and we can convene in the study."

"That is acceptable, my lord." Then, tipping his head toward the bucket, which held all of Orion's grooming implements, he said, "Though I have the utmost faith in your ability to handle this by yourself, may I attempt to help? Many hands make lighter work."

"Orion does not like anyone else touching him," Christopher warned. "Poor Plinkton gets nipped daily just for coming too close."

"I am sure I can manage." Harding bent to retrieve a brush and joined Christopher in tending to the beast. Orion, for his part, startled only a little, and when he turned his head to find Harding at his flank, gave him a gentle butt to his shoulder. Harding accepted this with a smug little look at Christopher.

"Well, he really is much improved, I suppose," Christopher rushed to say, filling in the silence again like a fool. His hands worked the comb in fast, jerky motions. "When he first came to me, Orion was not fit for any company. Now he's practically a gentleman."

The corner of his mouth lifted in that way that made Christopher's skin prickle. "Your influence, no doubt, my lord."

He sniffed, trying to concentrate on his work. "Harding, I have the distinct impression that somewhere deep inside that stony exterior, you are laughing at my expense."

"My lord, I would never."

Christopher doubted his sincerity, but for the sake of their fragile truce, he let it lie.

They continued brushing down Orion, and with the two of them it took no time at all. Soon the horse was groomed and sparkling and safely locked in his stall. Christopher gave him a scratch between his eyes as thanks for his relative calm. He hadn't bitten Harding once–quite a vote of confidence for Harding's character. Christopher wondered if perhaps Orion's instincts could be trusted.

He turned to the man with a rigid smile. "Shall we?"

Christopher led the way through the gardens and into the

manor. They entered the study, where Christopher took his seat behind the massive oak desk. He still sometimes felt like a child playing pretend when he sat there, in the place where his father had sat. Then Christopher noticed that Harding was still standing in the center of the floor, valise in hand, like a soldier ready for orders.

"Won't you sit?" He gestured to the chair opposite.

There was a brief silence during which he was convinced Harding would decline, but he eventually bent. "If you'd prefer, my lord," he said, taking the chair and placing the valise on the floor by his feet.

They sat there for a long moment, watching each other across the expanse of the desk. Christopher had assumed that Harding would get the discussion started, as he undoubtedly knew a valet's business better than Christopher did.

Yet Harding only sat, and waited, and stared, though all of it was done very politely.

"Well," Christopher said, covering some of his nerves by fiddling with his desk set. Each item–penknife, inkwell, blotting papers–needed a slight tweak, in his opinion. "Erm, how shall we proceed?"

"Would you like to look over my references, my lord?" Harding suggested.

"Yes!" The enthusiasm and relief could not be wholly excised from his voice. "Yes, that would be an excellent place to start. Let's see them."

Harding bent and opened his valise to retrieve a sheaf of papers from its black maw. He placed the neat bundle, tied with string, on the edge of the massive desk. "Each of my previous employers has been gracious enough to furnish me with these letters, save for my most recent one, who unfortunately passed away due to old age. In his stead, his son kindly wrote this recommendation." Harding unknotted the string and placed the topmost letter, a crisply folded thing of gorgeous cream stock, on Christopher's blotter.

Christopher reluctantly plucked it from the desk as if it were a nasty creature that might snap at his fingers.

The missive indeed contained a glowing recommendation from a Mr. L. M. Pentagraff II, because of course it did. It wasn't as if Harding would be daft enough to bring references with him that stated, *Eh, maybe don't hire this one. He sneaks the port and oversleeps on Sundays.*

The entire exercise felt rather pointless. Christopher leafed through the rest of the stack, trying to project a confidence he did not feel. "You've certainly held quite a few positions," he said just for something to say. There were at least five letters from former employers, along with an envelope stamped with a wax seal from Cloy & Bellow. Christopher cracked it open and skimmed it. More of the same: *You'll find herein Mr. Harding's impeccable references, which we have, where possible and to the best of our ability, confirmed with the appropriate persons.* Christopher lifted his head and pinned Harding with a look. "Is this a normal number of masters to have served at your age?"

Harding seemed unperturbed at the notion that he might be a serial valet, hopping from one employer to the next without a care in the world. "I can only speak for myself, my lord, but I do not think it unusual. One's position may come to a natural end for many reasons, as my references state." He nodded at the pages still in Christopher's hands.

"How old are you, anyway?" Christopher shuffled through

the pages and found the earliest reference from a viscount up in Yorkshire dated eight years prior—Harding had been his footman and acting valet when the usual man was indisposed. He glanced again at Harding's face, handsome but still in the bloom of youth. "You can't be more than a year or two older than me, surely?"

"I will be nine and twenty come this winter," Harding said. "I am not certain of Your Lordship's age."

Christopher's heart tightened at the very mention of it. "Five and twenty this September," he mumbled, then dropped his gaze to the papers again. In only a matter of months, he would either be married or destitute. He forced himself to focus on the task at hand. "It will be strange to have a manservant who isn't old enough to be my grandfather. Plinkton the butler is getting on in years, you see."

If Harding was annoyed at this line of conversation, he did not show it. He only tilted his head as a curious bird might before saying carefully, "Have you never employed a valet before, my lord?"

"I have not." Christopher chanced a smile, knowing it wouldn't be returned by such a dour thing as Harding. "I'm not sure what my lawyers told you, but—"

"They imparted the necessary facts."

Christopher blinked. "Did they?" His smile, as yet unanswered, grew. "Now I'm curious. What facts did they feel were necessary?"

Harding's chair creaked, though he didn't seem to shift an inch. Old furniture, as old as the house itself. "That you lived alone at Eden Abbey; that you required a valet for an imminent trip to London; that the position might extend beyond that should I prove myself useful but there was no guarantee; that you are young with no wife or children; and–" Here Harding hesitated for the first time, though his hesitation seemed to have less to do with nerves and more to do with the careful consideration of his next words. "That you had somewhat eccentric habits. My lord."

Even after all these years of living with a well-kept secret, Christopher still felt his heart stop at the phrase. "For example?" he asked, his voice strangled.

"Misters Cloy and Bellow suggested to me that you may, for example, be accustomed to dressing yourself," Harding said. The sour look on his face deepened, his lip curling faintly.

Christopher bit down on the curse that lay on his tongue. "Ah. That." He supposed they knew, having looked over his financial records in the course of their work, that Christopher had not kept a valet all these years. His solicitors were privy to a good deal of his personal business, of course, but he could only hope Cloy and Bellow weren't spreading word of his habits around London.

And he prayed they did not guess the reason behind it.

Harding crossed his legs. As long as they were, it took some time. "I was certain I had misunderstood them, sir." It was a leading sort of statement. It made Christopher smile again.

"No, no misunderstanding, Harding. It's true; I am accustomed to dressing myself and I would continue to do so should I take you on as a valet."

The frown on the man's face was barely perceptible and only there for a flash of a moment, but Christopher saw it all the same.

"May I ask why, my lord?" Harding intoned.

Christopher spread his hands. "I will do you the courtesy of being frank. I do not require a valet, and yet I find myself in need of one, if only for appearances' sake."

"Your visit to London," Harding said, proving that the intelligent gleam in his eye was not just for show. "You don't wish to appear in society without the requisite trimmings, is that it?"

"Exactly." Christopher neglected to mention that he would also be in the market for a wife, and potential wives would expect an earl to travel with his valet. That particular piece was Christopher's to puzzle out, and he did not wish to delve into the details of the thing. "If I'm not tossing around pots of money as I should, people might not take me seriously. Isn't that a funny conundrum? You would just be for show, Harding."

Those expressive eyebrows rose again. Christopher was beginning to wonder if Harding communicated exclusively through his brows, and how long it might take to learn that language. "For show, my lord?"

From his tone, it was clear he wanted to tack on something to the effect of *Like a commemorative plaque?*

Christopher waved away his indignant protest. "There might be small tasks here and there that you might be able to handle for me, but as far as my wardrobe is concerned, I do not need any assistance."

Harding frowned. "You're paying me a wage anyway; I may as well dress you while I'm here, my lord."

Christopher leveled a wry look at him over the polished wood of the desk. "Your work ethic is to be admired, of course, but one might consider not looking at a gift horse so closely." He shuffled the references back into a neat stack. "Is the arrangement acceptable to you or not?"

Harding seemed to take an age to answer. When he did, his soft voice formed his words so delicately and so prettily that Christopher had to wonder what sort of etiquette training they were putting valets through these days.

"The relationship between a man and his valet should be based on trust and mutual understanding. However, I do not expect such sacred things to spring up overnight. If you prefer to dress yourself, my lord, as your valet, I can only strive to be of service to you in other ways and hope, in time, that we reach a point where you trust me to do it for you. I am very good at what I do, Lord Eden. Could you possibly imagine yourself allowing me those duties in the future once I have proved myself to you?"

"Possibly, Harding, possibly," Christopher prevaricated.

It wasn't wholly a lie; anything was possible. Christopher *could* imagine. His imagination was excellent, and if pressed, it would produce a picture of Christopher being dressed like a doll by Harding in some frightfully boring costume of black on black with perhaps a smidge of grey for color. Of course, in this imagining, Christopher was not constrained by his singular secret and there was no need to be anxious about allowing another man to dress him.

He moved his inkwell an inch to the left in what he thought was a rather self-possessed gesture. "If that's settled, then I do not foresee any problems with your employment here at Eden Abbey." He settled back in his chair, relieved to have finished the interview. "Shall we, erm, begin now? Is that acceptable?"

"Certainly, my lord." Harding sounded almost amused at the question. Christopher was going to have to get used to being silently laughed at by this bastard. At least Cook and Plinkton had given him plenty of practice already. Speaking of which–

"Ah, one more thing: the butler, Plinkton, is getting on in years, as I've said. He's been here since before my father was born, and I wager he'll still be here when I'm long gone. There may be times when you may need to pitch in while we're at Eden Abbey. Lighten his load. Is that all right?"

Harding's face, which normally seemed cut from living rock, softened into something almost human. "You worry for the butler's good health, my lord?"

"Of course I do. The man practically raised me," Christopher said. "And he's older than Moses. So would you be able to lend him a hand once in a while?"

"Sir, you needn't ask. Under your employ, I will follow all orders to the letter."

"Good." He cleared his throat and reached for his penknife, nudging it another scant inch to align with the edge of his blotting papers. "So, erm, what now?"

"Shall I acquaint myself with the household, my lord?" Harding said. "Perhaps settle in?"

"Yes! An excellent notion," Christopher enthused. "Why don't I show you–" He rose from his chair, ready to play guide to the new addition.

"No need, my lord. I can find my way, I'm sure." Harding stood, valise in hand, and gave a grave sort of bow. He went into the hall and turned toward the door that led to the back stairs. His footsteps barely made a sound on the old floorboards. For a moment, Christopher wondered how he knew his way around the Abbey without so much as a cursory tour of the place, but he reasoned that most old estates were likely built along the same lines, and Harding could probably make an educated guess as to the direction of the kitchens.

Must be nice, he thought, knowing your business as well as that.

Christopher listened to his assured, quiet footsteps receding, then gave a sigh. He flopped bonelessly back into his chair, shaking his head at himself. He was probably the only gentleman in all the land who had sought out a lazy valet on purpose. Just his luck that he'd managed to hire one who was competent, tireless, and, damn it all, far too handsome.

Christopher groaned and put a hand over his tired eyes, rubbing at them distractedly. Why hadn't he instructed Cloy & Bellow to send him a valet with grey hair and wrinkles and a face that looked like a hatchet?

Oh, yes. Because Christopher has specifically told them not to. Like a fool.

As always, he had only himself to blame.

Chapter 3

Christopher stayed cloistered in his study for the remainder of the morning, conscious of the fact that his new manservant would be flitting about the Abbey. Christopher did not want to make more of an ass of himself than he already had and thought it best to leave Harding be. He tried concentrating on some correspondence that he had been neglecting of late, though he ended up reading the same sentence again and again. His mind was too distracted by the sound of Plinkton's voice echoing throughout the halls and Harding's answering murmurs. The words were muffled, but it was obvious enough that the old butler was showing the new man about the place. Probably pointing out all the relevant bits, Christopher mused, like which stairs always screamed when you trod on them wrong or where one could feel the perennial draft.

He wondered what Harding must think of the house's little quirks. Christopher was seized with a sudden desire to ensure the man did not think ill of Eden Abbey. Though it was old and crumbling, it was his home. It felt like he was showing some vulnerable, fleshy part of himself to a mere stranger.

This was troublesome, as Christopher had spent years avoiding exactly that, and for good reason.

It would be impolite to say the almighty creator had erred in his making, but privately Christopher couldn't help but think that someone somewhere along the way had made a real hash of it. If things had gone as they should have, Christopher would have been allowed to wear the clothes he liked and live the way he wanted from the very start, regardless of his shape. As it stood, he had been shoved into petticoats and taught to work on his embroidery with clumsy fingers for the bulk of his childhood. That was behind him now, thank god. But should anyone discover his origins, Christopher thought it likely that he would not only have his title and lands stripped from him, but he would doubtlessly be sent to some madhouse and forced back into womanly trappings.

That, he knew, was to be avoided at all costs. Even if it meant shutting himself away from the world for the rest of his days, Christopher would keep his secret safe. Not even Plinkton or Cook knew the truth of the matter, for reasons that inspired no pride in Christopher.

This did not weigh on Christopher as much as one might imagine, however. The fact of his singular make often faded from his mind in the face of day-to-day concerns. It was a vital fact, to be sure—one that meant Christopher would always remember to lock his bedroom door when he was in a state of undress, for example, not to mention complicating his search for a fiancée—but it was not his entire life. Especially not when his estate was at risk.

Christopher made one more attempt to read the letter from his steward (yet another plea for Christopher to consider investing his remaining funds as his late father had, in textiles and shipping and what have you) before giving up on the thing. He didn't plan on replying, anyway; his childhood tutor had been a Quaker and a fervent abolitionist, and Christopher was not about to cast aside the lessons he'd learned at the man's knee. What he needed was a little nourishment. He left the study and went in search of something to eat. With the weather as decent as it was, he had half a mind to filch a pie or something from Cook's larder and eat it in the garden.

He was so engrossed in planning this little outing in his head that he didn't notice James Harding at first. The man was standing in the main hall, valiseless now, his hands clasped behind his back while he contemplated the family portraits on the wall. He, too, seemed as lost in thought as Christopher had so recently been. Christopher cleared his throat to catch his attention.

Once he had it, he scarcely knew what to do with it. Harding's dark eyes swept over to him, resting there like a bird on a branch, light as anything. "My lord," he said. "I couldn't help but notice—" He nodded at the paintings.

"Ah. Yes." Christopher looked at the portraits. It had been a long time since he'd done so with any real intent to study them. He was startled to see all the little details anew now that he was actually taking them in.

The painting of Christopher's parents was an old one, commissioned at the very start of their marriage. His father sat in an armchair with a spyglass across his lap and a peevish look on his face, like he was annoyed with the artist and ready to give him a stern lecture. His mother was standing behind him and to the left, the white bird of her hand resting limply on his shoulder. Her gown was a watery, pale thing, more of an impression than a color. To Christopher's mind, it looked like she was attempting to calm her husband.

"I always thought this was a poor likeness of them," he said. He wasn't sure where the thought came from or the inclination to share it with his cheerless new valet, but once he began speaking on the subject, he could not stop. "They look so unhappy here, but my memory of them is quite the opposite. Mother was always laughing; she had a lovely laugh. And my father was always giving her reasons to showcase it."

If Christopher concentrated, he could smell the harbor air of his childhood, rife with humanity, and see the spires of Philadelphia from the hill where their house sat beside the river. There had been different birds there, and different trees, but the same sound of his mother laughing at something his father had said while they sat close on the chesterfield in the parlor. What excellent years they had been, that time spent abroad.

"I am sorry that this portrait does not do them justice," Harding said, breaking him from his reverie.

Christopher smiled, though he did not feel like doing so. "I am, too. But it's the only portrait of them I have, so here it is. There were others, of course, but they were lost when—" He stopped. Swallowed. The sound of water rushed into his ears, and for a moment he feared he might lose his balance entirely. He placed a hand against the wall to steady himself. The feel of cool stonework beneath his palm grounded him in the present.

"They were simply lost," he said in a soft murmur, and decided that would suffice.

"I see," Harding said. His gentle tone made it seem possible that he did, indeed, see and knew better than to press the issue. He turned again to contemplate the imposing wall of cold stone and the other painting that hung there.

This time, Christopher had to force himself to look. He raised his eyes to the portrait and tried to see what Harding was seeing: a boring picture of a rather ordinary girl of nine, her blond curls arranged in an elegant fall over one shoulder. She was dressed in a gown of dark navy dotted with seed pearls which gave the impression of a night sky, and in her hand was a fan, closed and dangling quite uselessly. The only noteworthy aspect was her eyes—a piercing, almost desperate stare of ice-cold blue, as if the girl were pleading silently with the viewer for some kind of succor.

Christopher coughed into his fist, finding his throat suddenly dry. "My sister Catherine," he offered. "My twin, in fact."

"Yes, I can see the resemblance, my lord," Harding murmured. He continued staring up at the painting, his gaze no doubt roving over the nose, the chin, the lips, and mentally comparing them to Christopher's. "She's lovely."

"She's dead," Christopher said.

He took a fiendish sort of pleasure at seeing the composed man twist in the wind at these words.

Harding was silent for a long moment, concern creasing his handsome features before he finally said, "My condolences, my lord. I did not know."

"That's surprising. I thought everyone was aware of the tragedies heaped upon the Winterthrope family."

"I am not so well-informed, I suppose," Harding said. He executed a deep bow. "Forgive me, my lord. Perhaps I should have made inquiries before coming to Eden Abbey, if only time permitted."

Christopher waved away the notion. "Please, it's actually very refreshing not to have someone tiptoeing around the thing." Plinkton avoided the subject entirely, and Cook had a habit of pursing her mouth and making a rapid sign of the cross whenever she mistakenly mentioned the late Winterthropes within Christopher's earshot. His earlier glee at Harding's discomfort faded in the face of the man's sincere apology. It was the first chance he'd ever had, he realized, to tell the story—or rather, a version of it—on his own terms. He nodded at the portrait of the late Lord and Lady Eden. "You see, my father had some business interests in the States some years ago"—ghastly business, as it turned out, which Christopher had only discovered when he first took up the title and saw the accounting ledgers, hence the divestment that his steward so despaired at—"and when my twin and I were about ten years of age, it was decided we would accompany him there."

"Is that where you developed your sense of independence, my lord?" Harding asked, raising a cool eyebrow.

"The likelihood has occurred to me." Christopher smiled, pleased at the notion, but his gaze landed on the portrait of the young girl, and the smile slipped away. "At any rate, a fever swept through the city one summer before we had a chance to decamp to the country. It claimed many victims, including my parents."

"Your sister as well?" Harding asked in that gentle way of his.

Christopher shook his head. "No. That came later." A wave of dizziness washed over him. For a moment, the floor seemed to roll beneath his feet like the deck of a troubled ship. His throat worked, and he found that even now that he had the chance, he could not finish the story. It was all rather mortifying. These episodes normally happened without an audience, and Christopher sternly reminded himself to breathe so as not to draw Harding's notice. He turned away from the portraits and clapped his hands. "Well! Enough of this morbid talk for the moment, eh, Harding? I came this way to raid Cook's larder, so I'll be off."

"I would be happy to wait on you while you take your midday meal, my lord," said Harding, floating behind at a polite distance.

"No need; I always wait upon myself. I find it best that way," Christopher said cheerfully as he pushed through the green baize door that led belowstairs. Cook's scrumptious meat pie was calling his name. Unfortunately, so was his annoyingly solicitous valet, who followed close behind. And just as he was catching his breath, too.

"Lord Eden, if I may," Harding said, his footsteps crisp on Christopher's heels, "I could not help but notice there is no portrait of yourself hanging in the main hall."

"Hm?" Christopher glanced over his shoulder as they descended the stairs. "Ah, that's true, I suppose."

"Have you never sat for one?" Harding asked.

"Oh, I have," he replied breezily. "I believe the painting is stored somewhere in the attic. It's the twin to my sister's portrait. Mother had us sit for them before we left England."

"You don't wish to display it?"

Christopher led the way into the kitchen. "Ha! The last thing I want to see every day is a painting of myself in a skeleton suit. Can you imagine? What little authority I have in the household would disintegrate. Cook would laugh for hours." He turned his attention to opening the larder door with enough care that the hinges wouldn't creak and alert Cook, wherever she was lurking.

Harding waited behind him, playing lookout without being told. No doubt trying to be useful, as he'd promised. "Have you considered commissioning a more recent portrait of yourself, my lord? A man of your stature should have one on display."

"I haven't, and I won't," Christopher said, finding a clean plate and helping himself to a hefty slice of golden pie left over from Cook's dinner the night before. "The thought of sitting for a portrait bores me." He did not mention that it also filled him with dread that the artist, after making such careful study, might see something in his face and bearing that gave him away. "I think I will leave the walls to the honored dead." He turned and swept past Harding with the pie and a fork in hand, heading for the kitchen door that led outside.

Harding, for reasons Christopher could not fathom, continued to follow. "My lord," he said as they left the house and stepped into the little side yard where Cook kept a few scraggly herbs, "if you are anxious to appear in society as a gentleman of means with good prospects, you may want to consider things like this. These details are easily managed. I can commission a portraitist upon your arrival in London, if you so desire."

"I do not desire," Christopher said waspishly. He used his

hip to knock open the little gate that led from the kitchen yard to the rose garden. "Some details cannot be borne, Harding. No one needs to look at my face that badly."

"Your betrothed may wish to, my lord," Harding said.

Christopher whirled, nearly upsetting the pie from its china plate. "My *what*?"

"Your betrothed. You intend to acquire one imminently, do you not?" Harding stood tall and dark, looking like a black heron stalking amongst the plants.

"How did you know that?" Christopher demanded. "My solicitors didn't tell you, did they?" Such a breach of confidence would be beyond the pale.

"No, I made the assumption myself," Harding said, still looking as placid as a pond. "You are a man who famously prefers to live in the country year-round, so I'm told, yet you've arranged to stay in London for an extended period during the Season. You are suddenly concerned with giving the impression of a conventional earl who employs the usual amount of servants. These facts, combined with your age, made me think it likely that you are considering marriage. It was not a great leap of logic, my lord."

Christopher boggled at him. "Are all valets masters in the art of deduction or is it just you?"

Harding considered the question seriously, his hands clasped behind his back and his chin dipped to his chest. "I'm not sure, my lord."

With a roll of his eyes, Christopher stomped into the garden to set his plate upon a stone bench. Harding followed, as he'd predicted. It was as disconcerting to have him for a shadow as it was to have said shadow somewhat understand the shape of Christopher's secret plans. He could only pray Harding would not puzzle out all the sordid details.

He had it on good authority that he was not the first man in history who had been forced to marry for the purpose of claiming an inheritance. He had heard rumors—written in the more gossipy columns of his men's fashion magazines—of miserable women tied to husbands who barely knew their names or faces, married just to fulfill some legal stipulation. Christopher abhorred such practices.

Though he wanted no part of their sisterhood, Christopher liked women well enough. Having nearly been one himself, he had more sympathy than usual for the fairer sex. Therefore, he had no intention of luring an upstanding lady into a marriage without first giving her all the facts: that he could not sire children for her, that he was a man of unusual make, and that she would need to take his secret to her grave. In return, Christopher was prepared to offer her whatever she required, such as an understanding that she would be able to conduct her own affairs discreetly and with Christopher's blessing. Most importantly, she would need to understand that Christopher would have no romantic designs on her whatsoever, as the necessity of this marriage had soured him on the idea of love entirely.

True love, the soft kind with longing gazes and tripped heartbeats, was all well and good for other people, but it was not possible for him.

"Listen to me, Harding, for I will only say this once." He turned and crossed his now empty arms over his chest. He wished he was just a little bit taller so that Harding did not loom over him as he was doing now, but there was nothing for it. "You are not to share this tidbit of information about the young master with anyone, do you understand? No one knows that I hope to find a wife in London, not even Plinkton and Cook, and I would prefer to keep it that way."

Harding's frown was so small as to be imperceptible, but Christopher had become an expert at cataloging them in a short span of time. "Surely it is no secret that a man in your position and at your age would be thinking of marriage. It is not a shocking development in the least."

"No, but it is very private," Christopher said, "and I value my privacy above all else."

Harding inclined his head. "I am beginning to understand that, my lord. I will not breathe a word of this to anyone."

Christopher sniffed. "See that you don't." He glanced down at the pie on the bench, wanting nothing more than to sit and eat in the sunshine as planned, but loath to lose what little commanding presence he had. He wished Harding would just leave already.

Harding, though, seemed content to stand there in the garden until the end of time. "May I ask, my lord, is there a certain lady who has caught your eye?"

"What?" Christopher nearly choked on his tongue. "No. God, no. I haven't–"

"Because if there was a specific lady you wish to pursue, I could keep my ears open once we arrive in the city to . . . assist in your cause, my lord."

"The entire thing is theoretical at this juncture, I assure you," Christopher said. He could feel his damnably fair cheeks flaming with embarrassment. "I don't have my heart set on any particular person."

"I see." The very corner of Harding's lip lifted at this pronouncement. "In that case, my lord, I will await any updates on the matter from you, should you see fit to share them."

"I want to eat my lunch now," Christopher said, trying and failing not to sound like a petulant little boy. "Could you . . . ?" He made a shooing motion with both hands.

"Absolutely, my lord."

And with a bow, Harding at last fucked off.

Christopher all but collapsed on his stone bench. This valet would be the death of him.

Chapter 4

After a long day of avoiding everyone, especially his new valet, Christopher was ready to retire to his room with a glass of brandy.

Retiring to his room with a glass of brandy was one of Christopher's favorite things to do. He held the glass beneath the circle of his fingertips and in his other hand carried a book. It was Ovid, in the original Latin, and Christopher was eager to dive into it. He had always had a knack for languages, and poetry was a true weakness of his.

He set his accoutrements on the bedside table before adjourning to his dressing room, where he slipped off his coat and hung it in its appropriate spot. He was about to unknot his cravat when he heard a distinct shuffling noise coming from the room next door.

Christopher froze, his hands still at his throat. That room should have been empty. No one had gone into it for at least a decade, as far as Christopher was aware.

Yet, in the ensuing silence, he heard it again clearly: footsteps, the thump of things being moved. Either there was a prowler or the Eden ghost was back, and Christopher was not certain which he preferred. A prowler at least might be reasoned with, but in his experience, ghosts never listened.

He grabbed a walking stick from a stand in the corner of the dressing room and hefted it in his hand. The door was at the back of the dressing room, and Christopher noted that the row of slippers he usually kept in front of it had been moved aside. With his heart racing, Christopher took hold of the doorknob and breathed deeply.

He threw the door open wide and charged forth with his walking stick aloft, ready to beat a thief.

There was no thief. There was only Harding sitting motionless in a straight-backed chair, watching him with an unimpressed look. He was in his stockings, a boot in one hand and a polishing cloth in the other. "Did you require something, my lord?" he asked.

Christopher stood frozen in the doorway with the stick still lifted above his head. "Harding?" he yelped. "What are you doing here?"

Harding looked about the tiny room with his brow pinched. "I live here, my lord."

Christopher felt he was on the verge of a nervous attack. He lowered the stick to his side and groaned. "Please, forget the 'my lords' for a moment. You needn't bother with them when it's just the two of us."

Harding put down the boot and stood politely with his hands clasped behind his back. "It's not easy to forget that sort of training, my lord." At least he had the decency to wince at his misstep.

Christopher closed his eyes and reminded himself that screaming in frustration was a response unbecoming of the Earl of Eden. "Right. Of course. To return to my original query: What do you mean, you live here?" He opened his eyes to see Harding glancing around the tiny room as if the question was some sort of joke, or perhaps a test.

"These are the valet's quarters," he said slowly. "This is where I am to sleep, is it not? If you have need of me, it's better that I'm close at hand."

Christopher vacillated. He'd known in a sort of vague way that the room was, indeed, traditionally meant to house the earl's valet. Christopher had fuzzy childhood memories of his own father's valet emerging from the room like a spirit from a crypt. He could not for the life of him recall the man's name.

James Harding was nothing like that nameless man. He was entirely too memorable, every part of him: name, looks, annoying habit of figuring out Christopher's plans, etc. The thought of such a man sleeping so near to Christopher's own bed with only the dressing room between them made Christopher break into a sweat.

Christopher's unique situation made this arrangement impossible. If Harding was allowed to traipse in and out of his master's bedroom at all hours, there was a chance he might catch Christopher in a state of undress. Normally such a thing would be standard for a man and his valet, but for Christopher it would spell disaster. Even his current state of half dress—coat off and shirtsleeves bared—was already much too dangerous.

"There must be empty rooms belowstairs that would be more comfortable," Christopher pointed out. "You needn't live in this tiny closet on my account."

"These are valet's quarters, sir," Harding repeated. "They are meant to contain your valet." He pointed to the various dust-covered tins of bootblack and what looked like sewing notions in worn cases. "Everything I require to tend to your wardrobe is already here, and more importantly, should you need me–"

"I won't need you," Christopher insisted. "I can function perfectly well on my own. We've discussed this."

"Should you need something after you retire for the evening," Harding plowed ahead, ignoring him, "I will be right here, ready at a moment's notice."

"What could possibly happen that would require you at a moment's notice in the middle of the night?" Christopher propped his hands on his hips. "If I should lose a button on my flies or misplace a pot of hair oil, it's not exactly a disaster of epic proportions, is it? There's nothing that cannot wait till morning, my dear fellow."

Harding did not give up an inch of ground. "My lord," he said slowly, "I understand that employing a valet is a new experience for you. Giving up your privacy, even a sliver of it, must . . . chafe. But the whole point of my being here is to be of service to you. So if you would rather not know I am here," he met Christopher's gaze with something like steel, "I will be a ghost to you, and I promise you will never see but glimpses of me."

Christopher sighed and looked away. "Don't be ridiculous. That is not what I meant."

"Then pray tell, sir, what you desire."

Christopher faced him again, looking carefully. Harding endured his gaze with a straight back and shoulders set. It gave Christopher the strangest sensation, not unlike what he'd felt when Orion had first come to Eden Abbey as a temperamental horse in need of training. Except now, Christopher was the unruly stallion and this man, this impossible mirage of a man who looked so dour, he was the one offering a calming hand, palm up and flat. And would wait for Christopher to take it.

"All right. Here is what I desire." Hesitation colored Christopher's words. He chose them carefully so that they would be as truthful as he could manage, yet reveal nothing. He had enough sins piling up against him, after all. "I am set in my ways at this stage, and I do not want to give up my privacy, as you say. Yet I can see that the idea of taking a room elsewhere—or doing anything too out of the ordinary—gives you pause. You're clearly a man who prides himself on doing his job to the letter." Christopher licked his dry lips. "I propose a compromise: you may make your bed here in the old valet's quarters if you truly wish to, and I promise I will call upon you if I ever do need your assistance. But you will not leave this room in the mornings unless and until I call for you. Is that clear?"

Harding's thick black eyebrows winged upward like startled crows. "That is . . . rather backward, my lord. My day should by rights start much earlier than yours. While you are still abed, I should be—"

"What? Selecting my ensemble for the day? Readying my creams and hair oils? I told you, I dress myself, Harding, and I will continue to do so no matter how many valets I keep about the place." Christopher crossed his arms over his chest. "There would be nothing for you to do for me first thing in the morning anyway."

"Still." Harding frowned. "The thought of lying in bed whilst you begin your day is . . ." He stood up even straighter, if such a thing were possible. "It's abhorrent to my sensibilities, my lord."

The image was abhorrent to Christopher as well, if only because it conjured a damnable palpitation in his head and chest. His mind, which was turning traitor just like his horse, briefly wondered if Harding was the type to sleep nude.

"Noted," Christopher said in a strangled voice. "It changes nothing about my desires. Either you agree, or you can find another room."

Harding gave a frustrated scoff. "You would have me be a prisoner here."

"Oh, don't be so dramatic. I am allowing you another hour or so of sleep for no less pay." Christopher stuck out his hand. "Are we agreed?"

Harding narrowed his eyes at him, but eventually clasped his hand and shook it. Rough palms, Christopher noticed. Likely from a lifetime of scrubbing and polishing. They weren't so bad, actually. "It will be as you say, my lord."

They went to bed much earlier than grown men really needed to, but since further conversation seemed rather awkward, there was no other choice. Christopher lay in his too-large featherbed with its too-soft pillows and too-heavy bedclothes and wondered if Harding was in his own bed, staring up at his ceiling in much the same way. The thought led to other, less appropriate thoughts, and Christopher pulled a pillow over his face to muffle the ensuing groan. He prayed that sound did not carry. If Harding could hear him, that would be unfortunate. Not only because Christopher was often the victim of terrible dreams, but because he was a man much like any other and indulged, as many men did, in that shocking practice of self-gratification. He didn't think he was very loud when he brought himself off, but he couldn't say with absolute certainty that he was completely silent. He wondered idly which would be the lesser embarrassment of the two–frightful visions or onanism–should Harding indeed overhear him. It was an impossible decision. They were equally mortifying, albeit for different reasons.

Christopher flung the pillow from his face and forced himself to stop thinking of his panicked mind, and his own right hand, and Harding two doors away in his own little bed, and anything at all, really, until sleep finally took him.

That first morning, Christopher awoke in the usual way, in a panic and covered in sweat. The dream dissolved as soon as he opened his eyes; though he could not remember the exact details, he still felt the sensations.

Quite annoying, but he marshaled his courage. He flung the bedclothes back and got himself upright, stuffing his bad dreams into the sea chest in the back of his mind, the one that was labeled WINTERTHROPE–TO REMAIN LOCKED AT ALL TIMES.

He instead focused on the task of washing and dressing himself, despite knowing that his vulnerable, nude form would only be one thin door away from James Harding. He stood in his nightshirt in the dressing room and stared at said door, waiting to see if it would indeed creak open, and whether Harding would break his solemn oath. Christopher cleared his throat, but heard no response from within the valet quarters. He shifted in his slippers, considering. He'd worn his bandages to bed the night before despite the discomfort; he'd have raw patches of skin along the edges of the bindings from where he'd thrashed in the throes of his dream, no doubt, but he hadn't wanted to risk being caught out by Harding.

He hadn't even known the man for a full day. He couldn't possibly trust him, not with this.

He knew, then, what he would need to do to ensure that Harding was being truthful in his promise to not exit his quarters until given express permission. He cleared his throat again, louder this time, and stamped one slippered foot against the floorboards. No valet emerged from behind the door.

Christopher coughed, a terrible, hacking thing that, for all that it was false, sounded extremely alarming.

That got him a response, at least. From behind the shut door came a tentative, "My lord?" Harding's voice sounded even softer with the wrappings of sleep and disuse.

With feline indifference, Christopher reached out to grasp a rack that held a smattering of his winter scarves and cloaks. He tipped this away from the wall and watched it crash to the floor with a loud bang.

"Lord Eden!" came the cry from within the valet's quarters. Twin thumps sounded against the wood of the door, and Christopher imagined it was Harding's palms making contact with the barrier between them. "Are you well? What was that?"

"What was what?" Christopher returned brightly as he began slamming every drawer in his dresser.

"I heard a noise. And coughing. Are you in any distress? What is that racket?"

Christopher did not answer, only kept banging. The stocking drawer especially made a delightful sound.

"Please, sir, if you do not answer me, I will have no choice but to open this door," Harding called.

Christopher plucked his dressing gown from its peg and wrapped himself up in its warm velvet embrace, ready in case his valet proved to be a lying scoundrel. Another layer of armor was always a good idea.

The door did not budge. From within the depths of his lair, Harding's voice came out in a muffled, tense thread. "My lord, is this a *test*?"

The smug grin that had taken up residence on Christopher's face dropped off.

"I don't appreciate being baited like a lapdog being taught tricks. My lord." Harding sounded like a man pushed to his limits.

It seemed like a very childish game, all of a sudden, to tease Harding like this. Christopher could not even manage to form a reply. He walked to the door, reached for the knob, and then retracted his hand. He'd never allowed a single living person to see him in only his nightclothes, not since—well, since it mattered. Half a lifetime of caution was not so easy to throw to the wind, no matter how disappointed in you a valet sounds.

Christopher swallowed and spun around, leaning his back against the damned door. He felt exhausted, like he could crawl back into bed and sleep the day away. He heard a thump behind him in the region between his shoulder blades. His imagination conjured an image of Harding pressing his forehead to the door. Perhaps he was tired too.

"Sir, I understand my presence in your life is a drastic change, one that will take time for you to become accustomed to. And I know you must have your reasons for wanting me to stay in this room until you allow me out. But you must realize, I cannot possibly be expected to remain here if I have reason to think you are in distress. What sort of man would I be if I did that?"

"I have terrible dreams sometimes," Christopher found himself saying to the ceiling. "I'm not sure, of course, but I might cry out in my sleep occasionally. It's not—though I may sound troubled, I am truly in no danger, and I would be embarrassed if you were to fly to my bedside at the smallest whimper."

"Then let us agree," Harding said. "If I hear you cry out, I will not come. I will only come if you call for me."

Christopher blinked hard, tears coming unbidden to his eyes. What a thought, having someone he could call for. How long had it been since he'd done such a thing? In the cradle? How could he explain that he would never call for anyone, not even in his darkest hour? That in those moments, he was completely alone by necessity? There was a reason Eden Abbey was so empty of life, and it hadn't occurred to Christopher until that moment to expect anything different. He sniffed and ran the side of his hand under his nose.

Harding continued. "But if I hear this sort of thing—the coughing, the crashing, something that cannot be explained by a bad dream—I will not wait for your permission."

Christopher nodded, even though he knew he couldn't be seen. "Agreed," he said. "My apologies, dear fellow. I don't know what came over me." He lifted the lapel of his dressing gown to his face to dab the wetness from his eye.

"No apology needed," Harding said, and the warmth in his voice seemed to suffuse the door between them. Christopher felt the back of his neck heat. "We are both navigating new waters. It takes time and frank discussion for a man and his valet to understand each other."

"You didn't open the door," Christopher said. It felt important, somehow, that Harding had kept himself locked away. "You kept it shut."

"Well, unless there was a burglar loose in the house who was ransacking the dressing room while simultaneously causing you to cough, I thought it unlikely my services would actually be required."

Was that a hint of a smile he heard in those words?

Christopher slumped more of his weight back against the door, letting out a barked laugh. "Next time I'll make sure my acting skills are up to snuff," he said.

"Please don't." There was a short silence from Harding's side of the door, and then, "May I come out now, my lord?"

"Ah." Christopher's gaze swept around the disordered dressing room. "Not quite yet, sorry. I still need to dress."

"Very good." The creak of worn bedsprings marked Harding's retreat back to his narrow bed. "Please let me know when you are finished."

"Right! Yes. Good," Christopher said, and hurried to restore the rack he'd tipped over.

Once he'd put the dressing room more or less back to rights, Christopher rushed through the rest of his morning routine. He chose a tawny pair of buckskin breeches with the matching waistcoat and cream-colored coat. It seemed strange to be knocking about the room in silence when Harding was waiting patiently behind the door, so he began talking as he dressed. Nothing of great consequence, mere pleasantries and musings made aloud.

"The weather looks especially fine at the moment," was his opening foray. He finished freshly rebandaging his chest and ducked to look out the small window just above the vanity table to confirm. "Yes, just a few clouds in the sky. Orion should have a good run of it this morning."

There was a slight pause whilst Christopher wriggled his muslin shirt over his head and stuffed the tails into his riding breeches.

"Do you take the horse for a ride every morning, my lord?" Harding called through the door. His voice sounded a bit strained, as if this sort of idle talk was quite new to him. Christopher felt a surge of gratitude; he would have felt like an ass if his ramblings had gone unanswered.

"Yes, as a matter of fact. Rain or shine, it does not matter to Orion. He will eat up the ground in any weather." He shrugged into the tan waistcoat, the one with the chased silver embroidery that resembled palm fronds, and began buttoning it up.

"May I ask, my lord, where you found such a creature?" Harding asked through the door.

Christopher's hands paused on his topmost button. A serene sort of smile took over his face. "A nearby farm. Their plow mare had birthed this colt that—well, Orion just refused to be told what to do, even at that early age. I'd heard they were going to sell the little hellion for dog meat, and I just had to have a look for myself."

"You must have had an instant bond with the animal, sir."

Christopher snorted. "Not even close, actually." He finished with his buttons and grabbed up his cravat. "He tried to stomp a hole in my foot. I found him an awful little thing and told the farmer he was best rid of him as soon as possible." He laughed as he twisted his knots at his throat. "But then, as I was walking back to the Abbey, I thought, Well, just because he's ornery and foul-tempered, does that really mean he should be sent to the butcher? Cook and Plinkton can be some of the most foul-tempered people I've ever met, yet I can't imagine my life without them. So I turned around and went back to the farm, where I proceeded to offer a grotesque amount of money for him." Christopher slowed his movements, finishing with his cravat. "I appreciate creatures who are wholly themselves, I suppose. I wouldn't want Orion to lose his independent streak. He's not at all ashamed of it, and for that, I cannot help but be impressed."

There was another bout of silence in which Christopher wondered if he'd spoken too freely, if there was some clue in his chattering that might give Harding pause. But the moment soon passed, and Harding called out, "Are you nearly done dressing, my lord?"

"Oh! Yes." Christopher pulled on his coat of cloudlike cream with the self-styled buttons. "Emerge from your prison, my dear fellow. The young master is decent now."

The door opened to reveal Harding, the long, narrow shape of him filling Christopher's field of vision.

Christopher blinked. He had been expecting more of the same immaculate black clothing that Harding had worn the day before. He had not been expecting . . . this.

"What on earth are you wearing?" he cried.

Harding glanced down at himself. Affixed to his person was the livery of the Eden household–at least, the livery that used to be worn by all the male footmen in Christopher's dim childhood memories. It was a uniform that spoke of a bygone age: starched white stockings that showed the shape and sturdiness of the calves, knee breeches that clung to the thighs, and a surcoat of rich purples and blues (the colors of the Winterthrope family crest, a rabbit rampant) buttoned nearly to the throat. And to top off the bizarre ensemble was a powdered wig, curled at the sides and no doubt clubbed at the back.

"It's your livery, my lord," Harding replied.

"Yes, I can see that! Why are you wearing it? It's dreadful."

Harding gave him a look. "It's traditional. I acquired the ensemble from Plinkton last night." He held out his arm to examine a sleeve. "I admit it was rather musty from being stored in a chest for so many years, but I gave it a good beating to get the dust out and made a few adjustments to the fit. Once we are in London, I suspect it will add a certain amount of gravity. Do you not approve?"

"No, I certainly do not approve." Christopher wrinkled his nose and gave one powdered curl an experimental tug. The wig shifted a bit off-center, the false hair feeling crispy under his fingertips. No doubt it had once belonged to a footman, back when Eden Abbey employed dozens of them. It had likely been sitting in that chest since the day the last earl and his family had left for America, leaving a skeleton staff behind. "You should wear your own clothes, honestly."

Harding sighed. "If I do that, I might be mistaken for . . ." He searched for a word. "Your peer, my lord, and not your valet. It would be embarrassing for all involved."

Christopher made a gesture that encompassed the entire estate. "And who, pray tell, would even be around to make such a mistake? No," he shook his head, "I cannot abide this pageantry. At least not when it's just the two of us, here at the Abbey."

Harding glanced to the heavens as if asking the divine for strength, then said, "Shall we compromise once more, my lord? I will wear my own clothes when it is unlikely any outsiders will come to call, but I will wear the livery if I accompany you in public."

Christopher considered these terms. He hated inflicting a powdered wig on a fellow human being under any circumstance (thankfully they were becoming less common by the day), but he had to concede that having a manservant in livery togs in London would certainly be fashionable. The entire point of employing James Harding, after all, was to show all of society—including a potential wife—that Lord Eden was as normal and unimpeachable as an earl could be.

"We are agreed," he said at last. "Now will you please change into something more suitable for riding? I'm going to saddle Peaches so you might join me. I promised Orion we'd visit the seaside, and I don't want to disappoint."

"Peaches?" Harding floundered like a flat fish. "Join you?"

"Yes, is that acceptable? You said you were well acquainted with horses."

Harding opened and closed his mouth a few times, lending more credence to his fishlike appearance. "My lord, I would be happy to accompany you, of course. It's only, in my previous positions—this is highly unusual, I would say."

Christopher was going to pretend at being not unusual for months; he didn't see why he should have to get an early start on it. He turned on his heel and called over his shoulder, "Up to you, of course. I'll be in the stables in half an hour should you decide to meet me there."

Chapter 5

Harding met him at the stables.

Their ride was nothing short of pleasant. Christopher had wondered if the addition of Harding would hinder his enjoyment of the peaceful morning, but instead he found it to be quite the opposite. With Harding riding Peaches (a chestnut mare with the personality of a warm slice of cake) beside him, Christopher was in his element, talking a mile a minute about his horses and the surrounding countryside, pointing out Peaches's ability to sidestep dips in the road without being told, or expounding on some local legend concerning a nearby wooded bower. Having gone so long without companionship—at least, that of someone his own age—it seemed he was starved for it. He wondered just how pathetic it was that he was essentially paying a man to be his friend.

As with most things that gave Christopher an uncomfortable feeling in his middle, he dismissed the question and locked it away in his proverbial sea chest.

"Would you mind," Christopher asked as they headed south, "if riding together in the mornings became a regular habit?"

"Do my skills appear so rusty that you think I need a chance to polish them?" Harding did not smile per se but allowed his eyes to soften as he glanced over at Christopher.

Christopher gave him a shrug in return. "You said it, not I."

There were only a few days left before they would need to leave for London, but Harding and Christopher spent them well. It was only sensible, Christopher thought, that they get to know each other, if for no other reason than to be able to present a decent picture of master and servant when they arrived in the city. And if getting to know Harding meant spending more time with the man, well, all the better. Christopher was delighted with each tiny scrap of information he was able to gather about his new valet: that the first horse he'd ever ridden was a bay named Ferdinand; that he had strong opinions on trousers and breeches; that he would prefer to add a few darker colors to Christopher's wardrobe ("One single coat of navy, my lord; would that be such a burden?"); that eating walnuts made his face and hands puff up like someone had taken a bellows to him; and that he preferred dressing in dark colors not because he thought it suited him, but because it allowed him to fade into the background as a servant should.

"Well, it does suit you," Christopher informed him while they rode together one morning. "If I could order you to wear nothing but black for the rest of your days, I would. But I know you will insist on wearing that dreadful livery when we go to London." He shivered dramatically just for the sheer pleasure of watching Harding attempt to hide his smile.

After they turned the horses around to head back to the stables, Christopher realized that, as many tiny bits of information as he'd managed to wheedle from Harding, he still did not know much. The man was cloaked in mystery, and it seemed only natural to want to relieve him of his outerwear.

"You said you worked as a stable boy in your youth," Christopher said, glancing over at his noble profile. "Where are your people from, Harding? Were you raised in the country?"

"No, my lord. I was born and raised in London," came the soft reply.

"London!" Christopher's imagination teemed with thoughts of a whole gaggle of Hardings living in some gloomy rookery, squeezed shoulder to shoulder, each one as handsome as Harding was. "You must be looking forward to our sojourn, then. I suppose there will be many evenings where I will be out and about with no need of you; plenty of opportunities to visit with family."

"Actually, my lord," Harding said with strange delicacy, "I have no family left to speak of."

"Oh." Christopher deflated, feeling a right ass. Here he was, himself quite alone in the world, and it hadn't even crossed his mind that Harding—or anyone else for that matter—might be in the same boat. "Oh, I'm sorry, dear fellow."

"There is no need for apologies. You couldn't have known." He guided Peaches around a fallen log with a deft hand.

Christopher ached with curiosity to ask about the circumstances of this tragedy, but propriety held him back—as well as the carefully guarded look on Harding's pinched face. He attempted instead to lighten the mood. "Well, perhaps there are old friends or acquaintances that you might meet while we are in the city. Or there are other things you can do for entertainment. I mean it, Harding: a free evening is not to be squandered. I don't want you moping about the house waiting for me to return from a ball or—"

"Take care, my lord," Harding said all of a sudden, and swung Peaches into action with a quickness that seemed to surprise even the horse herself. In the blink of an eye, Harding had placed his own mount on the path before Christopher's, effectively blocking his way. He also reached over (not far, as their horses were nose to neck) and laid his hand on Christopher's where they had his reins in a loose grip. The touch seemed designed to reassure Harding that the young master was held firm, but it also served to produce a noticeable hitch in Christopher's breathing.

Christopher did not know what to make of it at first, but then saw where Harding was focusing his intense gaze: there was a steep gully just ahead on the path where the earth had washed away, leaving only a few bits of bramble to hide the treacherous pitfall from hapless travelers.

"Excellent eyes, Harding," Christopher said, breathless. One false move and Orion might have broken a foreleg. "I'm very much in your debt."

"As long as you are safe, my lord," said Harding, "there are no debts between us." He seemed belatedly to realize his hand was still resting on Christopher's person, and he jerked it away with a quickness normally reserved for the touch of hot coals.

"We should return to the stables soon, at any rate," Harding said, bringing Peaches around.

"Yes." Christopher hoped to god the croak in his voice wasn't too obvious. "Return."

Chapter 6

The next few days continued uninterrupted in terms of Harding settling into the Eden estate. He familiarized himself with the grounds, with Christopher's wardrobe, and with the quirks of the house. The two of them became more familiar as well, though Harding still resisted calling Christopher anything other than "Lord Eden" or "my lord" or, when feeling particularly frisky, "sir."

Christopher knew he was more informal than most with his servants, but he really couldn't help it. It was in his nature. He'd always felt more comfortable around such people–the "salt of the earth," his father had called them–than with those of his own social station. There were simply fewer dangers when conversing with the serving class, he supposed. With members of the ton, one had to be always on guard, especially in Christopher's situation, where one wrong move could expose his most private secret. Of course he liked chatting with Cook more than he did the Marquess of Bumplishborne; Cook was too busy with her work to bother with things like collecting evidence of Christopher's abnormal origins.

It was this attitude toward the serving class that made Christopher insist quite firmly that Harding take an evening off every so often, and since there was not much to do about the manor until they needed to leave for London, he didn't see why Harding shouldn't start right away. Thus, Harding was expelled from the dusty halls of Eden Abbey one pleasant Friday evening with orders not to try sneaking back upstairs to rearrange Christopher's sock drawer. He went with only a little grumbling, and Christopher felt very pleased with himself about it. He took his simple supper belowstairs with Plinkton and Cook as was usual, then found himself at loose ends.

He did not want to read. He did not much feel like replying to the scant few letters that still needed his attention before they left for the city. It was too late to take Orion on yet another ride. And it was too early to go to bed.

The last few days, his attention had been wholly taken up by James Harding, and now that the man wasn't there, Christopher realized he was actually very bored.

"I think I will take myself on an evening ramble," Christopher told Cook as she cleared away his empty dishes.

"Really?" She frowned at him. "The weather's foul tonight, m'lord." She nodded to the fan-shaped window over the sideboard, where drizzle was sticking to the windowpane.

"If I wait for the weather to improve, I will be stuck inside for half a year." Christopher gestured to Plinkton. "My hat and stick, if you would. It's just a little rain, so no umbrella. It would only slow me down."

"As you wish," said Plinkton, and within moments Christopher was crossing the lawn on his way toward town.

The air was damp with the kind of rain that is heavier than a mist but not heavy enough to do anything but cling to one's sleeves and eyelashes. Christopher blinked away the drops as he contemplated the new upheaval in his life. Harding, stony but pleasantly efficient. Stubborn as Orion had been as a yearling. Now sleeping on the other side of his dressing room wall, no doubt able to hear every creak and groan of Christopher's floorboards. All because of some loathsome expectation that valets must be kept as close as a faithful hound, or some kind of indispensable pocket watch. They might as well share a bed at this rate.

Christopher tried very carefully not to consider what sharing a bed with Harding might entail.

The rolling hills of Eden at last gave way to the flatter ground of the town, and Christopher reached the outskirts of it just as the sun was making its miserly way toward the horizon. With all the clouds, though, it was already a hazy kind of night that fell over him. Market Eden, too, seemed ready to go to bed early. Every shop was closed for the day and only the occasional light glowed from the windows of the modest homes that lined the main thoroughfare. No one else was on the road, and Christopher felt, not for the first time in his life, that he might be the only living creature in the world.

His loneliness abated as he rounded a bend and saw the village inn lit up at the end of the lane. He smiled at the familiar sight. The place was unfortunately named Eden's End, and the innkeeper had been compelled to replace the sign stating so numerous times over the years, as local youths were wont to scrawl a helpful "TAIL" in the center of it as a lark. Christopher eyed the most recent sign—free of any vulgarity so far—and thought it would be easier if the proprietor just changed the name to something else. But Eden's End had stood on this spot long before any of Christopher's ancestors came to this place, and he suspected it was a point of pride for the villagers to hold firm even after so many years.

As he walked closer, he could make out silhouettes of patrons standing in the windows, their mouths and arms gesturing like lively puppets. Christopher felt the knot in his chest unwind a bit. Here was life. Here was some measure of proof that he was not alone.

As he drew closer, Christopher could hear music pouring from the tavern, some country reel that had been popular these last few years; he'd heard it at village fêtes before. The figures in the windows were dancing, he realized, mugs of beer in hand. Laughter flowed forth, and he found himself admiring the scene. It didn't much matter to him that he wasn't a part of it. Lord Eden was so rarely a part of any happenings in the world, but it gladdened his heart to see the good folk of his bit of country enjoying their evening. He stepped closer to get a better look.

A new figure flitted across the window, one that was achingly familiar even after so little time to memorize it. Christopher blinked, but the vision did not abate: there was Harding, wearing a simple coat of dove grey, his shirt collar hanging scandalously open. He was reeling with the best of them, passing one girl then another along the line. The mug of beer in his hand never spilled a drop despite all the hopping and clapping the dance required; Harding merely clapped his free hand against his thigh, which gave him a chance to drink deeply before dancing off again. His dark hair hung in his eyes, damp in the close environs of the tavern, where steam clung to the windows. Harding swiped a lock of hair back behind his ear while turning to laugh at something one of the village girls had said. It was muffled behind the pane of glass and under the swell of the fiddle player, and Christopher dearly wished he could hear that laugh in full. He hadn't the faintest idea what it would sound like and was rather miffed that the girl at Harding's side did.

Christopher knew in an abstract way that his servants had lives and interests outside of their duties at Eden Abbey; he even encouraged the old guard to leave the grounds with a very generous full morning off on Sundays and free evenings thrice a month. And yet he had not imagined that James Harding, that dour undertaker in his dark suits, that absolute lunatic who complained about not being worked hard enough, would let his hair down in such a raucous manner. If pressed Christopher would have guessed that Harding's personality was more like his own: a bit of a homebody, perhaps, content to spend a quiet evening in front of the fire with a good book or a tipple of sherry. This scene proved him wrong. Harding appeared to be the life of the party. Christopher watched as the dance drew to a close and the revelers broke formation to conduct loud, happy conversation. Yes, there was Harding at the very center of their attention, receiving titters from girls and older ladies alike, and slaps on the shoulder from the men. Seeing this easy intimacy made something burn inside Christopher's gut.

If he was jealous, which was absurd, it was only because he had never experienced such casual fun with the folk of Eden Market. A certain distance had to be maintained. Oh, Christopher could have barged into Eden's End, ordered a round for the house, and inserted himself into the dances if he cared to, but that would only put a damper on everyone's spirits. No one wanted to drink and dance with their landlord.

Yes, Christopher told himself as he watched Harding through the window. That was the sort of jealousy it inspired in him. Nothing more.

He should have made his exit right then. He should have walked back to the Abbey and left it at that. But Christopher stayed frozen on the spot even as Harding turned toward the window to sip at his mug. His eyes lifted just as he began to drink and he met Christopher's gaze through the glass. Harding paused with the mug at his lips, and they both stood there, one inside and one without, their eyes widened in surprise. Christopher could see the hazy outline of his own dumb face staring back at him in the window's reflection, overlaid atop Harding's.

There was nothing he could do to erase the awkwardness between them, so Christopher did the only thing he could and raised a hand weakly in greeting. Harding moved back into action as well, like a clever automaton given a windup, and lifted his mug in a little toast.

No one else saw Christopher standing there, and before anyone could, he did what he should have done at the very start and departed, walking quickly back toward the estate. The wind had picked up, and Christopher wrapped his greatcoat tighter around himself, fighting the chill that suffused his whole body. He was no stranger to loneliness after all these years, but it still managed to surprise him, the way it filled his throat and threatened to choke him. That feeling was his only companion for the long walk back to the Abbey.

Chapter 7

Christopher insisted on helping pack for London. He knew his wardrobe better than anyone else, he pointed out to Harding, and would remember to include things like his summer stockings and dancing slippers in the heavy baggage. Unfortunately, Christopher was also a creature who loved to be distracted, and when Harding unearthed a trove of snuffboxes from a dusty drawer, the Right Honorable Earl of Eden became preoccupied with examining each piece in the little collection.

He sat atop a tower of three trunks that had already been packed to the gills with shirts and stocks. His feet dangled several inches from the ground as he laid out each snuffbox beside him on the trunk lid. Harding had had the foresight to ask Cook for a pot of strong tea to brace them throughout their task, and this sat within easy reach on the vanity. Christopher held his teacup and prodded at one of the snuffboxes, a pretty little thing done up in green and pink enamels.

"None of them have been used, really. I've never acquired a

nose for snuff myself," Christopher said. "They just keep popping up. Christmas gifts, most of them. Ah, this one I received upon completing my studies at Cambridge." He held up a tiny bronze box that had a few scenes from the *Iliad* painstakingly painted on its faces as if it were a piece of ancient pottery. "My Greek professor was so glad to be rid of me, the occasion warranted it."

Harding stared at it. "A fine box indeed, my lord," he mumbled before turning back to his work.

Christopher set it back down among its brothers. "I don't suppose we need to take any of these to London with us, do we? Or should I carry some snuff just in case others may wish to partake? I'm afraid I don't know the etiquette."

Harding was hard at work over at the dressing table, pawing through the various drawers and decorative boxes the thing held. He did not answer, nor did he even appear to have heard. He seemed to grow more agitated as Christopher watched, the tense line of his shoulders rising to meet his ears.

"Harding," Christopher said once he'd swallowed another mouthful of tea, "is something the matter?"

"I'm not sure, sir," said Harding. His quick hands kept up their task of opening every possible lid of every decorative box to examine its contents. "I saw them here last night," he murmured to himself. "I could swear I did."

"Saw what?" Christopher asked idly. He poured himself yet another cup of tea and blew on the surface, sending steam flying.

"Your sleeve buttons, sir."

"My sleeve buttons?" Christopher frowned. "You mean

my cuff links?" He'd thought only Plinkton and other men of advanced age still called them sleeve buttons.

"Yes, those." Harding flung open another box. "I placed them *both* right here last night." He pointed to the single cuff link—a curled shape of silver scrollwork with a lapis inset—sitting all alone on a tray. "I wanted to make sure you had something suitable to wear on our journey, and I didn't want them packed away by accident."

Christopher refrained from reminding Harding that he needn't choose anything for Christopher to wear, but if the man wanted to be included in the selection of accessories, he supposed that was harmless enough. "And now one is gone?" Christopher guessed, calm as anything.

"I can't find it anywhere." Harding turned to him. His fine, elegant hands were wringing before him. "I assure you, my lord, I will find it if I have to turn all of Eden upside down and inside out."

"It's fine." Christopher began stacking the snuffboxes into a little pyramid. "The ghost probably took it, is all."

There was a long beat of silence that enveloped the bedroom, into which Christopher took a loud slurp from his teacup. The brew was really quite good.

"A ghost, sir?" Harding finally asked. His tone seemed to indicate disappointment, though it wasn't clear whether that disappointment was in his master's mental state or in the possibility that this was merely a jest.

"Mm." Christopher searched for Harding's teacup and found it abandoned on a shelf behind him. He retrieved it and set about refilling it from the pot. "It takes things from time to time."

"I was not aware there was a ghost in residence at Eden Abbey," Harding said.

Christopher swallowed. This was not a topic one wished to broach if one wanted to keep a good, decent man in his employ, but he supposed the conversation needed to be had at some point. He only hoped Harding was not overly frightened by the occult. "Oh, yes. We're well and truly haunted here," he said with false cheer. "Rather famously. I'm surprised Cook or Plinkton haven't mentioned it." He handed the refreshed teacup out to Harding by the lip of its saucer.

Harding took the tea from him instinctively. "Perhaps it slipped their mind," he suggested in a cool way.

"Then let me be the one to inform you," Christopher said, turning back to his own teacup. "This is not the first time some little bauble of mine has gone missing, and I doubt it will be the last. Last year the ghost claimed my watch fob right off its chain. That one stung, I admit, but I've gotten used to losing a trifle here and there, just as Cook has made peace with hunks of butter and leftover pies going missing from the larder. It's all a part of life here at Eden, so please don't be too concerned about it. I promise I won't suspect you of filching treasures from my bureau." He frowned. "Although now that I've explained the situation to you, I suppose you could start filching and I would be none the wiser."

"I have no plans to filch, sir," Harding said with the appropriate amount of gravity.

Christopher eyed him. "I pay you enough to keep the temptation at bay, then?"

"More than enough," Harding assured him. "And anyway, I'm no thief. It would never occur to me to take a sleeve button.

Especially if it meant separating the set." He shivered, holding up the lone silver button so that it glinted in the morning light. "It breaks one's heart to see it come to this."

Christopher felt a wave of fondness wash over him. His valet certainly was something else. "Try to soldier on, Harding. It wasn't even my tenth-favorite pair."

"If you say so, my lord." Harding turned to the dressing table and hummed in thought. "I must confess, I don't personally believe in ghosts, and I'm a bit shocked you do."

"It's not so surprising, I should think," Christopher said, "especially when you consider that I spent my most tender years treading these halls." He set his teacup in its saucer with a merry rattle. The ghost was best left ignored, in his experience, and he had a lot of experience in ignoring it. "Now, let's see what else there is to pack." Christopher pushed himself off the trunk lid, but the drop was farther than he'd realized. He gave a manly yelp as he slipped down the trunks toward the unforgiving floor. It seemed inevitable that he would crash in an ungainly heap.

Just as Christopher had made peace with that, he felt strong hands clutch at his hips, disrupting the fall of his cutaway coat but, more importantly, saving him from an ignoble tumble. His breath caught, and his pulse thundered in his throat.

Christopher blinked up at Harding, his savior, just as the tips of his shoes touched the ground. "Ah," he said. Like a complete bacon brain.

In his defense, Harding was staring at his lips the same way he stared at particularly modish cravats in Christopher's trunks: like he was about to caress them to ensure they were properly cared for.

"Are you all right, my lord?" Harding asked. He smelled of tea and the crisp scent of bootblack. This close, the little mark on his cheekbone seemed positively indecent. He must have realized his hands were still attached to Christopher's person, for he removed them at once, letting him drop lightly onto his feet.

Christopher cleared his throat and tugged his coat back into place. "Yes, of course. Excellent catch, Harding. Your reflexes are fairly feline."

"Thank you, my lord."

"That was the second time you've managed to save my neck from a tumble. I'm beginning to think it's a habit with you." He chanced a laugh, hoping that it would cut through the awkward air that had overtaken the room.

Harding, instead, looked quite stricken. His hands, the ones that had so recently clutched Christopher by the waist, balled into fists at his side. He looked down and to the left, where the teapot still sat atop a trunk.

Harding grabbed at it like a lifeline. "I will fetch a fresh pot. Excuse me, sir," he said, and disappeared like the very ghost Christopher had warned him about.

Chapter 8

At last the time came for Christopher to leave Eden Abbey for London.

The coach ride was as tedious and uncomfortable as coach rides always were. Christopher wished he could pass the time reading, for there was little else to do, but if he so much as glanced at a piece of writing whilst in a moving carriage, his head became heavy and his middle queasy. The only thing to do was stare out the window when the sun was not too much in his eyes. Even some conversation would have been welcome during those dreary hours, but he had no conversational partner. Harding was riding with the heavy baggage in a separate cart. He had insisted on playing escort to the valuables, though Christopher had his doubts that his willowy valet would be much of a deterrent to any highwaymen who wished to help themselves to Christopher's effects. Perhaps Harding was hiding some dashing proficiency with a sword or pistol, but Christopher doubted it.

There were other things to think about on the journey (like his impending marriage) but Christopher was content to confine himself to mere daydreams of Harding running through a host of ruffians, mostly shirtless. And sweat dappled. Harding, of course, not the ruffians.

After a day and a half of changing horses and eating at questionable roadside taverns, the coach finally rattled into London and took Christopher to his townhouse in Bloomsbury.

On the rare occasions that he came to London, Christopher found Bloomsbury perfectly suitable, slightly removed from the hubbub of Mayfair proper. The townhouse was modest when compared to the other city dwellings of the ton, host to a mere seven bedrooms and only two sitting rooms. It was decorated in a staid manner befitting a noble family: a few pieces of art on the walls, harmless still lifes in oils, one portrait of a great-grandfather that was quite ugly. The only real notable item in the entire house was the sweeping black shape of the grand piano, which took pride of place in the more formal and spacious of the two sitting rooms simply because there was nowhere else it could possibly fit. Christopher supposed he could have it shipped back to the manor, but he knew it would only sit unused in a room where no one ever touched its keys. Though he used to be able to play quite well in his youth, he didn't dare attempt it these days lest someone note his proficiency. Winterthrope men were not given piano lessons, traditionally, only the women.

Christopher took off his pale kid gloves and laid them on the sideboard as he surveyed the entry hall. A maid came to collect them along with his hat and stick. Plinkton had engaged a few girls to ready the townhouse and see to its upkeep during his stay, and Christopher could find no fault in their work. The furniture was free of dust and the floors were polished to a sparkling shine, not only for Christopher's sake but in preparation for its sale. Judging from its neat appearance, surely it would be only a matter of time before it attracted a buyer.

That was one hurdle, at least.

Christopher went to the window at the front of the house, twitching back the curtain and watching the endless stream of humanity going up and down the street. Still no sign of the baggage cart, but he suspected Harding wouldn't arrive with it for another few hours.

He settled against the windowsill to watch the street. There were so many people here. At Eden Abbey, Christopher could go from one end of the week to the other without seeing another living soul apart from his few servants, but here, he could lay eyes on a hundred new faces all within the span of an hour: matrons with their bonnets perched on their heads, workmen carrying their heavy loads, children with shiny faces and sticky mouths. Here were people of every race and creed, a teeming city of thousands, humanity at its most manifold. Christopher sighed against the windowpane. Hadn't some poet said it was possible to feel quite alone while being surrounded by a multitude?

Then Christopher's gaze found a familiar face in the sea of strangers, and his heart gave a happy leap.

Shuffling down the lane in front of the townhouse was Horace Chesterfield, an old friend of Christopher's from his Cambridge days. Christopher rapped his knuckles against the windowpane as Chester passed by, and as intended, his head whipped up at the noise. When he spotted Christopher in the window, his long face rearranged itself to accommodate his surprise.

"Winny!" he cried. "Lord Eden! When did you get into town?"

Christopher unlatched the window and lifted the sash so he could converse more easily. "Just arrived, dear fellow," he said. "Will you come in and have a glass of something with me? I must have some brandy somewhere."

Chester frowned with regret. "No time to chat, I'm afraid. I'm supposed to meet my father in—" He slipped his timepiece from his waistcoat pocket and consulted it. "Well, ten minutes ago, actually," he said with a mournful look. Now that he was not in motion, Christopher could note the changes in his old friend. There were the usual signs of aging, of course, a tempering into manhood, but more notable was the pall cast over his every word. In days gone by, Chester had always had a spring in his step. That spring was now missing entirely.

"Ah! I don't want to keep you, then," Christopher said, though he couldn't hide his disappointment.

Cambridge had been a harrowing experience for Christopher, but Chester had been a balm to him during their time there. Although he relished the chance to attend those hallowed halls of learning, and Christopher's studies in the classics put him in a near fit of rapture, there was the social aspect of his schooling to be considered. While many of the other Cambridge lads gallivanted along and forged bonds of intimate friendship—some more intimate than others, though they always claimed to have grown out of such boyhood larks—Christopher had held himself apart from that crowd. He would blame his decision to withdraw from the world even at that young age to his singular manhood, which he could not allow the other boys to discover, but in truth the entire enterprise did not appeal. He preferred to spend his school days reading Latin in the stacks, not stealing goats from the local farms whilst drunk.

Christopher was lucky, then, to find a kindred spirit in good old Chester. Horace Chesterfield was the fifth son in an old, old family—titled, but not landed due to the quirks of history. He was an odd, romantic sort, and even as a boy he could spend days scribbling in some notebook, not lifting his head unless Christopher tossed a piece of toast in his direction. He applied himself to his classwork in the most middling of ways, but Christopher, being more friendly with him than anyone else at Cambridge on account of his toast deliveries, knew that Chester contained hidden depths. The man was a poet, or would be if his father would allow him to publish under his own name. Chesterfield the Elder—Lord Gatt was his unfortunate title—had a vendetta against poets and thought having one in the family would do them no favors. As it was, Chester languished in obscurity, printing his stanzas anonymously to no great effect. Christopher, who had an eye for poetry, thought Chester's lines very good indeed. It was all fairly moody stuff: ravens and widows and the drumbeat of horse hooves. If he could only be allowed to tarnish the Chesterfield reputation the tiniest bit, Chester could have made a mint as a gentleman poet. Such verse, when flowing from an aristocratic pen, was all the rage.

"I wish you would detain me if only for a moment longer," Chester called up to the window, misery suffusing his every word. "Anything to delay this luncheon. Papa is no doubt in a mood to harangue me about finding a job in a clerk's office. Or joining the navy." He screwed up his face in disgust, much to the consternation of an older woman passing by. Christopher thought it likely that her son was on board some ship at that very moment, poor sod.

"Well, we must find time to catch up while I'm in London," he said.

Chester seemed to try to summon some enthusiasm for the notion. "If my father lets me live past this afternoon. Are you coming to the Leftmores' ball this Saturday?"

"I don't know the Leftmores," Christopher reminded him. He knew *of* them, but had never made their acquaintance. "I don't know anyone, you'll recall." His friend was sometimes a bit forgetful, as most poets are.

"Everyone knows the Leftmores," Chester insisted. "I have a cousin who's just now engaged to one of their nephews; I'll drop Mrs. Leftmore a note later today and make certain you're invited."

"Oh." Christopher chewed at his bottom lip. He'd thought that angling an invitation to some of the Season's most lavish events would be more difficult. Although he knew he needed to attend parties if he was to find a wife, he'd had an idea that it would take more time than this. Now it seemed he did not have a moment to steel himself. A week would have been welcome, or a month. Or a lifetime. Still, he couldn't be ungrateful for his friend's efforts. "I'm in your debt, Chester. Thank you."

"It's nothing!" He gave his watch another sorrowful glance. "I'd best be going. I will see you at the ball, all right? Good afternoon!"

And with that, he allowed himself to be swept up in the tide of the crowd.

Christopher reluctantly ducked back inside and shut the window. He stood there, drumming his fingers on the windowsill, and thought. It was a Tuesday, which meant he had a few days to prepare himself for the ball. He would have to send word to his tailor. Christopher owned a lavish wardrobe, but the one thing it lacked was modish formal wear, as he never attended events that required it. That would have to change.

"Shall I prepare a bath for you, my lord?" asked a maid who materialized from the ether for the sole purpose of giving Christopher a terrible fright.

Once he'd recovered his wits, he realized a bath would be just the thing. "Yes, please. I really should get out of these traveling clothes." He felt coated in dust from the road, but worse than that, his trousers, while excellent country wear, were all wrong for strolling through the city. He was glad he'd had the foresight to pack a more genteel ensemble in his traveling case along with a few necessary odds and ends, like his linen bandages. He could bathe and change and turn into the presentable young city-dwelling master before Harding even arrived.

He would also have to find a suitable hiding spot for said bandages, as he didn't have any armoires with secret compartments in the London residence. Beneath the mattress was one option, he supposed.

After he was made clean and orderly, Christopher conducted

a few necessary errands. He sent a boy with a note to the Brothers Charbonneau in Savile Row to apprise them of the matter of his formal dress. Once that was accomplished, it was time for his appointment at Cloy & Bellow to begin the excruciatingly tedious work of selling the townhouse. He was kept at the solicitors' for hours, signing an unending parade of papers, and did not return to Bloomsbury until it was well into the dinner hour.

As he ambled up the lane, he saw that the cart carrying the heavy baggage had arrived. It stood outside the residence with a truly huge pile of trunks and crates teetering in its embrace. Harding, clad in the absurd livery and powdered wig, was loudly directing a few strapping men to unload it.

"To the master bedroom with that one, please," he bellowed, his normally soft voice reverberating down the lane. "That one is meant for the sitting room–no, not the east one, please, the western one!" People on the street stopped and stared at the hubbub. Christopher could hear their low murmurs of wonder as he passed them by. Harding spotted him in the crowd and executed a low bow, still speaking much too loudly. "Ah, Lord Eden, how was your journey? You've found the residence prepared to your liking, I hope?"

"It's lovely. What's all this?" He waved the head of his walking stick at the scene, including the sweaty workmen and the very public show of unpacking.

Harding's voice dropped to its usual near whisper. "I thought it might behoove Your Lordship to have word of your arrival spread quickly. I made it a point to pack a bit more than was strictly necessary–"

"A *bit* more?" Christopher eyed the massive trunk that was being carried past them, one of dozens.

"All the better to reinforce the notion that Your Lordship is not only a man of means, but intends to stay in London long enough to, say, conduct a proper courtship." Harding looked very pleased with himself, the corner of his lip curling just so.

"Or to see me into my old age. It looks like I'm about to set up camp for an entire army." He turned back to Harding and frowned at his stockinged calves, shown off to great effect by the old-fashioned knee breeches. "Did you actually travel in this ensemble? I can't imagine anything more uncomfortable. Wait—yes, I can. You didn't change behind a hedge on the way, did you?"

Harding gazed at him placidly. "I do not undress behind hedges, my lord."

More's the pity for the hedges, Christopher thought, but held his tongue. He gave the growing crowd of onlookers another glance. The more working-class members were starting to drift away, commenting not at all quietly about the display of excess, a sentiment Christopher shared and felt faintly embarrassed about. As those people departed, more folks dressed in the elegant trappings of the ton seemed to take their places. Christopher could hear them and their servants whispering about the reclusive Lord Eden finally returning to London. Harding must have heard them as well, for he arched his brows in Christopher's direction as if to say, *Isn't my ingenious plan proving effective?* And it was, damn him.

Christopher felt a heavy weight growing in the pit of his stomach at all this attention. Any one of those whisperers might share the news of his arrival with his future wife. It made one queasy to think of it. He made his way quickly up the front steps to the townhouse's door, dodging the porters as he went.

"I believe I shall dine in tonight," he called to Harding over his shoulder. He couldn't abide the thought of dressing for dinner at an exclusive London club, not now. "Have the kitchen girls slap something together, will you? Nothing too rich; the carriage trip has left me with little appetite."

"Very good, my lord," Harding called to his retreating back, sounding more smug than he had any right to be.

Chapter 9

That night, Christopher went to sleep at his usual early hour despite the city still teeming with noise and life. With his predisposition for bad dreams, he found it useful to go to bed early; it allowed him to snatch at least an hour or two before the dreams overtook him. If he was lucky, he could fall right back asleep until the next bout, and so on until sunrise. This time, however, Christopher's dreams were not of the terrifying variety.

Instead of the deck of a pitching ship, he dreamt of the woods surrounding Eden Abbey. A sliver of lucidity came to him as he stepped along the mossy ground, his mind surprised at the change of scenery. "This is new," he murmured in the dream. "I wonder why . . . ?"

He caught a glimpse of black out of the corner of his eye and turned to see Harding walking alongside him as if it was the most natural thing in the world.

"Oh, dear god," Christopher said, "am I really dreaming of you?" Such a thing was inevitable when he was spending so much of his waking time with the man, he supposed, but it was still a bit much.

Harding, for his part, merely inclined his head in polite affirmation.

It must be exhaustion, Christopher told himself as they tromped through the forest like children. The introduction of James Harding into his heretofore quiet and boring life was a big change; one's brain wanted to spin these sorts of things into poetic meaning. Though Christopher did not believe in fortune-telling and augury, he could concede that his dreams had fashioned Harding into a symbol.

Why he was now holding the hand of that symbol, he couldn't rightly say. He looked down, startled, as he realized Harding's work-roughened palm was resting against his, their fingers entwined. It was warm and dry, and he gave it a little squeeze just to make sure it was really there—well, really there in this dreamworld.

He faced forward, swallowing hard. "It's a matter of exposure," he said aloud to the woods. "A sleeping mind tends to populate one's dreams with the things one knows best. We've been spending too much time together, is all."

"If you say so, my lord," said Harding, who appeared to be just as smug in dreams as he was in reality.

"Even if I did have designs on your person—which I most certainly do not, as I am a gentleman," Christopher rushed to say, "it's not as if anything could ever come of it. Not only are you a man, but you are my manservant, not to mention the matter of my unique situation." He supposed he should feel some measure of fear in mentioning the thing aloud, even if it was only a dream, but in the hazy confines of their private forest, Christopher felt it was the most natural thing in the world to say.

"Very true," Harding agreed, much to Christopher's consternation.

"So then why are we here?" he demanded.

"Would you rather have another awful dream instead?"

Christopher considered this as Harding assisted him over an extremely charming babbling brook. "No, I suppose not. This is much more pleasurable." Something tickled his mind, the sort of thought he would never allow himself in his waking moments. "Although–"

And in a flash, there they were in the middle of Oxford Street. It was the busiest and most horrible street in all of London, as far as Christopher was concerned. Carriages rattled nonstop and there were more bodies crammed onto it than the thing could safely hold. And yet, because it was a dream, Christopher stood untouched by the flowing crowds. Harding's hand was still in his, and with a tug he was led down, down, down to lie atop the thin black line that was Harding's body.

"Look here!" Christopher cried as he was positioned astride those narrow hips. "I don't care if it isn't real! I'm not going to fuck you in the middle of a street!"

"Why not?" Harding's eyes danced with that queer sort of humor that meant he was having a silent laugh at Christopher's expense. "No one seems to mind."

Christopher looked around and saw it was true. Not a single passerby was giving them a glance. It was as if they were invisible to the world around them. "Damn my excellent imagination," Christopher muttered.

"Shall I?" Harding asked, even as his hands reached for Christopher's lapels to shove his coat down his arms.

"Now wait just a moment—" Christopher could not help the panic that gripped him by the throat. He was not sure what would be revealed here if Harding undressed him. Like any healthy young man, Christopher had had his share of scandalous dreams in the past, and the chances of his body appearing as it actually was in waking life were even with his body taking on the shape he wished it would be. Yet those dreams had been so ephemeral and never involved his real acquaintances; this one felt different, and Christopher was seized by the notion that he might disappoint this dream version of Harding somehow.

"It's all right," Harding was saying. "It doesn't matter to me what you look like."

"It matters to me." Christopher grabbed his strong wrists but could not wrench them away as they worked open his waistcoat buttons. "Stop that this instant!"

Harding sat up so that Christopher was balanced in his lap, his capable hands holding him tightly by the hips. His mouth hovered over Christopher's, and for a moment, they merely breathed each other's air. "I'm not permitted to dress you; I'm not permitted to undress you," Harding murmured. His lips brushed against Christopher's in not quite a kiss. "What am I permitted to do, my lord?"

Then, in the usual manner of dreams, their clothing vanished. Christopher screwed his eyes shut and refused to look. He didn't want to know. He didn't want to see.

"Aren't you curious?" Harding whispered in his ear.

He shivered. "Harding . . ."

And then that clever mouth was at his neck, his throat, moving along his jaw as their bodies pressed together. A carriage passed by, much too close, the wheels a mere inch from Christopher's head.

"Harding, no," he panted. "Harding! Ah, Harding!"

"My lord?" Harding said, though his mouth was occupied with nuzzling the point where Christopher's neck met his bare shoulder.

"Harding," he whimpered, and was on the cusp of allowing the dream to run its course, his own dignity be damned, when a harsh shake woke him.

He lay there in his bed, flat on his back in a daze, and blinked up at the dark ceiling. He was covered in a fine sheen of sweat over every inch of his skin, and fine tremors ran through his limbs.

Harding–the actual Harding–swam into view above him, his handsome face pinched in concern. "Lord Eden!"

Christopher yelped and tugged the bedclothes, which were already providing him with all the necessary cover, right up to his chin. He had not worn his bandages to bed. Would his chest's shape somehow be apparent? "What are you doing? You're–I'm–you're supposed to stay in your room all night!"

Much like the master's suite of rooms at Eden Abbey, Christopher's bedroom in the townhouse featured a connected dressing room and valet's quarters, and their previous arrangement regarding Harding's confinement still held.

"You called out for me, my lord."

Christopher blinked. "I did?"

Without deigning to answer, Harding reached out and brushed a lock of sweat-soaked hair from Christopher's brow. In his agitated state, Christopher at first thought the gesture held some note of affection, which made the tremors in his limbs even worse, but soon Harding pressed his palm to Christopher's forehead and he realized it was only for practical reasons that his valet had initiated the touch. "You're a tad warm, but you don't feel feverish. Did you have another terrible dream?"

"Y-yes," Christopher stammered, for he could not tell the truth. "Yes, I must have– Did I really call for you? I didn't intend to."

Harding's cool palm fell away. Christopher tried not to miss it too much. "Perhaps I was in your dream this time, my lord."

"Perhaps. I . . . don't recall." He couldn't look Harding in the eye after what he'd just dreamed. He looked away, his whole face flaming hot. "I am sorry to have disturbed your sleep, dear fellow. Go back to bed; I'm fine, truly."

"If I may be so bold, my lord, you don't seem fine."

Christopher slid his gaze back to Harding, who was hovering at his bedside and dressed in a hastily knotted dressing gown over what looked to be a rather voluminous nightshirt. If his undressed state was not enough to convince Christopher of his sincere worry, there was also a frantic look in his eyes for good measure.

"It happens often enough." Christopher swallowed. "I'm used to it."

"Will you be able to go back to sleep?" Harding asked after the silence had stretched out another moment. When Christopher hesitated to answer and add another lie to the pile, Harding took the initiative. "Why don't I make you a cup of warm milk, my lord? That might help."

"Yes," Christopher agreed. Anything to get Harding out of his bedroom when he was in such a state. "Yes, why don't you go down to the kitchens and get a pot going? I'll join you in a moment."

"Your Lordship can stay in bed if you—"

"I think a little ramble around the house will do me good." Christopher shooed him away. "Go. I'll be down shortly."

Harding reluctantly went to the door and, finding it locked, turned the key in the latch with a quizzical look over his shoulder.

"Right behind you," Christopher said with a wan smile in lieu of explaining why he locked his bedroom door at night.

Harding sketched a bow and disappeared.

Christopher flopped back onto his pillows and grabbed a spare one to press over his red face. "Oh, dear god above." His body was still alight with the memory of that damned dream. What sort of employer—what sort of *man* was he, to have entertained such provocative notions about Harding? How could he calmly sit at a kitchen table with him now, sipping hot milk like nothing untoward had occurred?

He removed the pillow and took a deep breath. Dreams were just dreams, he reminded himself. They were not real and therefore meant nothing. He would stuff this dream down into the sea chest to join all his anxieties, which he'd been ignoring for nearly a decade. And anyway, one dream about the man, however scandalous, hardly meant that Christopher's heart was fixed on him. What he was feeling was obviously jealousy. He wanted to *be* James Harding, not be intimate with him. The dream was merely a metaphor.

Christopher slid his palm under the loose collar of his nightshirt and felt his heart rabbiting in his chest.

An extremely affecting metaphor.

The soft sounds of someone moving in the kitchen below floated to Christopher's ears, and he heaved himself out of bed with a sigh. If he didn't keep his word and venture downstairs, no doubt Harding would come looking for him. He locked the bedroom door anew, stripped off his sweat-damp nightwear, bound his chest with speed, and dressed in a fresh nightshirt, shrugging into his banyan for good measure. He stepped into the house slippers Harding had placed neatly by the door for just such an occasion and made his way down the stairs toward the smell of warm spices.

Christopher paused in the kitchen doorway to watch Harding moving about the room. Several candles had been lit, not to mention the cookstove fire, above which a pan of milk simmered, and by this light Christopher saw that his loyal valet was not perfectly put together. His black hair was mussed, hanging in his eyes as he fiddled with some jars of what looked like cinnamon sticks and bits of clove. The collar of his mud-colored dressing gown was turned up in the back; Christopher's fingers itched to reach out and coax it flat.

He looked, in a word, human. It was rather refreshing—and achingly domestic.

Harding's deep brown eyes flicked up to the doorway and saw Christopher standing there like a frozen fool. "Have a seat, my lord," he said, and pulled out one of the chairs that surrounded the simple kitchen table.

Christopher sat. There was a cloth-covered something on the table near his elbow, and he twitched back the fabric to find a lump of uncooked dough. The morning's bread, he assumed, and left it well alone. He felt suddenly like an interloper in his own house; though he owned the place, this room was meant for his staff. He was infringing on that. He wanted desperately to go back to his bed, if only to lie awake until the sun rose.

Harding plunked a mug in front of him. "Drink that," he said—ordered, really. It should have rankled, to have such a bully for a servant, but Christopher found he was happy to do as Harding said.

He lifted the cup to his lips and took a sip. The milk was warm and gently spiced, like a soothing tea. He hadn't been given warm milk since he was a child; Cook had supplied it then in droves. He drank more deeply and watched Harding over the rim of his mug as he puttered about the kitchen, putting things away and tidying up.

Christopher lowered his mug and wiped away the inevitable milk mustache with the back of his wrist. "Aren't you going to have some?" He glanced at the pan on the cookstove, still half full. "You're awake at this god-awful hour too, after all."

"His Lordship may want the rest," Harding said.

"His Lordship is content with the one cup. Go on." He nodded at the pan. "Drink it before it cools."

Harding hesitated before apparently deciding that Christopher meant what he said. He fetched a clean mug from a high cupboard and deftly poured the remainder of the milk into it with not a drop spilled. He cradled the drink in his fine-boned hands and leaned back against the counter, miles away from the table.

"Will you sit?" Christopher nudged the chair opposite him out from under the table with his foot. "Propriety be damned. I'll break my neck looking up at you."

For a moment, it seemed Harding would decline and remain standing until the world ended, but then he relented, folding himself into the chair much like an umbrella being closed. "Your neck, of course, takes precedence, my lord," he murmured.

Christopher flushed, remembering exactly which parts of his neck had received attention from the dream version of Harding minutes ago. He covered his awkward blushing with a deep drink from his cup.

They sat there at the table in silence for quite some time. After Christopher's face returned to its usual temperature, the atmosphere felt almost companionable. It was deathly quiet, not a thing stirring in the house or in the street. Christopher heard the faint chime of the clock in the hall: three in the morning.

Harding, shockingly, spoke first. "My lord," he said, his thumbnail worrying at a chip in his mug's handle, "I understand you are a private sort of man, and I would never intentionally pry, but these dreams of yours . . ." He lifted his calm gaze to meet Christopher's wide-eyed one across the table. "If you ever wished to speak of them to someone, I would be a willing ear to you."

Christopher opened his mouth, then closed it. He couldn't possibly tell Harding the truth of that night's dream, of course, so he was forced to continue acting out the farce. Still, he couldn't bring himself to hold Harding's gaze, staring instead into the depths of his mug. "They're nothing to worry about, really. I've had them practically all my life." He drained the last dregs of milk from his cup. "It's just one of those tedious things I must bear."

"Must you bear it alone?" Harding said.

Christopher fussed with his cup, turning it this way and that on the tabletop for lack of anything else to do. "I always have. I don't see why I can't continue doing so."

"Lord Eden," Harding sighed, "I have only been in your employ a short while, but I have never heard you scream in your sleep as you did tonight. I worry that your bad dreams are worsening."

Christopher's teeth ground together in his mouth. Oh, the irony! In truth, the last few days had been fairly excellent in terms of his sleep; the bad dreams had been minimal. And yet he could not say so, given how he had recently acted in the throes of Morpheus-induced passion.

"Possibly," he conceded, though the small lie burned in his throat. "It, erm, comes and goes."

Harding pinned him with a look. "Is it the upcoming ball at the Leftmores' that's caused it?" he asked. He had naturally been apprised of the expected invitation as well as the upcoming trip to the tailor's in preparation. "I noticed the event has inspired not a little anxiety in you, my lord."

"Anxiety? In me?" Christopher could not help the way his eyes skittered away to regard the transom above the kitchen door. "Why do you say that? Just because I'm going to be attending my first ball since I came of age where I will no doubt be exposed to the judgment of all of London society and be introduced to my future wife, all while being expected to *dance,* doesn't mean I should be feeling anxious, surely."

"It is good to see your lack of sleep has not affected your sense of humor, my lord," Harding said in that bland tone of his.

Christopher felt his gaze drawn to Harding's like dew to a windowpane. He detected a faint lift in Harding's mouth that meant he found something amusing. "One of these days, my dear fellow, I might even make you laugh. The bells of St. Paul's will ring out, I'm certain."

Harding's face took on an admonishing shape. Of course he wouldn't be deterred by a few silly jokes. "I wish you wouldn't place so much importance on the events of a single night, my lord. You may be introduced to a charming lady, or you may not. You're still young; I know you must be eager, but you have plenty of time to find a wife."

"Eager!" Christopher cried. "That's a fine word for it." His mouth immediately pursed closed. Did he always have to allow his tongue to get away from him like that? He stared into his empty mug and wished it contained something more to drink. Preferably something alcoholic. He turned the cup around and around in his hands instead.

Harding waited for a measure of silence before saying, "Am I correct in thinking a more appropriate word would be 'terrified,' my lord?"

Christopher dredged up a smile from the depths of his soul and plastered it on his face. "Perceptive as usual, Harding." He preferred to skirt the truth of the situation–that he would need to find, somewhere in London, a lady who could be trusted with his secret–and so offered another morsel of fact instead. "I have very little experience with the fairer sex, you see. Not many eligible women traipsing around Eden. Why, I've never even held a lady's hand, let alone . . ." He trailed off, wondering what exactly it was about this midnight tête-à-tête that made him so prone to sharing more than was strictly proper.

Perhaps it was Harding's placid nature, for he responded with a completely blank expression and no judgment in his voice: "Have you never had a kiss, my lord?"

Christopher opened his mouth to deny it, but found he could not. It was already painted on his face, clear as day, he felt. "I admit I have not yet had the pleasure," he said, and it came out sounding less like the saucy throwaway comment he'd meant it to be and more a forlorn sigh. He cleared his throat and cast about for some excuse to take the spotlight off his non-existent love life. "What about you, Harding? Have you kissed any women?"

It was an impertinent question for a man to ask his valet, and yet Harding seemed unbothered. "I have."

"Ah." Christopher shifted in his creaking chair. He thought of all the village girls he'd seen Harding dancing with that one evening in the tavern; surely they lined up for his kisses as they did for their turn at being his dance partner. "Many?" he asked, and if his voice squeaked a bit, it was only because his throat hurt from his earlier screams.

The corner of Harding's mouth was flirting with an upward curl again. No doubt he found Christopher's virginal inquiries very entertaining. "A sufficient amount," he finally said. Despite the self-effacing turn of phrase, he seemed suffused with a confidence that Christopher could only dream of.

And had, come to think of it. He tamped down on that line of thinking.

"It's a shame this is not something that can be practiced," Christopher said, his words punctuated by nervous laughter. "I hate to think of inflicting my unlearned self on the poor girls." His mind supplied a vision of how Harding might prove instructive in such matters, a thought that most assuredly had to be beaten back with a stick and locked away in the mental sea chest before being thrown into a lake. He shouldn't even be having this conversation with his manservant; he certainly couldn't ask him for instruction in how to kiss properly!

"I do not think you have any cause to worry," Harding said. "You are a man of excellent comportment, grace, intelligence, and looks–"

Christopher went warm all the way from the tips of his ears to his toes. "Oh, really now!"

"–but most importantly," Harding charged ahead, "you are gentle and kind. Any number of women will be happy to make your acquaintance should you desire it."

Christopher knew, but was too polite to point out, that Harding was likely only saying these things to ingratiate himself further so that he might be allowed to maintain his position beyond the Season. Still, it was a pretty piece of flattery, as false as it surely was.

"Thank you, Harding," he said quietly, certain a blush was once again painting his cheek. "Shall we go back to our beds? We can get a few more hours' sleep, if we're lucky."

"Let me scrub out the pan and cups first. The serving girls would be miffed if I left dirty dishes for them to wash in the morning." Harding levered himself up from the table with a faint scrape of his chair.

Christopher stood as well and collected their two mugs. "Then, by all means, we should put everything back in its place so the girls are none the wiser." He said it in a jocular manner, but in truth he very much wanted to keep his midnight drink with Harding a secret. Habit, he supposed. The less people knew of his life, the better. It wouldn't do for the temporary staff to whisper about why Lord Eden was up at this god-awful time of night, drinking milk.

He took up a position next to Harding at the water bucket. "Hand me a rag. I will dry as you wash," he said.

Now it was Harding's turn to give him an incredulous look. "You do not honestly expect me to allow Your Lordship to dry the dishes?"

"It's either that or His Lordship sits on his rump and watches you do everything yourself. I want to get to bed before sunrise, so please." Christopher held out his hand. "Rag."

Harding stared at him with a stubborn glint in his eyes, looking more formidable than a man holding a dirty pan had any right to be. Christopher stared right back. This battle of wills might have gone on for the remainder of the night, but Harding at last gave a deep sigh and surrendered a dry cloth to Christopher.

"I will never understand why you think you must play at being a servant, my lord." Harding said. "You don't need to prove anything to me."

"Oh, just shut up and scrub," Christopher said.

Chapter 10

The following morning, Christopher received a note at breakfast that had been hand delivered by the tailors' apprentice. Florid writing filled every inch of the page:

My dearest Lord Eden–

So you finally return to grace London and myself with the perfume of your presence! I am aware of the ball you have mentioned, as well as what every man of quality plans to wear on the evening in question. Your own formal attire, though hastily constructed, shall be a jewel among pebbles, if I may be so bold. Despite your tardiness in placing such an order, I believe the result will delight you. I took the liberty of cutting your coat quite daringly, as I'm sure you will agree anything else would be a waste of your waist. The buttons you may find some quibble with, but I assure you they will be de rigueur within a month's time in this country; already they have overtaken the continent. I doubt you will find any fault with the breeches. I won't hear any arguments about them, not that I expect any from a man of taste such as yourself. As for the final trimmings, I leave the decision on fabrics and color to you. Please come to the shop today so that you may approve my excellent suggestions. If you arrive closer to midday, we will likely have more time to ourselves.

Yours in haste,
É

Christopher shook his head and muttered fondly, "Ah, Étienne, never change."

He glanced at one of the serving girls, who was delivering his eggs and kippers on a plate, but she gave no sign of having heard him. She merely plopped the food in front of him and disappeared. Christopher sighed as he picked up his knife and fork. What he wouldn't give for a simple morning bun and a cup of strong tea, not this weak stuff the temporary staff had brewed for him. Alas, he was not at Eden Abbey and so could not breakfast with Cook and Plinkton as he preferred. He was stuck here with this very competent but not at all familiar staff, and so was forced to eat his eggs in the informal dining room like a normal earl would.

He ate quickly to get it over with.

"Will we be visiting your tailor this morning, my lord?" a voice suddenly said at his elbow.

Christopher choked on a kipper in surprise. Harding helpfully poured more tea into his cup so he could wash it down. After Christopher had regained his ability to swallow, he asked, "Where exactly do they teach you servants how to move so silently? It's not natural. Please, for my sake, try to make a sound once in a while."

"My apologies, my lord. I will try." Harding nodded at the note sitting next to Christopher's plate. "I overheard the messenger boy at the door. He told the maid he was from the Brothers Charbonneau. Am I wrong in thinking you will be fitted for your new clothes today?"

"Wonderful deduction as usual," Christopher muttered around a piece of toast.

"Then I shall change into my livery so I may accompany you," Harding said. He was wearing his normal ensemble of too-much-black at the moment.

Christopher gave him a wild look. He hoped he wasn't sporting any crumbs on his face from the toast; he wanted to project an air of authority. "Accompany me? Why should you accompany me?"

"I am your valet," Harding said simply. "Is this not one of my duties to assist in your tailoring decisions?"

Christopher tossed the final tiny triangle of toast back onto his plate. A visit to his tailor—a *private* visit—was one of the only joys London had to offer him, and he was not going to give it up, not even to accommodate Harding's work ethic.

"My dear fellow," Christopher said, "I will go to my tailor alone and that is final."

Less than an hour later, Christopher was turning his curricle faster than was strictly safe onto Savile Row with Harding, damn him, sitting right beside him on the narrow seat.

"Are we at risk of missing your appointment, my lord," Harding asked as they jostled over the cobblestones at breakneck speed, "or are you incapable of driving at a sedate pace?" He held his tricorn hat as well as the wig beneath firmly against his head lest the wind whip them away.

Christopher gave a mirthless harrumph. "You insist on joining me only to insult my driving? Don't you have other things to do today? Surely you're not finished with all the unpacking." He maneuvered the horses–fast, but not as fast as Orion–around a plodding team of donkeys attached to a dog cart, narrowly avoiding a screeching cat that bolted across the lane.

"I am, actually," Harding rejoined, "and I believe I am wholly necessary when it comes to your wardrobe."

Christopher heaved a groan of frustration and brought the curricle to a skidding stop along the curb. He turned to his valet with the reins still tight in his hands. "Harding, I have been a patron of the Brothers Charbonneau since I've been out of leading strings. I have never once required a chaperone whilst shopping."

"My lord, it's my privilege to guide you in choosing new pieces. It has been quite some time since you last visited London, and the fashions–"

Christopher gave him a withering look. "Do you find my current mode of dress so unfashionable?"

Harding's gaze roamed Christopher's person at the question. Christopher bore it as well as he could, refusing to blush or stammer at the attention. He wondered what Harding might see when he looked at him like that. Probably a strange sort of dandy who insisted on wearing his pale colors when everyone knew jewel tones were all the rage; who had tied his cravat in a pattern he had devised himself after studying the latest examples; and who wore his boots with just a mite more heel than most young men would.

"No, my lord," Harding finally said. "I only meant you may find it useful to have my opinion before making selections."

"I am perfectly capable of ordering my own clothes."

"Then at least allow me to make the acquaintance of your tailor, sir," Harding said, "so that if there is some detail I must see to or some last-minute order that must be placed, he will know me as your valet."

It was a sensible request. Christopher knew from long afternoons spent at the Charbonneaus' shop that other gentlemen's manservants practically treated the place as a guild hall. They were constantly flitting in and out, speaking in that truncated way that efficient workers did. "My lord needs four more like the last two," for example, or "His Grace wants it in velvet after all; can you manage that?" The three brothers who owned the toggery were on a first name basis with practically every valet in town. It would be odd for Harding not to be introduced, at the very least.

And Christopher was already pushing the boundaries of odd.

He gave a sniff and tossed Harding the reins so he could tie up the horses. "Very well. Have you ever had any dealings with the Charbonneaus for your former employers?"

Harding alighted from the curricle and made use of the wrought iron post at the roadside. "No, sir."

"Well, be forewarned. They are quite French."

"I had assumed so, given the name."

Christopher hid his smile. No one could be prepared for just how French the Brothers Charbonneau were, and it was frankly adorable that Harding thought he was.

He leapt down from the seat and marched in the direction of the storefronts. "An introduction, Harding, but then you must go away and let me be fitted in peace!"

"Another excellent compromise, my lord," Harding said, keeping up with Christopher's pace easily on his longer legs.

The shop was like most on the Row: a well-kept little storefront with a sign in gold letters swinging above the entrance. Christopher was about to push his way inside, but Harding beat him to the door and held it open for him as he entered. Inside, the shop was crammed with bolts of fabric in every hue and texture lining the walls and stacked on tables. Several dress forms held works in progress, pieces of coats and trousers coming together to form exquisite clothing. The scent of clean linen and wool filled the air, and Christopher inhaled deeply. It smelled of home, or as near as he could get in this city.

"Étienne?" Christopher called into the reaches of the shop as he removed his hat and gloves. "I got your note."

A small blur of ruffles and silk rushed in and grabbed Christopher by the hands. "Lord Eden!" Étienne kissed him twice on both cheeks before kissing him squarely on the tip of his nose. "It's been far too long!"

Christopher accepted the greeting with good grace. "Hello, Étienne," he said warmly.

Of the three brothers, Étienne Charbonneau was the youngest and the most shameless. He was a delicate man, even smaller than Christopher, with a head full of dark curls and a perpetual glint of laughter in his eyes. When Christopher had first ventured into their shop all those years ago, it had been with great trepidation. Just out of Cambridge, he had gone to nearly a dozen other tailors in London that week only to find that none would suit. They had all been very talented, of course, and more than polite when showing the Earl of Eden the fabrics they kept on hand and the sketches of various styles they offered, but Christopher could not imagine allowing any of them to touch his person in the intimate way a man's tailor must when procuring his measurements. He'd almost been convinced that he would be forced to wear a potato sack for the rest of his life—but then he had met Étienne, who could rightly be called Christopher's confidant.

The youngest Charbonneau had been minding the shop on his own that fateful day, when Christopher, younger and much less wise, had crept in to ask tentatively after some new braces. Étienne had taken one look at his outmoded coat and held his trusty length of measuring tape aloft.

"You are the Earl of Eden, yes?" he'd said. "Every tailor in the city has tried to fit you for a new wardrobe, but each time you— What is the phrase? Run like rabbits."

"Well, I—" Christopher tried to say. "I didn't quite run." He picked up one heeled foot. "These shoes scarcely allow it."

"Come." Étienne had stabbed a finger in the direction of the back dressing rooms, which were hidden behind a length of blue velvet curtain. "You are too good-looking a man to be wearing that."

"Now, wait a moment!"

Christopher had been bundled into the dressing room before he even knew what was happening.

"I have seen everything," Étienne promised him. "Short, tall, fat, thin: there is no type of man I have not measured."

"Are you absolutely certain of that?" Christopher muttered.

Étienne had leaned in close and placed his hands on Christopher's cheeks, causing him to gape like a landed fish. "Whatever the source of your anxiety, my lord," he said, all flighty pretense evaporating, "I assure you, there will be no judgment on my part. I am the very soul of discretion. Your tailor is like your priest." His eyes darted about the confines of the space. "This room is a confessional. Whatever happens here, the world will never know."

Somehow, for some reason, he found himself believing Étienne. "I see," Christopher had said, though with his cheeks squished as they were it came out a bit muffled.

Étienne dropped his hands. "Now! On which side do you dress?" he asked in a perfunctory manner. "Left or right?"

"Neither," Christopher said. It was the boldest word he'd ever spoken, and his heart felt as if it would pop out of his throat as he uttered it. "I dress on no side whatsoever."

Étienne did not miss a beat. "Ah, so your lines will be without fault. Excellent. A clean silhouette is truly the ideal. Excuse my reach, my lord." And he placed his hand high up on Christopher's thigh, right in the crease where his leg met his trunk. Étienne's tongue poked from his mouth in concentration as he ran the measuring tape down Christopher's inseam.

Christopher held his breath. He had never fainted in his life, but he thought he might now. Fortunately, Étienne was quick and his touch professional. He soon stood back with the tape slung around his neck.

"Your shirt, please, sir." He gestured to the billowy expanse of snowy linen that Christopher was still wearing.

Christopher regarded him with narrowed eyes. "I am not a violent man," he said slowly.

Étienne's eyebrows winged upward. "I should hope not, my lord."

"But if you breathe a word of this to anyone, I will shoot you in the street like a dog." He paused. "And then shoot your brothers for good measure."

"Does His Lordship carry a dueling pistol with him today?" Étienne asked with a distinct lack of concern.

"Well, no–"

"Then I think we have nothing to fear. Now come." Étienne plucked Christopher's shirttails from his trousers.

Christopher stripped his shirt off the rest of the way, revealing the bandages beneath. Étienne looked at them for a moment, then shrugged. "I would recommend the thicker linen, my lord." He grabbed a bolt from its place on the wall and held the tail of the fine fabric to the light. "You see? Quite sturdy. Even if you were to find yourself without a waistcoat for some reason, it would offer you more modesty, I think."

"Monsieur Charbonneau–" Christopher began, smiling.

"Please, Monsieur Charbonneau is my eldest brother. Call me Étienne, I insist."

"Very well. Étienne." Christopher held out his arms. "I would very much like to be fitted now."

That had been many years ago, and many measurements

later, Étienne was still the only person with whom Christopher felt wholly safe (though even he did not know the entire story of how Christopher had come to be the Earl of Eden).

Christopher now turned to regard Harding over his shoulder. The man appeared largely unmoved by the display of continental affection, though Christopher thought he detected a slight raise of his thick brows. *French,* he mouthed soundlessly, feeling somewhat smug about it. Then, clearing his throat, he turned back to his tailor. Their hands were still clutched between them. "Allow me to introduce my valet, Mr. James Harding. He may call on you from time to time as my proxy."

Étienne's gaze swept up and down Harding's form, lingering on his legs. Christopher gave his fine-boned hands a little squeeze in warning, and those eyes snapped back to him. "A valet? You? Oh, my dear." He switched from his accented English to rapid-fire French, which Christopher followed as closely as he could given that it was only his second tongue. "I never thought I would see the day. Is he to attend the fitting as well?"

"No, of course not," Christopher returned in his serviceable French. "This is a temporary arrangement, just for the Season."

"Do not tell me 'of course not' when it is not so clear!" Étienne darted another look at Harding, who seemed to be taking all this in stride, standing there placidly. "I, for one, would seek to make such an arrangement last as long as possible. Those calves, Christopher." From his inner coat pocket, he extracted a fan made of delicate lacework and unfurled it to beat the air near his face. "Thank god above for these uniforms, eh?"

"Étienne! Stop staring. What would Bernard say?" Bernard was the third son of a family of well-to-do merchants as well as Étienne's lover. The two had a long-standing arrangement, though of course they could only meet in secret, usually under the guise of a fitting.

Étienne made a gesture that could only be described as Gallic. "My Bernard would agree with me, of course. We both have eyes."

Christopher rolled his. "Be that as it may, if you could refrain from being a complete strumpet for just a moment," he said, still in French, "I would appreciate it. That is my manservant you're talking about."

"So territorial." Étienne sighed, darting another scandalous glance at Harding's legs. "Though who could blame you?" The tailor had never tried to hide his own particular persuasion from Christopher, a show of friendship that Christopher greatly appreciated, but in this moment, he did wish the full force of Étienne's thirst for strapping men wasn't being directed at Harding. There were a thousand others he could leer at, after all. A decidedly nasty part of Christopher's mind pointed out that, as working men, Harding and Étienne had much more in common than Christopher did with either of them, but he told that voice it could go to hell. This one was out of bounds—and he conveyed that message to his tailor with a withering glare.

Harding gave a polite cough into his fist. "Shall I wait outside, my lord?" he asked. His voice held a frosty note to it.

Christopher had a moment's panic where he thought perhaps Harding could parse their French, but he realized it would be exceedingly rare for a servant to have been exposed to such education, and so he relaxed.

"Yes, why don't you find a public house and have something to eat?" he suggested. "I'll be a while with Étienne."

Harding gave the tailor a cool look that seemed to indicate his dissatisfaction with his master spending a minute more in his presence, but his face soon returned to its implacable mask. He gave a bow and a murmured "My lord" before departing.

Étienne watched him leave with much interest. Once the door had shut, he stuck his elbow into Christopher's ribs and switched back to English. "It took you ages to get a valet, but if that is the result, perhaps it was worth the wait."

"You're incorrigible," Christopher said, but his judgmental tone was marred by the laughter that bubbled up from within him at his friend's antics. He gave Étienne a playful shove. "Now tell me: Is it ready?"

"Your ensemble for the ball? I must still have your opinion on the colors, Lord Eden."

"No, not the ensemble—let's worry about that last." His eyes darted around the shop, but he didn't see any sign of Étienne's brothers. "The *other* thing."

"Ah yes!" Étienne rushed back into the depths of the shop, and Christopher followed with his heart thrumming. "My brothers are having their midday meal as well, so we won't be disturbed."

They passed huge bolts of fabric of every pattern, the stacks reaching the ceiling or leaning along the wall in neat rows. Christopher would have normally allowed himself the pleasure of touching each one and feeling the fine softness of expensive material against his fingertips, but today he had a more pressing goal. He followed on Étienne's heels as they slipped into a tiny, cramped room that served as a private workshop, where Étienne could practice his craft away from his older brothers' prying eyes. Among other practices, of course.

"Here we are," he said, moving aside some heavy stacks of cloth to reveal a small chest on a high shelf. "Remember, this is just a trial fitting. It may take a few more before I achieve perfection."

"I'm aware. Now give it here." Christopher could not hide his eagerness, bouncing in his well-heeled boots.

Étienne handed over the garment with quiet reverence, like a mother holding her child out for the vicar at a christening. It was a nondescript piece of cloth, just a plain, pale thing that any casual observer might mistake for a particularly rough and unforgiving chemise. But Christopher unfolded it like it was the most precious silk brocade.

"Oh," he said in a whisper. "There it is."

The garment was shaped as a waistcoat might be, except instead of a row of buttons down the front, there was a series of small hook-and-eye closures along the left side, where the panes of cloth met under the armhole. The whole thing was constructed out of canvas, with very little give in the structure. Christopher set it aside atop a pile of silver buttons and immediately began untying his cravat.

"And I will be able to put it on and off it by myself?" he asked with undisguised glee.

Étienne bobbed his head. "That is my hope. Let us see, my friend. Come, come."

He took Christopher's coat and helped him slip out of his waistcoat and cravat. Once Christopher's shirt had also been removed, Étienne very decently turned his back, feigning some pressing need to fold the shirt in a neat square while Christopher unwound the bandages from his chest. During their long association, Christopher had often bared his body in front of Étienne, and he could do so without too much distress, but it was a near thing. Étienne, bless his soul, gave Christopher what privacy he could in such trusted moments.

Christopher completed the laborious task of unwrapping his chest and quickly shrugged into the new garment. Étienne had a tailor's ear for the slightest shift in fabric and must have heard the canvas settling into place, for he spun around with a wide grin.

"How does it feel?" he asked.

Christopher's fingers fumbled with the many closures along his left flank. "Hold on. I have about a thousand of these to do; must there be so many?"

"Unfortunately, for the sake of the structure, it must." Étienne stepped forward and reached for the hook and eye that kept slipping from Christopher's grip. "May I?"

"I need to be able to do it myself," Christopher pointed out. "It's not as if Harding will be able to assist me every morning, you know."

"You will, you will. With practice, my friend. For now, we must check the fit."

"Oh, all right," Christopher relented, dropping his hands and allowing Étienne's masterful fingertips to fiddle with the closures. "Good lord, you're quick."

"Practice," Étienne repeated. "I cannot tell you how many girdles I have put on and taken off my clients. The theory is much the same." He finished with the final hook and gave a little cry of triumph. "Let us look at you." He spun Christopher around to face the opposite wall, where a full-length mirror stood half covered with scarves of sumptuous silk. Étienne plucked the scarves away, letting them fall to the floor, and Christopher at last saw himself in the new garment Étienne had designed especially for him.

His breath caught. The piece itself was unadorned, no lace or ribbon, exactly as Christopher had requested. The canvas was taut with not an inch of give. It was not what he would call a flattering piece of clothing–the tight fit meant that some of the more squishy flesh under his arms bulged where the armholes met it–but it served its purpose wonderfully. Christopher's chest was completely flattened, and unlike the loads of linen bandages, this binding waistcoat was thin, unlikely to be noticed beneath his layers of togs. Best of all, the discomfort he felt around his middle was greatly reduced. The bandages tended to squeeze at his ribs until they creaked, not to mention the chafing. This garment still produced the welcome tightening sensation across his upper body, but it wasn't painful.

"How many can you give me?" he blurted out, turning this way and that to admire his much-reduced silhouette in the mirror's reflection.

"Six or seven, I should think," said Étienne. "It is not the sewing that is the issue, of course; it is quite a simple thing to produce. The problem is finding the time to produce them without my brothers watching me." He rolled his eyes toward the ceiling and muttered a quick prayer in French to the Virgin Mary. "Mother, bless and protect the youngest sons, for they have the worst asses as brothers."

Six or seven. An absolute treasure trove, as far as Christopher was concerned. "Do what you can," he said. He placed a hand on his flat chest, gaze still on the mirror. "I will pay handsomely, I promise you."

Étienne flitted around him, nudging at this or that part of Christopher's body, humming at each seam. "I think I can improve the fit, if you would be so kind as to allow me to make some adjustments before I take it back?"

Christopher nodded. "I don't think I want to take it off just yet anyway," he said, and watched as his friend produced a needle and thread from mere ether and set to work, pins bristling between his lips.

"With this invention of mine," Étienne said between the pins, "you'll be able to dance all night if you like! And with no fear of bandages unraveling."

Christopher was not a complete failure on the dance floor, but he was not exactly looking forward to spinning away for hours in a press of bodies. Still, at least the new undergarment would make the thing slightly more comfortable.

Once the measurements were taken and the binding waistcoat was back in the hands of its creator, Christopher dressed himself anew. He and Étienne then made themselves at home atop piles of velvets and silks in the private workshop, judiciously opening a bottle of good wine that Étienne kept on hand for just such an afternoon.

"So," Étienne said as he poured for them. "This new valet of yours." His eyebrows did something that Christopher was fairly sure was obscene.

"He has a name." Christopher flicked a piece of stray thread from his knee, an unavoidable consequence of sitting in a tailor's domain. "I'll have you know Harding has proven very capable. Though he balked at first at not being able to dress me, I believe we have settled into something of an understanding. He's been invaluable these last few days. Oh, and his horsemanship isn't bad at all!" His head popped up and his eyes shone. "Can you credit it? He's been accompanying me on my daily rides back at the Abbey."

"A valet who can ride." Étienne pulled his mouth into a considering pout. "I can imagine. Impressive, no?" He didn't bother suppressing a devilish giggle.

Christopher grabbed the nearest handful of cotton batting and flung it at his friend's ridiculous face. "Can you try not to be lecherous for a single moment?" he cried as Étienne only laughed harder. "You make it sound so tawdry when it's anything but."

Étienne gasped in mock offense and held his cup of wine close to his chest. "Are you honestly telling me you do not notice how handsome this Harding of yours is? Even if you do not share my love of men, certainly you can appreciate them from afar. Like a painting. Or well-cut coat."

"Of course I've noticed," Christopher said. "I even had a bit of a, erm, pleasant dream about him last night."

Étienne practically crowed at this. "A nocturnal visit, eh? And you call me a lecher—you're the one lusting after your luscious man!"

"Yes, I suppose I am. Though I–" He ran his fingertips around the rim of the teacup that was serving as his wineglass. Even with Étienne, his closest companion, he wasn't sure if he could be entirely candid on this subject.

Étienne leaned forward on one elbow, his eyes wide and delighted. "Yes, my dear Lord Eden?"

A sigh blew through Christopher. If he couldn't bare his soul to Étienne, then to whom would it ever be bared?

"I worry," Christopher said carefully, "that it makes me less of a man."

Étienne gave a little frown and snuggled farther into his pile of silks. "Do you think I am less of a man for taking Bernard into my bed?" he asked.

"No, of course not," Christopher was quick to say, "but my case is different."

"Because of how you are shaped?" Étienne asked.

"Precisely."

Étienne drank his wine deeply, his eyes fixed on the cloth-draped ceiling of the little workshop as he contemplated this. Finally, he said, "There are all sorts of men in this world, my dear Christopher. I have seen them in the altogether countless times. Their manhood has nothing to do with their *manhood,* as far as I can tell."

Christopher's face flushed. "Étienne!"

"What? I do not name names! I'm merely saying, why should you be held to a higher standard?"

"Point taken," Christopher said. He paused in taking another sip of wine to watch Étienne drain his cup. "So you don't think it means I'm not a real man if I want–that? With another man, I mean."

"Oh, my dear." Étienne scoffed. "'Real men.' There are no real men, I think. There are only the men who pursue their desires and those who ignore them. And you, Lord Eden, have pursued more than most. Don't forget that, eh?"

"Thank you, Étienne. I shan't," Christopher said. He raised his teacup in an impromptu toast. "But I'm still not going to fuck my valet. Delectable as he may be, my energies are better spent on more important things. I have a duty to the earldom, after all."

"Duty!" Étienne groaned. "I am so bored by duty. Can we not get drunk and go swim in the Thames right this moment instead?"

"I'm afraid not." Christopher swallowed the last of his wine and set the cup on a stack of orders. "I have a reputation to uphold, such as it is." Not to mention he couldn't swim.

Étienne gave him a look. "Since when do you care for your reputation, Lord Eden?"

"Since I received a letter from my solicitors regarding my father's will." He sighed and told Étienne the entire story. It lifted some of the burden from his shoulders to share the truth with someone, though he hated thinking of his imminent and unwanted marriage. "So you see," he said as his tale drew to a close, "I need to find a willing bride, and quickly."

"I have a suggestion for you, then," said Étienne. He folded his hands behind his head. "Miss Verbena Montrose."

Christopher waited for more information following this pronouncement, but none seemed forthcoming. "Who is that?" he finally asked.

"Who is–?" Étienne sputtered, sitting upright. "You really

have been away from London for too long. She's all anyone's been talking about. Every man who comes into the shop—" Étienne made a puppet with his hand, snapping its mouth open and closed. "Miss Montrose this, Miss Montrose that. So lovely! So charming! Such a wit!"

Christopher frowned. "If she is as popular as all that," he said, "then I should seek another. Surely she would never accept my proposal if she is entertaining so many legitimate ones."

"Ah, see, that is the problem," Étienne said. "She has not had any offers yet. Her father lost his money on some business scheme, so no man has dared make a move. She is determined to find a husband, however. If she could only find one who did not care for her nonexistent dowry . . ." Étienne trailed off meaningfully.

Christopher groaned. "She's desperate, you mean." He didn't enjoy the idea of taking advantage of the poor girl's financial need.

"Not desperate; it is too early in the Season for that. But it makes me wonder if, given her ambition, Miss Montrose might be amenable?"

Christopher hummed in thought. It wasn't the worst idea he'd ever heard. "Do you think she will be at the Leftmores' ball this Saturday?" he asked.

Étienne looked at him with deep pity in his eyes. "My dear, everyone will be at the Leftmores' ball this Saturday. Well." He waggled his head. "Everyone who shares your station, I mean."

"Then I will strike up a conversation with her there, see if she seems the type to—" Christopher shrugged. "Keep secrets, I suppose."

“She will likely do that and more if it means becoming Lady Eden,” Étienne said with a knowing cock of his brow. “Now, shall I show you your ensemble for the ball?”

Christopher let out an long-suffering sigh. “I suppose you must.”

Chapter 11

The official invitation arrived the next morning. Christopher watched from an armchair in the sitting room as Harding bore it to him on a silver salver. He picked it up between thumb and forefinger like it was a particularly noxious insect.

"Smells of anise," he muttered. He so hated anise.

The Leftmore invitation came engraved on the creamiest of card stock with the names unfurling in dainty calligraphy. Every detail spoke of opulence and taste. *Your Attendance is Most Anticipated,* it read.

The threat was implicit: show up or be shunned.

Christopher had no intention of being shunned until after his wretched marriage, and so he would go. More importantly, everyone who was even a middling member of the ton would be in attendance. Christopher's future wife, he was certain, would be there. If not Verbena Montrose, then someone else. All he had to do was find her.

But first he would need to be seen about town. He headed

to his dressing room to change. A ride in St. James's Park, he thought, would not only soothe his frazzled nerves, but announce to all and sundry that the eligible young Lord Eden had arrived in London, if they hadn't already been informed. He could only hope that the whispers that reached the ears of ladies such as Verbena Montrose were flattering ones.

He chose as his riding ensemble a waistcoat of fine silk the color of Eden Abbey's sun-bleached stones and a velvet coat in the most delicate shade of peach. He wore shining buff leather boots with tassels dangling from their tops. For his cravat, he attempted a new knot that reminded one of a flag in the wind, perfect for an active gentleman. Christopher gauged his appearance in the looking glass and wondered if he might ever catch the eye of someone like Harding, or if such daydreams were not worth entertaining.

A knock sounded at the dressing room door, startling a gasp from him. He clutched at his chest in embarrassment, as if he could take hold of his galloping heart and make it stop. As he was fully clothed, he opened the door to find Harding himself standing there.

"Please, don't knock so loudly, Harding. Have mercy on the young master. A tap would suffice, or a light rap. You could even whistle, if you know how."

"Apologies, my lord," Harding said as he strode into the dressing room. "I'm afraid I do not know how to whistle."

"You can learn, surely." Christopher shot his cuffs.

"Perhaps His Lordship can teach me," Harding offered with an amused curl of his lip.

"No, he certainly cannot. I've absolutely no idea how to

whistle." Christopher puckered his lips and made an ineffectual blubbering sound. "But it seems like one of the things a valet should know, does it not?" He turned back to the mirror and adjusted the wings of his cravat once more. "Harding, I want you to tell me honestly: What is your opinion on these clothes?"

In the mirror's reflection, he could see Harding's brow raising at being asked for his thoughts. "You wear them well, my lord," he said. "If I may?" His hands hovered at Christopher's shoulders, and Christopher assumed there must be a bit of fluff or something stuck there. It was almost sweet of Harding, he thought, to be asking permission for such an innocent thing.

"Please," he said. But Harding did not reach for any fluff. He reached instead around Christopher and rearranged the fall of his cravat. With his extra height, it wasn't an impossible endeavor, but still Christopher felt the intimacy of the thing like a gunshot to his chest—arms around him, Harding's breath on his cheek as he leaned forward to see better, his scent surrounding him. Leather and bootblack and something like fresh linen. Christopher stared down at the hands working at his throat, then looked up and saw their joined reflection in the mirror, Harding's face pinched in concentration beside his own slack-jawed visage.

Christopher shut his mouth with a snap.

"There." Harding retreated, leaving the cravat in a more perfect windswept formation. "That should hold through a dozen rides, should His Lordship so desire."

Christopher touched the delicate shape of the knots at his throat, watching it bob beneath his chin. It was endlessly fascinating to him, the ways in which beauty and softness still suffused his life even now after living ten years of it outside petticoats.

"Thank you, dear fellow," he said. "It's lovely. I suppose I must look my best for Verbena Montrose, after all."

Harding's left eyebrow made contact with his hairline. Christopher could follow its rise in the mirror. "Who, my lord?"

"Ah, she's this– She's a lady," Christopher explained.

"Yes, I gathered that much," Harding murmured, then set to work making tiny adjustments to the fall of Christopher's tail coat. "I thought you said your heart wasn't set on any lady in particular, sir. I was under the impression that your visit to London had more of an . . . exploratory nature." His tone, strangely enough, was the same cool one he'd used with Étienne.

"Oh, no, you misunderstand," Christopher said with haste. "I've never met Miss Montrose before. I don't have my heart set at all, really." He winced at his own reflection. "That sounds rather callous. Erm, perhaps I should explain."

"You need never explain yourself to me, my lord," Harding intoned. He sounded so serious, Christopher worried that he was about to whip out a penknife and make it a blood oath.

He sighed. Harding was already partway into his confidence, and he'd proven himself a stalwart manservant. And he was clever–Christopher had to admit that his cravats had never looked neater. There was also the matter of their late-night conversation, which was still ringing in Christopher's ears. With the exception of Étienne, he had never met a man with whom he felt so at ease. And since he had unburdened himself so recently in Étienne's company and still felt the wonderful effects in his lightened soul, the temptation to do so again was impossible to ignore. He decided that Harding should be privy to as many details as he could sensibly provide, such as the actual reason behind his sudden desire to marry.

"It's like this, Harding," he said. "I'm in a bit of a rush to secure a lady's hand. If it were up to me, I would be back at Eden Abbey in front of a warm fire with a good book. However, the previous Lord Eden had other plans." He gave a helpless shrug. "I'm to marry before my next birthday if I am to retain my title and inheritance. My father's will demands it."

Harding looked as startled as Christopher had ever seen him, which is to say, his eyes widened just a fraction. "I thought—so you have no interest in being married beyond this necessity, my lord?"

"Exactly, Harding. Trust me when I say that a wife is the last thing I want." He dusted a hand down his sleeve, but it was completely clean already, so there was no need. "I have it on good authority that Miss Montrose is the type of lady who might be interested in my proposal. I was hoping to make an impression this afternoon; even if she is not present on the promenade, word may reach her yet."

"I imagine a good many women would be interested, my lord," Harding said. He sounded a little miffed at the prospect.

Christopher shook his head. "I don't think so, not when I plan to be completely honest with the lady in question."

"My lord?" Harding inclined his head.

"About the marriage," Christopher clarified. He hesitated, but then forged ahead. In for a penny, after all. "I don't want the poor girl to sign the marriage contract if she thinks there is any possibility of . . . affection." It was a good enough euphemism, besides being literally true. Christopher didn't think it prudent to get into the details of why he wouldn't be sharing his future wife's bed or giving her children. "I expect this marriage to be in name only. My wife, whomever she may be, should expect the same."

This statement caused both eyebrows to climb Harding's face. "You sound very certain, my lord."

"Is that a hint of reproach I hear?" Christopher gave him an admonishing look in the glass. "I am certain. Love is for other people, Harding. It's not in the cards for me. It's only that I find myself in an inconvenient spot, and I wish above all else to project complete normalcy so that when I do propose, there will be no doubts about my respectability and fitness as a husband. The lady in question deserves that much, I think."

He turned away from the mirror, having fiddled with every part of his ensemble that could possibly be fiddled with. He found Harding standing much too close, and regarding him very seriously.

"Most men," he said carefully, "would not be concerned with the lady's feelings on the matter and would secure their marriage as quickly as possible using whatever means might be available."

Christopher frowned. "I suppose they might. One hears stories. Personally, I believe it is the height of cruelty to deceive a woman so." He thought of a very sad and alone Lady Eden shut up in the Abbey like a prisoner, her dreams of a loving marriage—or even a functional one—forever dashed. No, he couldn't stomach the thought. He shook his head. "That is not the sort of man I want to be," he said.

"And what sort of man *do* you want to be, my lord?" Harding asked.

The question took Christopher aback. He was not used to philosophical discussions before dinner. "I'm not entirely sure," he said at last. Their closeness reminded him, for some reason, of his last conversation with Étienne. Of what kind of man he was. But of course Harding was not referring to his taste in theoretical bedmates, only his morals. Christopher considered the matter. "A good man, if possible. But sometimes I fear I'm too late for that."

It was more than he'd meant to share, and the words hung in the air above their heads long after Christopher had uttered them. Harding's lips parted like he was about to say something else, but then the clatter of hooves came to a stop right outside the townhouse window, and he cleared his throat instead. "That will be your horse at the door, my lord."

"Good." Christopher gave himself a little shake to try to dispense with some of the heaviness that had overtaken him. He sighed deeply. "I'm off, then. Pray that this city nag is capable of a few turns around the park."

"I selected the creature myself, my lord. She is not as spirited as your Orion," he said with a slight smile, "but she will suffice."

"Excellent. Will you fetch the mounting block for me?" Christopher asked as he slipped on his tan riding gloves.

"Of course, my lord."

"It's a shame you can't–" Christopher sealed his lips shut.

"A shame I cannot what, my lord?" Harding asked.

Come with me, Christopher had been about to say. *Keep me company as I parade about the city. Talk to me about nothing in particular. Advise me on my situation, now that you know nearly all the truth behind it.*

An impossible desire, and equally impossible to speak aloud.

"Nothing," Christopher said in the end.

They left the cloistered world of the dressing room and marched out to meet the footman, Harding quiet at his side, Christopher's heart pounding in his throat.

Chapter 12

"Pour me a brandy, will you, Harding?" Christopher collapsed into his armchair with a pained groan. It was well into evening now, though the unseasonable heat was not stopping for anyone, even Time. Christopher was sweating in his clothes. He so hated to sweat. "And one for yourself," he added as an afterthought.

Harding paused in the middle of opening the decanter. "My lord?"

"Don't 'my lord' me like that, not after the day I've had." He rubbed at his tired eyes. There was far too much dust in this city. His nose especially felt clogged with it. His handkerchief would probably need to be burned; he had expelled a rather alarming amount of black soot into it over the course of the last few hours. And on top of the London air trying to murder him, Christopher had been expected to be sociable, which was a fate worse than murder in his opinion. "You have no idea how many times I had to bring that bloody horse to a halt to greet some 'dear old friend' of my father's or a 'distant but loving cousin' of my mother's. Lord above, you'd think my parents had connections to every single soul in the empire. Not that any of these people showed the slightest bit of interest in my well-being after their deaths, mind you! I deserve at least one glass of brandy, I should think."

"Forgive me, my lord," Harding said. "I was actually questioning why I should pour for myself as well."

"Oh." Christopher dropped his hands, letting them flop onto the chair arms. "Well, I suppose I didn't wish to drink alone," he explained. "If you would join me, I'd be much obliged." He tipped his head over the side of the wingback to look Harding up and down. "Do you drink? I suppose you at least drink beer," he said, remembering the night he'd seen Harding at Eden's End, "but if you'd rather not imbibe hard liquor—"

"No, my lord, I do not mind brandy. If you insist, I will join you." He righted another glass of cut crystal and filled it as well. "And I am sorry to hear that your ride in the park caused you so much distress," he murmured as he brought both drinks to Christopher on a silver serving tray.

Christopher chose one of the glasses for himself. "Thank you, Harding. You've really gone above and beyond what is expected of a valet."

"Sharing a drink at the end of a long day is not much of a hardship," Harding pointed out before taking his own glass, then stowing the tray back in its spot on the sideboard. He might have stood there all night, but Christopher waved him into the armchair opposite his own.

"Sit, sit. I'll get a crick in my neck staring up at you."

Harding folded himself into the chair, though he sat upright on the very edge of the seat as if anticipating the moment he'd be called upon to serve.

"Relax, if you can," Christopher said with a smile. He sipped at his drink and watched Harding forcibly sit back another inch in the plush armchair, his own glass clutched in one hand. Better. Perhaps the best they could hope for, given Harding's sense of propriety.

"So," he said, unspooling his first conversational gambit, "the Leftmores' ball is in two days' time. Do you have any opinions on what I should wear to this dreary affair?"

Harding smiled into his brandy as he drank. "Several opinions, my lord. I've already laid out a few options on the bench in your dressing room, if you'd care to look them over later."

Christopher gave a pleased hum. He sank even farther into the cushioned embrace of his chair. "If nothing else, at least I will get a chance to wear some of Étienne's latest confections. You did include the new coat with the silver buttons in your pile, did you not?" It was a coat of extraordinary make, just like Christopher himself, and he was eager to show it off.

"The alabaster silk?" Harding hesitated. "That particular coat is perhaps better suited to another occasion," he finally said.

"What?" Christopher sat bolt upright. "What do you mean? It's the perfect occasion for that coat."

"But my lord, the buttons," Harding said with a pained look. "The cut. It's– Well, in some circles, such as that of the Leftmores, it might be considered exceedingly . . ." He took a long, deep drink from his glass as if to buy himself more time.

"Exceedingly?" Christopher pressed.

"French," Harding finally said.

Christopher sighed and drank more brandy in a sullen manner.

"My lord, the entire point of your sojourn here in London is to present a perfectly normal picture of a young man so that you may find a perfectly normal wife," Harding said. "If you want to blend in with the crowd, as you say, then you mustn't wear that coat. In fact, I question whether you should wear white to the ball at all. The invitation indicated an avian theme."

"There are plenty of white birds," Christopher protested. "Doves! Swans! Those are exceptional birds, wouldn't you say? Why shouldn't I dress in my signature light colors?"

"I believe something darker might suit you–and the occasion, my lord."

Christopher scoffed. "You would shove me in a dour ensemble indeed. Black is for mourning, dear fellow, and I'm no widower."

Harding looked upon him with something approaching pity. "If you insist, my lord. I only thought to mention it, if only for the sake of the lady you will soon be wooing."

Christopher groaned. "Don't remind me."

"So you will proceed as planned?" Harding asked. "You are interested in a marriage in name only?"

"Well, what's the alternative?" Christopher tilted his head.

"You could marry for love," Harding said, "if it pleased you."

"Oh, I'm not so greedy as all that." Christopher waved a hand through the air.

Harding's handsome face creased in confusion. "It's not greedy to seek happiness."

Christopher pinned him with a startled look. "Isn't it?" he asked, his voice taking on a queer waver. "Isn't it just the height of greed?" He shook his head and forced a smile onto his lips. "There are many women in London who share my view, Harding. One should do what one can to oblige them. Time is not in my favor; I refuse to waste more of it chasing the ridiculous notion of love."

"In that case, you may as well–" Harding seemed about to say something, but shook his head and closed his mouth.

"What?" Christopher prodded. "Speak your mind, Harding. You have thus far done nothing but." This last he muttered into his glass as he drank.

"No, my lord," said Harding. "I overstepped." Yet instead of looking chastened by his lack of decorum, Harding exhibited a gleam in his intelligent dark eyes, like some sort of artist who was overcome with the urge to paint his muse.

Christopher noted it with wariness. "Harding, if I didn't know better, I'd say you had some sort of scheme in mind regarding my love life."

"Scheme, my lord?" Harding schooled his face into the very picture of innocence. Cherubs had nothing on this man. "I can't imagine what you might mean."

Christopher finished his drink with an unamused grunt. "I beg you, my dear fellow, please do not meddle in my affairs. The entire situation is stressful enough without my valet skulking about the place."

"I would never," Harding said with a strange amount of sincerity. "I only thought–" He licked his lips and leant forward in his armchair. "It might be nothing, or it might be a very elegant solution to your search for an unloving wife. I could make some inquiries—delicately—to determine the truth. If you would permit me?"

Well, how could Christopher refuse such a request?

He raised his empty glass with a sigh. "Carry on, then, Harding. But do pour me another first."

Chapter 13

Christopher arrived at the Leftmores' ball later than was fashionable, as he hadn't really wanted to come at all.

The Leftmore house was a sprawling monument of luxury built around a central courtyard that was, by the constrained standards of London, huge. The grand ballroom spanned an entire wing that bordered the courtyard. As Christopher entered and was announced, he saw towers of glittering cakes and sweet morsels, piles of tiny fruits dusted with sugar, and shining delicacies of unknown origin. Drink flowed as it was wont to do at these things, dispensed by black-clad servants who haunted the edges of the party, discreetly filling every glass. Lady Leftmore had decided on the avian theme for the evening: small birds flitted above the heads of the dancers in flashes of ruby red and deep turquoise, emerald green and the darkest purple. They gathered and tittered in the living boughs that had been installed along the high walls, chirping in strange counterpoint to the orchestra that was playing a waltz.

Christopher wondered how many guests would leave tonight's ball having been shat on. The thought made him smile to himself. And wish he'd brought an umbrella.

Dozens of peacocks were wandering about the room, and Christopher stepped over one, begging his pardon, to secure himself a glass of wine from a serving boy only too eager to be rid of it. He sipped slowly, knowing this would be his only drink of the night. If the society columns were to be believed, fêtes such as these often plied their attendees with wine and liquor until something frightfully interesting happened, and Christopher was resolved not to be too interesting tonight, his alabaster coat with the silver buttons notwithstanding.

"Winny," came a familiar voice, "you made it."

Christopher turned to find Chester wading through the flock of peacocks in his direction. He felt a surge of foolish relief at once again seeing a friend in the sea of strangers. They clasped hands and, for the first time in years, Christopher got a close look at Chester's face.

"Dear fellow, are you all right?" he asked. "You look peaked."

It was an understatement. Chesterfield looked as if he hadn't slept in weeks, his eyes ringed with dark circles and his eyes a bloodshot hue. He appeared pale and wan and underfed. And despite the brave smile on his face, his every movement radiated the foulest misery.

"I'm terrible, actually," Chester said, still smiling through clenched teeth. "I'm in love, you see."

"Oh no." Christopher clicked his tongue. "Bad luck, old boy. I do hope it clears up quickly." He knew from experience what this meant for Chester. Back in their Cambridge days, Chester would fall in love every week or so, and every time it would end in tragedy. Christopher supposed that this sort of thing fueled a poet's soul, and though he hated to see his friend tormented once again by love, he knew Chester would probably get a sonnet or two out of it.

"See here! You don't understand. This isn't another puppy dog infatuation." Chester shook his head. "It's the real thing, Winny, and it's awful. And she feels the same, which is worse!"

"What's the matter, then?" Christopher asked. "Simply ask her to marry you."

"I can't." Chester seemed to shrink another inch into himself. "Her father won't allow it. Says he won't let his daughter waste her life on some poet. Oh, she's too good for me, it's true!" Tears sprang to his eyes, and Christopher patted his arm in awkward sympathy.

"Who is she?" he asked.

"I can't tell you," Chester said glumly. "I'm sorry, but I care for her too much. I won't have her name bandied about."

"I would never bandy," Christopher said, "but of course I understand." He wondered if his friend was right, and that this time, the love he felt for this mystery girl was real. A younger, more brash Chester would never miss an opportunity to expound on his love's gentle voice or the color of her eyes. Perhaps he really had matured. Still, his misery was palpable. "It's a good thing you came to this ball," he said. "It's a chance to forget your troubles for a night, I suppose."

Chester looked at him askance. "Hardly. She's here."

"She is?" Christopher gaped. He glanced at one of the serving girls, who was ineffectually trying to shoo a peacock off a table.

Chester followed his gaze and sighed, slumping further into himself. "Not like that. She's here as a guest."

"Oh. Oh!" This was new. And a bit strange. "Don't you usually—? Erm." There was no polite way to say it, but Chesterfield was well-known for flirting with the working classes and ignoring society ladies. He'd always said they were the more "natural" of their species, a view that Christopher felt was a bit condescending. A lady could no more choose the circumstances of her birth than Christopher could, and so he chafed at the idea that one must be more attractive than the other.

"I know." Chester rubbed a hand down his face miserably. "Just my luck that the woman I fall in love with is—well, suffice to say, I am beneath her in every sense of the word." His eyes flicked up to the upper balcony that ringed the ballroom, where a swath of people were watching the dance floor in their bright finery.

Christopher did not examine the revelers above too closely, more concerned with keeping his old friend in one piece. He took him by the elbow and guided him away. "Come on, we can't have her see you like this."

"You're right, of course," Chester sighed. "I would hate to hurt any of her future prospects with my unseemly display of feeling." He lifted his gaze to Christopher's. "Oh, if only you could read her own poetry, Winny. She writes circles around me; I've told her a thousand times the world is poorer for not having her work published."

This, more than anything, convinced Christopher that his friend was not going through another silly, short-lived bout of passion. He truly cared for this lady, and it seemed supremely unfair that she should return his feelings and yet be barred from his company.

"Would it help distract you at all if I told you I need an introduction?" Christopher asked. "Though if you'd rather not become embroiled in my little melodrama—"

"Not at all. I adore your melodrama." Chester picked up his head and fastened on a brave smile. "Who is it you want to meet?"

"Verbena Montrose. Do you know her?"

"Of course. One of her cousins married my brother. She's practically family." He used his superior height to scan the crowd. "Ah, there she is." He tipped his chin past a pyramid of crystal goblets.

Christopher craned his neck, desperately trying to peer over the tops of the heads of the other revelers. Finally, he saw her.

Verbena Montrose was taller than he, though that wasn't exactly strange. Christopher refused to be cowed by the fact that the woman stood half a head above him in her dancing slippers. He was not the first man of short stature to attempt to woo, and he did not think it practical to confine his search to prospects shorter than himself—there weren't many young ladies of such minuscule proportions.

Her height notwithstanding, Verbena also possessed a lush head of hair in the strangest, most striking shade of red. Christopher was reminded of warnings from Cook regarding women with red hair—apparently she felt they were not to be trusted. When Christopher had tactfully pointed out that Cook herself was quite reddish in the area in question, Cook said that proved her point. Unlike Cook, however, Verbena Montrose had a willowy figure and a keen eye that seemed to settle on the faces of those around her with an air of amusement tinged with curiosity. She wore a gown of the color of mint dotted with dozens of crystals–more likely cut glass, Christopher noted–that caught the light and shone in constellations all along her hemline. Christopher was impressed with the cut and make of Miss Montrose's gown. It was elegant without being ostentatious, fashionable without being too costly. It spoke of a wearer with a good head on her shoulders.

It was something of a miracle that Christopher could even catch a glimpse of her dress, as the woman was surrounded by a thick knot of admirers. There were men offering her cups of lemonade, men fanning her, men bearing tiny plates piled high with offerings from the buffet table. Miss Montrose accepted all the attention as a benevolent ruler might, nodding and blushing prettily at her subjects, protesting that they needn't do this or that for her and then allowing it anyway.

Christopher gave a nod in her direction and whispered to Chesterfield, "Do you think you might introduce us now?"

Chester gave a weary sigh. "I don't see why not. Just because I am destined to a life of misery doesn't mean you should be." He led Christopher over to the throng and elbowed a path through. Despite his poor spirits, he managed to muster a little poetic flair in introducing Christopher to the lady.

"Miss Montrose, if I may present to you my bosom friend, the elusive and altogether mysterious Earl of Eden."

The throng of men surrounding the scene did not much like this turn of events and murmured as much to one another as they eyed Christopher's coat buttons. Christopher, however, was not about to be deterred by some ill-concealed whispers from the mouths of oily rakes.

He took Miss Montrose's gloved hand as she presented it and pressed a kiss to her fingers. "Please forgive Chesterfield, miss," he said. "I'm afraid he paints me as far more intriguing than I am. Though he did not, I see, do justice to your charms when he enumerated them for me."

It was a prettily done piece of flattery, and the assembled would-be suitors puffed out their cheeks at hearing it. Christopher paid them no mind.

Miss Montrose, for her part, smiled warmly. "Do you dance, Lord Eden?" she asked, taking him by the arm and leading him, somewhat strangely, away from the dance floor.

"I can," Christopher hedged. "I may not have had much practice, but I daresay I can make it through one reel without injury to myself or other innocent persons. Would you care to dance, Miss Montrose?"

"After that resounding endorsement?" She laughed. "I don't think I would, even if I were able."

"Oh." Christopher frowned. This was not going as smoothly as he had hoped. "Well, of course if your card is full tonight . . ."

She lifted her arm in a graceful sweep and showed him the dance card that dangled from her wrist on a length of white silk decorated with the requisite bird feather. Christopher could see that the card was completely blank. "I do not dance myself," she said. "I'm quite famous for it. Did you not hear?"

"No, I had no idea." Christopher groped for a polite rejoinder. "I would not have asked if I'd known you eschewed dancing. Sadly, I spend all my time locked away in my country estate, as you may have heard, and I am not privy to the latest news."

"Well, we must fix that, mustn't we?" she said. "Gossip is the currency of the realm, after all, and if you are deficient in it, I fear you will find yourself unable to move through the world."

They shared a laugh, although Christopher doubted she was joking. The mention of gossip and its undeniable power made sweat spring up along his spine, uncomfortable through his many layers.

"I would be much obliged if you would loan me some of that currency," Christopher said. Then he steered their conversation to safer waters. "May I ask–do you not enjoy dancing? Is that why your card remains empty? You don't seem to be lacking offers." He glanced over his shoulder, meeting the icy glares of approximately a dozen dandies who were following at a discreet distance.

"Oh, I enjoy it just fine." Miss Montrose tossed her fall of red curls over her shoulder. Her eyes continued scanning the ballroom as they made their slow circuit of the festivities. "Unfortunately, I have a weak ankle. My family doctor advised me to do my best not to aggravate it." She heaved a sigh that seemed to Christopher entirely theatrical. "It's really very tedious. How awful that I cannot participate in the dancing at these balls!"

"Is it?" Christopher looked back again at the angry storm cloud of young men who would likely be willing to kill Christopher if it meant taking his place at Miss Montrose's side. "You seem to have persevered despite this setback."

"It is kind of you to say so." She flashed him a smile, then looked away, then looked back again out of the corner of her eye. Ah, an accomplished flirt. Christopher found her more cunning by half. While he could admire such a woman, he also was a little bit afraid of her. Whether this weak ankle of hers was an actual affliction or merely a white lie, Miss Montrose had managed to snag the attentions of half the eligible men at the ball. And a few of the ineligible ones, if the appraising looks from a viscount Christopher knew to be betrothed meant what he thought they meant.

He gave the viscount a cutting glance as they passed, ignoring his attempt at a greeting.

"Oh, well done," Miss Montrose whispered as they swept by. "He's been a thorn in my side all evening. It's difficult to find a polite excuse to leave a conversation in my position."

"Tell me all about it," Christopher said. "In fact, tell me everything you think I should know. I put myself in your capable hands, Miss Montrose."

"Well!" She beamed, clearly gleeful at the prospect of dispensing her hard-won knowledge. "Do you see them?" She tipped her head minutely at a pair of men standing by the towering cake, conversing in hushed tones. "The Ashton brothers. As close as brothers can be, or at least they were. Now they're fighting over the same lady." She made a gesture across the room under the guise of waving off a flitting songbird, pointing out a statuesque woman in a jade gown. "Katarina Polova. They say she's the granddaughter of Bohemian royalty."

"Ah." Christopher looked at the lady briefly, not wanting to be impolite, but still curious about a woman who could tear apart two loving brothers. She was beautiful, he supposed, but no more beautiful than a hundred other ladies he'd seen in his life. There must be some hidden spark inside certain people, was his thinking, a thing that fueled desires and ignited them into flames. Perhaps he himself was immune—except, of course, where a certain valet was concerned.

Miss Montrose continued to chat as they walked arm in arm, pointing out people of note and explaining this or that bit of gossip that involved them. Christopher, for his part, made the appropriate sounds of surprise or disgust depending on the circumstances, wondering all the while what someone like Miss Montrose would say should his own secret ever be revealed to society at large. Would she call him a woman who thinks herself a man? An unnatural sort of girl playing at trousers and cravats? How long would he feed the whispers if that was the case?

"Oh," said Miss Montrose as they approached a group of revelers against the southernmost wall. "That poor dear. It breaks one's heart, doesn't it?" To her credit, Verbena Montrose sounded genuinely sympathetic to this unnamed person's plight, which was enough to pique Christopher's curiosity. He craned his head to survey the landscape and spotted what could only be the subject of Verbena's comments: a young woman, pale with jet hair collected atop her head in a fairly simple tumble of curls, surrounded by laughing people and looking as miserable as a human could with a glass of champagne in hand. She was not engaged in what seemed a lively conversation that surrounded her, merely glancing toward the doorways leading out into the courtyard every few moments as if yearning for a chance to escape.

Christopher quirked a brow in Miss Montrose's direction. "Who is she?"

Verbena blinked. Several times. "You don't know?"

"I'm afraid I am as ill-informed as you feared," he said.

"Well! Eden Abbey must truly be cut off from the world; everyone had heard that sad tale, I thought. It was in all the papers."

"I confess I do not read the London news with any regularity," Christopher said. For the sake of his own well-being, he'd long ago decided to stick to fashion magazines. The lurid tales of city life were too distressing to endure on a daily basis. "Please, enlighten me."

Miss Montrose led him away from the girl, waiting until they were a sensible distance before speaking in an eager whisper. "That is Lady Belinda Greene, youngest daughter of the Duke of Rushford. Though I suppose it is more accurate to say she is now the duke's only daughter."

Christopher felt his heart clench. "Oh, my word," he murmured. He forced himself not to glance back at the hapless lady, as he was certain she had endured more stares than was reasonable. He abhorred being stared at himself. "What happened?"

Verbena leaned in closer. "The eldest daughter, Lady Constance, went missing about—it must be a decade ago now." She dropped her voice to an even lower whisper. " 'She fled to Gretna Green,' they said. 'She'll be back in a fortnight, having married a secret lover.' Except she never returned, and surely must be dead." She shivered.

Christopher offered her a kind press of his hand, the only support he could give, as he agreed with Verbena's macabre assessment. After ten years, what other conclusion could there be?

Verbena gave him a grateful look in return, though it fell from her face as they passed within view of their topic of conversation. “Poor Lady Belinda,” she said. “The loss plagues her still. She can rarely muster a smile these days, let alone the strength to entertain any offers of marriage.”

Christopher caught another look at Lady Belinda as they passed by a glass cage that contained about a dozen unruly parrots, her sorrowful reflection captured in the faceted panes. His heart went out to her, though she was a stranger. “A hellish fate for one so young,” he murmured, feeling a growing sense of dread as he spoke the words.

“Yes,” Verbena said. “And one so sweet. We are acquainted, as we are of an age, and she has always been nothing but kind to me despite it all.” She shook her head. “Can you imagine losing a sister in such a fashion? Shrouded in mystery, without even the truth for comfort?”

The words stopped Christopher in his tracks, though he did not register the way his feet froze to the floor. He did not register much at all, in fact–at least nothing of the ballroom in which he stood. He was cognizant only of a phantom chill upon his skin and the swirl of unseen saltwater about his ankles.

“My lord?” The faint whisper barely penetrated the fog that had descended over Christopher. The scent of fine perfumes and sugared cakes faded. He could smell only the sea. He could hear only–

“My lord.”

Only a scream. The one locked away in his own mind.

“Lord Eden!”

Christopher startled at Verbena’s voice, brought back to the waking world in a rush of color and sound. The ball. The party. Christopher attempted to take stock of himself now that the attack of nerves was at its end. His breath was fast and hard like he'd just ridden a mile at a gallop. His hands shook with faint tremors and a cold sheen of perspiration was on his brow. Verbena regarded him with concern, her hand still tucked into the crook of his elbow. He gave the woman a shaky grin and retrieved his handkerchief to mop his face.

"My apologies, Miss Montrose," he said, "it seems all this excitement is too much for a country mouse like myself. Perhaps I have overindulged in the Leftmores' good wine."

Verena Montrose did not look convinced. A lady as clever as her wouldn't be. "If I have upset you with my somewhat morbid talk–" she began.

"No, please!" He patted her hand where it lay on his arm. "I am glad you informed me. I would hate to misspeak should I make the acquaintance of any Greenes."

Verbena was somewhat mollified by this if her pleased, tentative smile was anything to go by. "Shall we take another turn around the room?" she suggested. "I'm sure there are many more pieces of news I can impart, if you have need of them."

"I think I should take myself outside for a moment. Fresh air is what I need," Christopher said, and gracefully extracted himself from Miss Montrose's touch in such a way that it ended with them shaking hands. "Have an excellent remainder of your evening, Miss Montrose. I hope you find a suitable escort to not dance with you."

She favored him with a knowing look. "Enjoy the air, my lord," she said.

They parted just as the musicians struck up a new, lively tune and the dance floor flooded with all manner of revelry. Christopher headed toward the open French doors that led into the garden. Just before he stepped outside, he cast a glance in Verbena Montrose's direction, but her minty, sparkling skirt disappeared into the crowd. An extremely sharp girl, he wagered, one who would surely achieve what she desired, whatever that might be. All he knew for certain was that her designs would not include him. Miss Montrose was not a candidate for the title of Lady Eden. Anyone that well-informed and who dealt so deftly in gossip could not be his future helpmate, given his situation. He would say it was a pity, but he was certain she could do better than an earl anyway. A woman like that should settle for no less than a king.

He looked around the crowded ballroom for any sign of the topic of their erstwhile conversation, but Lady Belinda Greene was no longer standing against the wall looking depressed. Christopher could not see her anywhere, actually; she must have finally tired of the festivities and left for home.

Perhaps Christopher would follow her example soon. He could call for his carriage in no time; the hired driver and Harding, who had insisted on filling the position of footman tonight, were close by with the other guests' vehicles. The thought of seeing Harding soon—even a Harding dressed in his wretched livery—buoyed Christopher considerably. He stepped out into the cool night air in the courtyard. His pulse was still racing. A quiet moment in the garden would do him good.

He stood on the veranda and searched for constellations in the night sky just for something to do. It was breezy outside, a welcome contrast to the stuffiness of the ballroom, and Christopher could feel the sweat that had gathered along his back and under his arms cooling beneath his fine clothes. He dabbed at his temple with a handkerchief and wondered how much longer he would have to remain at the fête before he was able to make a polite escape.

A knot of young men tumbled out of the ballroom to ruin the muted quiet of the veranda. Christopher scowled at their antics; they were well and truly drunk, louder than Hades. He moved away before they could spot him and pull him into their inane conversation about some boxing tournament they planned to attend. Perhaps a brisk walk around the garden was in order.

Christopher was in the process of pretending to admire a stand of pink and red gladiolas when he heard whispers on the night breeze. As much as he was a novice at attending balls, even he knew that this was the sort of place where young lovers might meet in secret and exchange promises (or more) under the cover of darkness. Christopher didn't begrudge them this opportunity; though he knew love was not in the cards for him, he thought it only right that others should have the chance to woo. Propriety was less of a concern for him than most, given his own unique situation, and so his attitude toward trysting was rather more liberal than the average member of the ton.

Christopher had just resolved to leave the hidden lovers to their own devices, perhaps linger at the edges of the garden in order to engage any other wanderers in conversation so that he might keep the besotted pair from being discovered—but before he could station himself as their protector, he heard one of the voices more clearly. And recognized it.

The voice, that particular blend of soft and low, could only belong to James Harding. Now, though, his voice was strained in its fervent whispering: "That is why I had to see you tonight, Bee. Please, won't you at least hear me out?"

Bee? Christopher quickly stepped behind a topiary cut into the shape of a frog midleap, frowning at the diminutive. Whoever Harding was conversing with must already be on intimate terms with him, if pet names were being bandied about. The woman's–Bee's–voice replied in a rushed, breathless whisper such that Christopher could not make out her words, only her distress. From the cadence of her voice, though, and her upper-class accent, it was clear that she was no serving girl from the host's household. She was of the ton.

A red haze descended over Christopher's field of vision. The fact that his manservant was secretly meeting with a young woman filled him with the hot sort of rage he normally only felt when reading a poor translation of the *Iliad.* How could Harding dare to–? He only required one thing of his manservant, one simple thing! And that was discretion. Conducting a moonlit affair with a genteel woman right under the noses of the whole of London society was very much not discreet.

Christopher ignored the little voice in his head that put forth the notion that any circumstances that included Harding wooing someone would enrage him all the same. That was not the point. The point was– Well, Christopher was too angry to think clearly but he knew that Harding had a lot to answer for!

He edged closer so that he could make out the conversation.

The tremulous voice of the woman quavered as she said, "Not here. We risk being found too easily here."

"The house then." Harding's voice sounded as determined as it did when giving Christopher unasked-for sartorial advice. "Tonight. It's our only chance to meet alone. Leave the ball early. Beg off with some excuse."

"And you will come to Grosvenor Square?" The lady sounded doubtful. "You promise?"

"I swear to you, I will be there at midnight." A mere half hour from now, Christopher realized with a start. "Let me in through the side door, as we used to do."

Christopher frowned at that. So this affair had been going on for quite some time, then? He supposed he shouldn't be shocked. James Harding was well-liked by the people in the village, popular at Eden's End. He recalled the night he watched him dance through the tavern's window. How many other women had he . . . danced with?

Meanwhile, this Bee of his was making noises of agreement. "Midnight. I'll be at the door. Now go, before you're spotted or I am missed."

Christopher strained his ears but could not hear any farewell kiss. There were only footsteps: one set leading away, and another heading right for Christopher's hiding spot. He shrank back into the shadows of the shrubbery and waited. Soon the woman came into view, and it took all of Christopher's willpower not to gasp aloud.

It was Lady Belinda, the sad girl who looked no less miserable now that she had made plans for a midnight meeting. Indeed, tears stood in her eyes, and as Christopher watched, she dabbed them away with the silk handkerchief she retrieved from her tiny reticule. Christopher wondered if the shock of meeting his valet after, it sounded like, some time apart had shaken her nerves.

Whatever the lady's feeling, Christopher knew he could not let this stand. He watched as she made her way through the garden and back into the ballroom, no doubt to tell her father the Duke of Rushford that she had decided to depart early.

Christopher hurried to the exit. He could not allow this rendezvous to proceed at any price.

Chapter 14

It was no surprise to Christopher when he found his carriage sans Harding. The lone hired driver remained, smoking a pipe, which he quickly tapped out on his heel when he saw Christopher approach.

"Departing so soon, m'lord?"

"Yes." Christopher opened his own carriage door and mounted the steps without waiting for a helping hand. "We leave now."

"Ah, your man, Harding—he told me he had some business. I was to wait for his return." The fact that Harding had insisted on accompanying Christopher in the role of footman for the evening now made perfect sense. The sly devil.

"The plan has changed," Christopher said with steel in his voice. "We go to Grosvenor Square. *Now.*" He so rarely barked orders that the words sounded stilted, as if he were reading lines from a play instead of speaking for himself.

"Of course, m'lord." The driver swung up onto the seat and took up the reins.

Within moments the carriage was clattering down the cobbled lanes at a good clip. Christopher sat back against the plush velvet of the interior with his arms crossed over his chest, stewing over what he'd heard in the garden. How was Harding making his way to the meeting place, he wondered. It would take ages on foot. Perhaps he had hailed a hackney; his salary was generous enough to allow such an indulgence, but the sight of a man in full Winterthrope livery doing so in the middle of a ball . . .

It would draw attention, and that was the one thing Christopher abhorred above all else. He squirmed on the carriage bench, unable to get comfortable. After a moment, he realized it was not just his feeling of betrayal that was causing this, but a bundle of cloth wedged under him. He reached behind himself and pulled a lump of purple and blue silks from behind the cushion.

Ah. So Harding had at least swapped his garish livery for something more suitable to lurking, Christopher surmised. A small blessing, though it meant that the man had planned every step of this. Somehow, that rankled Christopher even more.

"Grosvenor Square, m'lord," called the driver as they turned onto the lane that led to the finest, most expensive addresses in all the city. Christopher was only vaguely familiar with the houses that lined the square, but he spotted one lone candle in a third-story window, the only light to be seen. That had to be Lady Belinda's window. All the other residents would still be at the ball.

He gave the order for the carriage to stop and told the driver to return to the stables. "The air is so fine," he said between gritted teeth, "I think I will walk home tonight." The last thing he needed was his coach driver catching sight of the scandalous scene that would soon unfold. The driver did not question this departure from the norm and wisely turned the horses, leaving Christopher alone on the pavement.

He glared up at the window with its single lit candle. As he watched, a silhouette passed by, long and thin with an enviable profile. Christopher recognized Harding's shadow as if he'd known it his whole life.

His valet, upstairs, alone with the daughter of a duke! His blood boiled. He had to put a stop to this nonsense, and quickly. Christopher marched up to the front door, which was decorated with a brass knocker in the shape of the Greene coat of arms, but before he could grasp it and give it a thorough bashing, he stopped. His sense began to overtake his anger. What exactly would happen if he banged on the duke's door in the middle of the night? Some sleepy servant would greet him, surely. And then what? Would Christopher demand to see Lady Belinda? Declare his intentions to halt a tryst? It would be the ravings of a lunatic. He'd be tossed into the street. No, he could not rely on the usual channels available to a gentleman visitor. He had to find another way.

He looked up at the window once more, the only rectangle of yellow light in the dark, and noticed that, unlike its neighbors, the façade of the duke's home was covered in a trellis upon which delicate vines were trained. Christopher stepped off the front stoop to get a better look. Yes, the trellis reached all the way to the third story. A man could, if he was nimble, climb the thing to reach the window with the lit candle.

Christopher glanced furtively over his shoulder. The square was deathly quiet and still. No other people were about. If he was quick, he wouldn't be seen. He might sully his faultless coat or snag the delicate fabric on a thorn—a thought that gave him no little pause—but there was nothing for it. The reputations of three people hung in the balance, and his ensemble, much as it pained him, sat on the lighter end of the scale.

"This is madness," he muttered to himself even as he reached for the latticework of the trellis that was affixed beside the front entrance. He tested it gingerly and found that it didn't immediately peel away from the brick façade. Having little experience in climbing trellises, Christopher could only imagine this was a good sign. He lifted his foot and stuck it awkwardly into a square of the lattice, clinging to some of the sturdier vines.

There was a slight creak of wood, and the vines tore away from the brick a jarring inch or two, but it held his weight. Christopher took a deep breath and began to climb, thanking his lucky stars that, for all his fears, a fear of heights was not among them.

As he left the safe haven of the earth and approached the lit window, Christopher realized he could hear voices, the very same from the garden. Harding's soft tenor, Lady Belinda's breathless whisper. As he struggled up the trellis, the voices coalesced into words.

"Nothing from you, not a word!" That was Lady Belinda. She sounded near to tears.

"You know such a thing was impossible." Harding sounded full of regret. "I could not risk it."

Christopher frowned as he grappled with an unruly strand

of vine that had somehow twisted round his ankle. Once it was dispatched, he stretched his arm up, fingertips just barely brushing the windowsill. So close!

"Is this not a risk?" the duke's daughter was saying. Christopher barely paid her any heed; his tongue was poking from the corner of his mouth as he attempted to go up on tiptoe. Damn his short legs.

"Under the circumstances, I thought the risk worth it. Bee, I think I know a way to solve most of our problems. If you would only listen—" Harding's voice was so serious, so determined, that Christopher was certain his valet was only moments away from sweeping the poor girl into his arms. He could not allow that to happen. He set his jaw and made another grab for the damned windowsill. His fingers found purchase on the ledge—just as the trellis under his feet gave a terrific groan.

Christopher's eyes flew wide.

He scrambled to drag himself up and through the thankfully half-open window just as the lattice and vines peeled away from the front of the house and crashed to the ground. The sound of the trellis splintering into pieces was somewhat drowned out by Christopher's yell. It was the sort of yell any reasonable man might make if he thinks he might be about to plummet to his death from a duke's windowsill. There was also the matter of the Queen Anne side table that was knocked over as Christopher made his appearance, scattering whatever unfortunate items had been sitting atop it. All in all, a downright cacophony.

Christopher found himself sprawled on a plush area rug. He lifted his face from where it had been mashed into said rug to find Harding and Lady Belinda staring down at him with matching looks of horror on their faces. That wasn't all they shared; now that he saw them side by side, Christopher noted that they both were possessed of a similar dark-haired, dark-eyed beauty. Damnably unfair, the two of them making such a fine set.

"Right!" Christopher scrambled to his feet. He put a finger in the air and hoped it lent some authority to his stance. Then he noticed a leaf out of the corner of his eye where it was stuck in his hair. He dislodged it and let it fall to the ground before continuing. "Aha!" he added, since it seemed the thing to do.

"My lord," Harding said as he valiantly tried to compose his face into something less shocked, "what on earth are you doing?"

"What am *I* doing? I could ask you the same question!" Christopher thrust his accusatory finger in Harding's handsome face. "But I already know the answer. You're conducting a . . . a . . . a tryst with this poor girl!" He flung a hand in Lady Belinda's direction.

The woman had turned the shade of milk at Christopher's appearance, but now she flushed as red as a warning flag. "What!" she cried. Then, lowering her voice to a hiss, "Who *are* you?"

Harding heaved a sigh and looked heavenwards. "Lady Belinda," he intoned, "please allow me to introduce my master, Lord Eden." He stooped to one knee and put the Queen Anne table to rights, gathering up all the bits and baubles that had scattered across the floor.

Lady Belinda did not seem to be in the mood to have the back of her hand kissed. She gave Christopher a shove just as he was getting his bearings. "You are lucky the servants of this house are such heavy sleepers, what with the racket you've made."

"It wasn't my intention—" Christopher began.

"I don't care. You must leave. Now!"

"Not without my valet," he shot back. "I will not allow him to besmirch your good name and my standing."

"Oh, for god's sake." Harding stood and pinched the bridge of his nose between his thumb and forefinger. "This is no tryst, my lord. Lady Belinda and I are merely—" He stopped then and glanced at the woman in question as if making a plea for help, but she didn't seem to have the words either.

"Don't you mean *Bee*?" Christopher cut his eyes to the woman, who stood with her arms crossed angrily. "That is what he called you, is it not?"

"I did." Harding strode in front of him as if to protect the woman from Christopher's glare. "A slip of the tongue. I worked in the Greene household as a young lad, you see. In the stables." He turned to the lady. "We grew up together. We're practically brother and sister, so you will understand the informality in our conversation." This was said in a soft, almost wistful tone that Christopher had never heard his valet produce. Then the moment passed and Harding bowed his head. "Please excuse my lack of etiquette, my lady."

"No, don't." Lady Belinda swallowed. "It's been ages since anyone's called me by my childhood name; I admit I have longed to hear it." She moved her gaze coolly to Christopher. "Your Lordship can call me Belinda, if you please. Since we're all on such informal ground here anyway."

"Then I insist you call me Christopher," he replied with acid on his tongue.

"Of course." The lady—Belinda—gave a textbook curtsy. "It would be my pleasure, *Christopher.*"

"Now that that's settled: can someone tell me what we're doing standing in the duke's home at," he consulted his pocket watch, "ten past midnight?"

"Allow me to explain, my lord." Harding stepped around him and sensibly drew the curtains. "I was about to tell Lady Belinda about your peculiar situation: that you are hoping to secure a promise of marriage this Season in order to fulfill the late Lord Eden's will. As it happens, she requires a suitable husband before her next birthday as well. The duke demands it."

"Oh. I see." Christopher felt his face turning a wonderful shade of red. One could roast chestnuts on his cheeks, he was certain. He turned to Belinda. "Erm, my commiserations."

"Yes," she said dryly. "Quite."

Christopher felt he might die of embarrassment, but he needed to be certain he understood the situation clearly. For once. He turned to Harding. "So you, ah, were going to propose that we . . . ?" He made a vague gesture between himself and the lady.

"Precisely, my lord. If Lady Belinda is amenable, I was going to suggest you two marry each other for the sake of convenience. That is why I needed to speak to her in secret."

Christopher screwed up his face. "Not a tryst, then?"

"No, my lord." Harding looked faintly ill at the prospect. "Not a tryst."

"Could we please stop throwing around the word 'tryst'?" Lady Belinda said. "It's making my skin crawl."

"My apologies." Christopher executed a hasty bow in her direction. "I should not have leapt to such tawdry conclusions."

"No, you shouldn't have," she agreed.

"And I am sorry for barging in like this," he added. Her stormy look made him reconsider mentioning the broken trellis. He straightened. "So! Erm. Would you be amenable? To the marriage of convenience, I mean."

"I'm not sure," Lady Belinda drawled. "It's difficult to say when you've made *such* an excellent first impression."

Christopher could only gape at this ready display of wit. He'd rather been expecting a wilting wallflower in need of smelling salts. At least, that had been the impression she'd made from afar at the ball. Up close, she was much more . . . lively.

"Bee," Harding said in a warning sort of way.

"Well, I'm sorry!" She huffed. "It's simply–"

Further argument was cut off by the sound of carriage wheels clattering in the street below and the voice of a footman calling out, "We have arrived, Your Grace."

The three of them froze.

"The duke," Harding said.

"That's not good," Christopher whispered.

Lady Belinda twitched a curtain aside and peeked out of the window. Their fears were confirmed if her pale visage was anything to go by. "If my father finds not one but two men in my bedchamber in the dead of night, I hesitate to give odds on any of us living to see the sunrise," she cried. "Get out of here immediately!"

Harding, always the practical one, moved quickly toward the window, but Christopher caught him by the elbow. "Erm, not that way, dear fellow," he said. "The trellis has met its maker, I'm afraid. Unless you plan on jumping from the third story, we'd better find another escape route."

Harding stared at him. "You broke the trellis?"

"Did you not hear it crashing to the ground earlier?"

"In all the commotion your entrance caused? I suppose not." Harding dragged a hand through his hair. "Why in god's name did you break the trellis?"

"I didn't do it on purpose! I daresay it's not designed to hold the weight of a fully grown man, no matter how petite one might be!"

"Gentlemen!" Belinda interrupted. "Time is short." Indeed, there were footsteps already upon the stair. "If you cannot run, you must hide."

"Hide?" Christopher gawked at her. "Surely you're joking." His pride demanded that he, the Earl of Eden, stand his ground.

Harding had no such compunctions, apparently. He crossed the room in two strides and opened the huge armoire that stood in the corner. Shoving dozens of hanging gowns aside as much as space allowed, he leapt into the maw of the thing and stuck his hand out, beckoning. "My lord, if you would follow me."

"What, in there?" Christopher squeaked. His pride was shrinking by the moment.

"Just do it!" Belinda said, shoving him inside the armoire.

"Now see here—" Christopher's protest went unheard as the armoire door slammed in his face. He was mortified to find himself squashed rather forcefully against Harding. The armoire, which on the outside had appeared to be so gigantic, somehow shrank to Lilliputian dimensions now. Christopher was trapped chest to chest with Harding in the absolute pitch-dark of the wardrobe's interior, and beneath the scent of fresh fabric and the feel of silk swiping along his brow, he could sense far more of his manservant than he had ever intended.

He tried to turn his head aside so that they weren't staring directly into each other's faces, but doing so caused a lock of Harding's hair to brush against his cheek, which in turn caused Christopher to shiver. Memories of his filthy dream flooded through him. He was achingly aware of every point of contact between their bodies. Christopher's only saving grace was that, being a man of unique construction, he did not have to worry about a cockstand giving him away in such a position. Small blessings, as usual.

"Your elbow is in my side," he murmured, trying and failing to put an inch of distance between them.

"If you could kindly move your leg—" Harding replied, jostling Christopher where their limbs had become inexorably tangled.

"Move it where, exactly?" Christopher asked.

Before Harding could offer a no doubt scathing suggestion, the bedroom door creaked open, and they both froze.

"Belinda!" The booming voice could only belong to the Duke of Rushford. "Are you already abed?"

"Yes, Father," came the softer reply, accompanied by some very convincing coughs. Christopher wondered if the girl had managed to throw a nightgown over her dress, or if the bedclothes were pulled all the way up to her chin to hide her finery.

"I was just about to drift off. I am so sorry I had to leave the ball early."

"Have you had anything to drink? A glass of milk? Lukewarm tea? I always have lukewarm tea when my stomach is upset."

Christopher stifled a groan; he could hear the bedsprings squeaking in a way that meant the duke had perched on the edge of his daughter's mattress. No doubt he intended to coddle the girl endlessly. Of all the fathers in London, Christopher seethed, must Belinda have the only one who cared about his child's well-being?

Harding must have felt similarly, for he gave a silent sigh of resignation, and the puff of his breath lit across Christopher's neck.

The voices of the two Greenes filtered through the armoire in a muzzy patter of conversation, up and down, back and forth. Christopher tried to block it out, but the only other thing that could hold his attention was Harding himself.

Harding, who was extremely solid for such a long reed of a man. It was too dark in the armoire to see anything, but Christopher couldn't help but feel the press of lithe muscle against him. There was a scent, too, that he could detect through the lavender sachets of the wardrobe. Hair oil, he decided. Harding wasn't the type to daub on cologne. It was very pleasant. Sandalwood, he would wager. Or perhaps frankincense.

Strange, that he had never noticed that before. Skin close and trembling, now he could notice nothing else.

His heart raced with more than the fear of discovery. He squirmed in the hot, close dark, trying to find a position that wasn't too compromising. An accidental brush of Harding's hand at his chest made him nearly jump out of his skin. He would have made a noise, possibly a loud one, if Harding had not clapped a palm over his mouth.

"Hush." Harding's voice was in his ear, caressing its way down his spine.

Christopher let his eyes fall closed. This was all too much. He couldn't breathe; there was no air in the wardrobe. He gave something like a whimper against Harding's hand, and something shifted between them. Harding's touch gentled, as if he planned to uncover Christopher's mouth, but perhaps he miscalculated in the dark. Instead, his fingertips ran along the warm seam of Christopher's lips, and Christopher, swaying in his hold, opened his mouth to let them in. Two fingers settled atop his wet tongue like it was the most natural thing in the world. Christopher stopped fidgeting and kept his eyes squeezed shut, concentrating on the salt flavor of Harding's skin.

"Hush," Harding whispered again, this time against Christopher's neck.

Christopher felt a shameful dampness in his trousers, and he prayed that Harding would not shift in such a way that it would become noticeable to him. He stayed as frozen as possible to ensure it. Only when Christopher was completely calm and still did Harding slip his fingers out of his mouth. He wiped them on his own trouser leg, and Christopher felt very strongly that he might expire from that gesture alone.

Finally, at long last, the duke left and the maids shut the door. Their footfalls faded as they walked down the hall, and then all was entirely silent. A long moment passed in which all breath was held. Then the armoire door opened, and Harding and Christopher tumbled out, gasping for air under the bemused gaze of Lady Belinda, who had been the one to free them. Christopher touched his own cheek and found it as hot as a coal. His only consolation was that Harding looked slightly affected as well. His hair was even a bit mussed.

Christopher hadn't thc faintest idea what the hell had just happened, but he found he wanted it to happen again.

"Apologies," Harding said when he at last faced Lady Belinda. "The perfume sachets are . . . overwhelming in such close quarters."

"Oh, be quiet." She shut the armoire with a click. She was still wearing her ballgown, though it looked as though she had managed to take off her slippers before leaping into bed under the guise of rest. Her stockinged feet paced the floor. "Now what?"

Harding spoke in a low whisper. "The duke and duchess will go to sleep shortly. When they do, and the house is quiet once more, we will slip out the side door just as I came in. The only bedroom we will pass will be the housekeeper's, and she sleeps like the dead."

"You know the workings of this house quite intimately," Christopher observed, still trying to catch his breath.

"As I said, I grew up here." Harding cast Belinda a nervous look. "Will you lock the side door behind us so there will be no sign?"

"No sign save for the broken trellis," she pointed out. "In the light of day, someone is sure to notice that."

"Oh, these things break all the time," Christopher said. "Everything in my own house is two minutes away from falling apart. Just say a very fat bird tried to sit on it."

"A fat bird?" Belinda repeated incredulously.

Christopher shrugged. "Or something to that effect."

The lady sighed and pinched at her nose just as Harding did when he was frustrated. They must have been very close as children, Christopher thought, to have picked up each other's mannerisms like that.

"I can't believe I'm going to marry you," Belinda muttered.

Christopher blinked. "Oh! Erm, you don't have to," he said.

"No, I shall." Her hand dropped from her nose. "James is correct. We both need to marry with speed, and I have no interest in marrying a man who expects me to fulfill the usual wifely duties." She pinned him with a look. "You don't expect me to carry out the usual wifely duties, do you?"

"I wouldn't dream of it," he stammered. "As long as you understand that I won't be providing any of the . . . usual husbandly ones."

"Then we are agreed."

They shook on it. Harding watched this all with a pleased smile teasing his lips.

"I have to admit," Christopher said as he retracted his hand, "I would not have thought that a lady such as you would be in need of suitors." As the daughter of a duke, her dowry was sure to be sizable. Not to mention her striking beauty.

"Oh, I'm not," she said. "It's only, I don't care to be married at all. Not in anything but name, not any longer." Her eyes took on a faraway look. "Love is a cruel thing, Lord Eden, and

I do not believe I shall have any part of it. If I cannot have what I truly desire then—" She shook her head. "I may as well participate in this farce of yours. At least this way, *someone* will benefit."

Christopher sensed there was a longer story behind this notion, but before he could ask, Harding pulled him by the arm to where he'd cracked the bedroom door open.

"The hallway is clear," he whispered. "We should leave now."

And so they did, exiting from the kitchen door at the side of the house and stepping carefully over the shattered bits of trellis that had landed on the pavement out front. It was strange, the way things could change over the course of a single conversation. Christopher had arrived at the duke's home filled with rage and ill-formed assumptions, and he was leaving with his valet, an engagement, and a lingering slickness between his legs. Not the evening he'd expected, not by half. And although he was still mortified by his manifold missteps, he was, on the whole, pleased by the night's events. He would need to take Lady Belinda fully into his confidence before the wedding, but if Harding trusted the girl, that boded well enough for now. Christopher cast a glance at Harding's handsome profile. His man had certainly worked a miracle; he deserved a raise, if money could ever be reward enough for saving the master's bacon.

"Again, apologies for my intrusion," Christopher said as they walked in the direction of his townhouse, "but all's well that ends well and all that. Thank you, Harding, for finding me a suitable wife." *And for sticking your fingers in my mouth,* went unsaid, though the sentiment was there. Christopher wished he could broach the subject, but it felt like one of those things that men shouldn't speak of aloud.

"The pleasure is all mine, my lord," Harding said, and if Christopher detected a glimmer of a smile at his valet's lips, it was surely a trick of the moonlight.

Chapter 15

The next few days required careful orchestration. Christopher was compelled to call upon Lady Belinda several mornings in a row, each time bringing her a little gift that would signify his intent to marry her. Harding was most helpful in suggesting certain items (a colorful pot of marigolds, for example, for the lady detested the usual cut bouquets) and dissuading Christopher from others.

"Not a volume of poetry, my lord. The duke has a well-known hatred for poets," he said when Christopher had produced the little book for inspection at the shops.

"Hates poets?" Christopher made a face. "Why all this hatred for poets? My friend Chester has a father who harbors the same ill will toward the breed, and I don't understand it at all. They're the most harmless creatures I've ever met. You may as well say the man hates cobblers."

"I've known quite a few cobblers who can inflict some small amount of harm, my lord," Harding said.

Christopher sighed and replaced the volume on its shelf. "No matter. If poetry is forbidden, I shall bring her something else. A folio of music? Does she play any instruments, do you know?"

"Several, my lord," Harding said, and guided him into purchasing a blameless pamphlet of cheerful tunes.

His visits to the Greene family went just fine. He was charming and deferential toward the Duke and Duchess of Rushford and played his part well when conversing with Lady Belinda. Belinda was a consummate scene partner, projecting a serene acceptance of Christopher's interest. Soon it was time to request that Lady Belinda accompany him on chaperoned outings, which the duke allowed with enthusiasm.

"I haven't seen her this content in a long while," the duke told Christopher one day in private as he escorted him to the door after his morning visit had concluded. "She must be fairly receptive, Eden. Do try to keep it up."

Christopher tipped his head back to tell the duke, who towered over him by at least a foot, "I will, Your Grace."

The very next day found him taking a sedate turn around the park with Lady Belinda at his side. The weather was lovely, and as a consequence, the pathways were simply jammed with members of the ton wishing to be seen on their own promenades. It was a slow parade indeed as Christopher and Belinda were obliged to pause every few steps to greet their passing acquaintances, from dour viscounts to a cheery Verbena Montrose in a handsome walking dress.

Miss Montrose did not much hide her curiosity regarding their courtship, which Lady Belinda assuaged with a promise that they would take tea together soon. As they parted, Miss Montrose observed that they made a "striking pair," which Christopher supposed was true. He had chosen an ensemble in shades of ivory touched off with a waistcoat of rich caramel and boots to match. Lady Belinda was wearing a dress one shade away from mourning clothes, a stark, haunting grey. They certainly made a memorable picture, Christopher mused.

He glanced over his shoulder at their chaperones. Trailing at a respectful distance were Harding and one of Belinda's maids. Normally an older sibling or aunt would be called into service for such a dreary job—shadowing young lovers and ensuring they didn't do anything inappropriate was a dull, joyless task—but as neither Christopher nor Belinda had many living relatives available, their servants would have to do.

Mary, the maid, seemed to be taking her duty very seriously if her hawklike stare in Christopher's direction was anything to go by. She met his gaze fearlessly, and in her eyes was a promise of god's wrath should he step out of line. Christopher gave her a pleasant nod in acknowledgment. He wished he could get Belinda alone for a moment to explain his unusual make and gauge her willingness to keep his secret, but Mary was making this impossible. Her distrust was only natural, however, as she was the only member of their little party who did not know that their courtship was all for show. Harding did his best to engage the girl in a bit of polite conversation as they strolled several yards behind their charges, but Mary gave him nothing but one-word answers at best, and at worst, an annoyed grunt. Christopher hid his smile and faced forward again.

"Your lady's maid is as protective as a bull pup," he said out of the side of his mouth to Belinda.

She gave a faint sigh and squeezed his arm where she held it. "Yes. She's been with us for many years." Christopher wondered if Mary had been employed in the household when the elder Greene child vanished. If so, it was no wonder the maid was keeping such a close watch on the duke's remaining daughter.

He endeavored to turn the conversation to a lighter topic. "Ah, so does she know Harding from his boyhood as well?" He glanced back again, but could detect no trace of history between the two now-silent servants as they marched along. "They don't look very friendly."

"Ah, th-that is," Belinda stammered, "Mary would not have known him well. His work was in the stables, not the house. It wouldn't surprise me if she doesn't recall him at all." Her ears took on a pinkish hue, and she turned away as if fascinated by some ducks swimming in the lake.

Christopher frowned at this. "If Harding spent all his time outside the household, how is it you two became so close? Do you ride?"

"Yes," Belinda said quickly, turning back to him. "I do—did. I don't any longer."

"What a pity." Christopher gallantly tried to hide his disappointment. "I would suggest you and I avail ourselves of some horses the next time I come calling, otherwise. Harding has accompanied me on many a morning ride back at Eden; he could tell you I'm a decent horseman."

"Could we talk about something other than Harding?" Belinda said, perhaps more waspishly than she intended, for her cheeks colored to match her ears and she again looked away. This time, there weren't even any ducks as an excuse.

Christopher pursed his lips and faced straight ahead. "Of course. My apologies."

Belinda held his arm in brittle silence as they walked onto a pretty little stone bridge that led to the other side of the lake. She paused in the middle of the bridge, and what with the hold she kept on Christopher's arm, he too came to a standstill. He turned to her with a questioning raise of his brow, noting how pale she'd turned. Over her shoulder, he could see Harding and Mary also stop some yards distant. With the crowds of people swirling around them, though, they were rather obscured from their chaperones' sight.

"Are you well?" Christopher asked in low tones. "Shall we get you out of the sun?"

"No, I– I'm sorry." Belinda shook her head, one black curl falling from beneath her bonnet to drape over her shoulder. Her eyes held a touch of desperation as she struggled for the words she wanted. Looking at her, Christopher couldn't help but see how lovely she was, despite her obvious misery. It made one feel protective. If he were a different sort of man, he thought, he might even grow to love her.

"I know this situation we find ourselves in is rather strange," he said gently. "You needn't apologize. Not to me."

Belinda looked bereft at this, and eventually said in a low whisper, "I'm afraid I am not a very good candidate for courting, not even for show. I'm no actress."

"That's all right. You're doing just fine." He gave her what he hoped was an encouraging smile, but it seemed useless in the face of her unhappiness. Her eyes went red and tears appeared at the corners. "Oh dear. Perhaps I spoke too soon." Christopher hastened to pluck his clean white handkerchief from his sleeve. "Tip your head back," he murmured. "There we are."

Belinda did as bidden, biting her lip to keep her sobs to a minimum. Christopher dabbed carefully at her eyes. He saw Mary surge forward two steps into the swirling crowd at the sight, and he called out to her in a cheery voice: "A bit of dust has gotten into Lady Belinda's eye! She'll be better directly. Come, let's get you out of this wind." He looped their arms together once more and led Belinda quickly down the slope of the bridge and through the knots of promenaders, ducking this way and that until he found a quiet bench nestled between some hedges, away from the crowds. He glanced over his shoulder and saw that they had lost their trailing chaperones in the confusion, though he doubted they had much time before Mary sniffed them out.

He guided Belinda to sit on the bench and gave her the handkerchief. Her tears were still appearing, one at a time, like crystals on her wan cheeks.

"Thank you," she murmured as she availed herself of the handkerchief. "I don't know what's come over me, really. Oh, that's a lie." She gave a humorless laugh and balled the sodden handkerchief in her lap. "It's perfectly clear why I'm so steeped in misery. Isn't it?"

Christopher flicked his coattails back and took his own seat on the opposite end of the bench. "Yes, I heard about what happened to your sister." He thought of the tepid condolences he'd been offered following the deaths of—well, his entire family. He had no desire to parrot such nonsense. "I, too, have lost loved ones, though I know saying so will give little comfort. Such wounds remain fresh regardless."

Belinda turned and stared at him, her lips parted in surprise. "Oh! You believe–?" She dropped her gaze to her lap, where her hands worried at the borrowed handkerchief. "Please do not think me too monstrous for saying so, but that is not the source of my current sadness. That was years ago. It pains me, yes, but in truth I have," she seemed to pick her words with extreme care, "made peace with it, of late. As much as one can, I suppose."

Christopher frowned at this. "If not Lady Constance, then what–?"

"I am in love." Belinda stared ahead, her spine straight as a walking stick. She seemed shocked that the words had even left her mouth. "It's awful. I love a man who is good and kind and beautiful, and I should be on his arm this afternoon instead of engaging in this absolute farce!" Fresh tears spilled down her cheeks, and she wept into Christopher's handkerchief.

A grimace crossed Christopher's face. He had very little exposure to women, let alone crying ones, and had no instinct whatsoever as to what he should do. He lifted a hand to lay on her shoulder in a comforting gesture, but then retracted it, unsure of whether it would be welcome. "I'm sorry. I didn't know," he said. "What is keeping you apart from this love of yours?"

Belinda's face surfaced from the damp linen of the handkerchief. It was red and puffy, but still quite lovely. "What else?" she snapped. "My father, of course."

"Ah." Christopher's mind turned the problem over slowly. It reminded him of his longtime friend Chester and his own recent troubles with love.

In fact—oh, piss and shit, he thought. Was that the reason he wasn't permitted to gift Belinda books of poetry?

"Please tell me it isn't Horace Chesterfield," he groaned.

A fresh wave of tears overtook Belinda at the mention of the name. "I'd felt so lost and adrift since—since that horrible loss was visited upon my family. But then I met Horace. He understood me completely. He wrote me lines upon lines that read like a mirror held up to my very soul." She turned to him, her eyes fever bright. "Do you know what that's like, to find someone like that and then be denied even their friendship?"

Christopher swallowed. He could, perhaps, commiserate. "Of all the bad luck," he muttered. "You poor thing. Why on earth did you agree to this plan of mine?"

"As I said," Belinda sniffled, "at least this way, one of us is made happy. And at least—" She seemed to vacillate. "Living in the same household as Harding again would be a comfort to me, of course."

They must have been exceedingly close as children, Christopher thought. But then again, he knew firsthand just how comforting Harding's presence could be, so he did not question that. Still, it broke his heart to see the girl so terribly sad, and he felt it was his duty to point out the flaw in her thinking.

"If one afternoon in the park with me is enough to make you burst into tears," he said softly, "how do you expect to survive a lifetime of feigning marriage?"

Belinda twisted the handkerchief between her fingers until

Christopher was certain she would rip it into shreds. "I don't know. Perhaps it will get easier. In time, the hurt will fade. Won't it?" She looked over at Christopher, her red-tinged eyes wide with pleading. He felt the urge to lie just to soothe her, but he knew he could not.

"Having never been afflicted with love, I have no idea," he said. He thought of how hopeless Chester had been at the ball, and how lovesick Belinda looked now. It wasn't right, he thought, that two people who clearly adored each other be kept apart. What's more, if she was as dear to Harding as she appeared to be, Christopher felt he should make some special effort to provide succor. "Yet I think," he said slowly, "if I am the cause of your distress, however unwittingly, I should take steps to help you."

Belinda shook her head. "How can you help me, Christopher?"

"By making sure you marry the right man." He sat up straighter, his resolve giving him spine. "My dear lady, I could marry any woman in the world, anyone at all, and my problems would be at an end. For you, only one person will do. Should we not ensure you are given a chance at real happiness?"

She regarded him closely. "I thought you didn't believe in love."

"Of course I believe in it. I just don't think I can wear it, what with my complexion." He deftly brought the conversation back to its safer topic. "Look, do you want to be Chester's wife?"

"More than anything," Belinda said.

Christopher clapped his hands. "Then let's make that a reality."

"My father would never agree to it."

"So you'll elope."

"But I am guarded so closely by our servants under the duke's orders. What chance do I have of reaching Gretna Green before being caught?"

"You managed to sneak away from that ball to meet with Harding. Together, we can manage to sneak you away for a bit longer."

"I don't see how," she said doubtfully. "You'd have to be the wickedest carriage driver in all of England to outmatch my father's horses."

Christopher brightened. "Oh, is that all?"

From directly outside the quiet of their little protected alcove came the sound of footfalls and a worried voice calling out, "Lady Belinda? Lady Belinda!"

Belinda sighed. "That will be Mary."

"Right. Not much time." Christopher took her by her slight shoulders so they could share a look. He hoped his face projected all the confidence he felt regarding her plight. "Let me help. I can talk to Chester; better yet, I can pass letters between you. We can make arrangements within the week, if you both have the courage to try. Will you?"

Belinda stared at him for a moment, clearly torn. Then, at last, she thinned her lips into a hard line and nodded.

"Good," Christopher said just as Mary, followed by a more sedately moving Harding, burst through the crowd some yards distant to find their little hiding place.

"There you are, m'lady," Mary cried. "You were gone all of a sudden. I was so worried!" She cut a glare in Christopher's direction, and he obligingly removed his hands from Belinda's person.

"My apologies. Lady Belinda was overcome by the heat. I thought it prudent to find a place for her to rest in the shade with all due haste."

Mary snapped her gaze to her mistress, an unspoken question hanging in the air. Clearly the girl was concerned about improper behavior unbecoming a gentleman. One word from Belinda and Mary would no doubt scratch out Christopher's eyes.

"I'm feeling much improved, Mary," Belinda said with a watery smile. "Lord Eden has tended to me with perfect alacrity."

"That is what worries me, m'lady." Mary cast Harding a sharp glance as if to say she blamed him entirely for his master's lack of decorum.

Harding cleared his throat and suggested they adjourn for the time being, seeing as Lady Belinda was not feeling well. Christopher agreed readily, helping Belinda up from the stone bench with a perfectly innocent outstretched hand.

"Let us plan for another, grander outing in the future," he said meaningfully. "Perhaps you would be so kind as to write to keep me abreast of your health."

"I will," Belinda promised, and with a look in Harding's direction that was full of regret and apology, she took Christopher's arm.

Once the lady and her maid were safely returned to Grosvenor Square, Christopher broke the news to Harding. They were walking back to Bloomsbury, and the day was still fine enough for the streets to be bustling with people and carriages. Christopher was glad that Harding was in his usual black attire and not his full livery, a concession he had only made because Christopher had pointed out that his duty today as chaperone meant he should stand out as little as possible among the ton in the park.

"Harding," he sighed, "I won't be marrying Lady Belinda after all, it seems."

The man looked up quickly from his contemplation of the pavement, his face a mask of shock. "May I ask why not, my lord?"

"She's marrying someone else."

"Who?" Harding demanded.

"Well, a man she loves."

"Chesterfield?"

Christopher inclined his head in acknowledgment.

Harding let out a noise that, in any other man's nasal cavity, might be called a snort. From him, it sounded far too wonderful to be called such. "The duke will never allow it."

"So you knew she had her heart set on another man?" Christopher asked. "And you proposed she should marry me anyway?"

"I knew she had given her heart away to someone she couldn't possibly marry. That is why I made the suggestion."

"I wish you'd told me," Christopher said. He wasn't angry, not necessarily. Only . . . "I'm rather disappointed in you."

Harding startled as if he'd been struck across the face. "My lord, I did not think it relevant. Truly. You have said so often that you don't believe in love–"

Christopher stopped in the middle of the pavement and faced Harding. "I have said it is not an option for myself. For other people, I am all in favor of it. And in the case of my bosom friend Chester and the lovely Belinda, I don't see why we shouldn't do everything in our power to see them happily wed."

Harding blinked twice. "If you mean to go against the Duke of Rushford, sir, you must understand the danger. Your own reputation is at stake, and you still require a wife."

"And what sort of reputation will I enjoy," Christopher said, "if I stand by and allow Belinda to be miserable for the rest of her days? You did not see her as I did today. Just the thought of being courted by someone who was not her Horace had her in tears. And Chester! He was inconsolable at the ball. I wouldn't be able to look at myself in the mirror if I married her. No, I must do something. It's what any decent man should do."

Harding stared at him. The rush of people around them seemed to fade into the distance. Christopher felt a lump in his throat.

"I know you and Lady Belinda are close," he said, "and that doing this would mean you may not see each other as often as you might wish. But will you help me?"

There was a moment where it seemed Harding might scoff and tell Christopher he was on his own when it came to his mad plan. Yet after the space of two breaths, he stood tall and gave a firm nod, just as Belinda had. "As any decent man would," he murmured.

"Wonderful." Christopher clapped his hands on his man's firm upper arms, holding him and giving him a friendly shake. He was overcome with affection for his loyal manservant in that moment, and had it not been for the very public thoroughfare they found themselves in, he might have given in to the urge to embrace him fully. As it was, he could only give Harding's lithely muscled arms a squeeze. "I knew I could count on you, Harding."

"Always, my lord," Harding said, with no hint of a smirk to make Christopher think he was only joking. "May I ask how you intend to assist our star-crossed pair in making their escape? The duke is on high alert for any signs of elopement, and I fear he will put a stop to any move we make before we make it."

"Well, here is what I was thinking," Christopher began, and he pulled Harding along by the arm so they could continue onward as he explained.

If they ended up walking arm in arm as, say, a courting couple or a pair of bosom friends might, well, it was only so that Christopher's whispered plan could be more easily imparted to Harding's willing ear.

Chapter 16

It took some time before everything was in place for the midnight ride to Gretna Green. That Scottish town just beyond the northern border had been host to many an eloping couple in its day, and though Christopher hated to follow a crowd, he felt it was the safest haven for their pair of lovers. Once they crossed the border, English law could not touch Chester and Belinda, and they could be wed in a hasty ceremony before the duke or god or the regent himself could say a word in protest.

But first, there were letters. Lots and lots of letters.

Harding's boots, Christopher noted, would need to be replaced, what with all the running he was doing about London, hand delivering their messages. The missives flew between Belinda and Christopher, between Christopher and Chester, between Christopher and various allies whose support would be paramount, and, with Christopher acting as middleman and Harding the courier, between the lovers themselves. Chester and Belinda tended to send each other long pages of verse, which Christopher was too gentlemanly to read in depth.

Plans were made, then refined. Christopher purchased a new landau specifically for the escape: something light and swift should they be pursued, yet sturdy enough to make the journey in one piece. He chose his team of horses with all due care, with less of an eye for their looks and more for their stamina and ability to move in perfect tandem. There was no question as to who would be the driver—Christopher would hear no argument.

If you know of anyone else in London who can out-drive the duke's best man, he wrote in one of his secret letters to Chester, *then please introduce us. Otherwise, leave it in my hands. I know what I'm doing.*

This was a lie, of course. Christopher had no idea what he was doing; he had never broken a law in his life—a written one, at least—and had no experience in assisting a couple to elope. Yet he was determined, and with Harding at his side, he felt they could not fail.

At last came the appointed night, when all parties were poised to flee.

Christopher stood on the northernmost corner of Grosvenor Square beside his new carriage, which sat with its roof pulled up to enclose the occupants. The weather had turned chill and the wind had picked up, but at least the sky looked clear. He tipped his head back to survey the stars and adjusted the fall of his ivory greatcoat. Harding stood just a few feet away, holding the horses. Dressed all in black, he looked like a ghoul come to collect souls. The thought made Christopher smile despite himself.

He checked his pocket watch by the light of the carriage lantern. Six minutes to midnight.

"She will come," Harding said, unbidden. "She will not miss this appointment."

Christopher hooked a brow at him, then peered up at the carriage window. The thick velvet curtains were pulled shut to conceal the precious cargo waiting inside. "I know," he said. "I do not doubt her." He bit his lip. "Nor you, dear fellow. I cannot thank you enough for what you're about to do for the sake of my friends."

"They are friends of mine as well," Harding said, "if I may be so bold as to make the claim."

"After tonight, you can be as bold as you please. There won't be much else bolder." Christopher glanced again at his timepiece. Four minutes.

He heard the light sound of footsteps upon the cobbles. Lady Belinda was early, then. Eager, as a bride should be.

He and Harding shared a look and a nod.

"Good luck, my lord," Harding said.

"And you." Christopher swung up on the seat and gathered the reins just as Belinda came around the corner. Her face was flushed, her hair escaping from its bonnet. In her hand was a small case.

"The footmen saw me leave!" she cried. Her voice rang out in the quiet of the night. "They're right behind me. We must hurry."

"Quickly, then! Get in!" Christopher called out. He whipped the horses, and they whinnied like hell was nipping at their hind legs.

The chase was on.

Chapter 17

Christopher had a head start, but not much of one. Within moments of whipping his team into a frenzy, he could hear shouts behind him calling for the duke's own light carriage to be brought. He craned his neck to look back at the rapidly shrinking sight of Grosvenor Square—and the handful of footmen in the lurid green Rushford livery shaking their fists at him. Christopher grinned and faced forward once more, leaning into the cold wind and snapping the reins along the backs of his horses.

His landau clattered down the cobblestones for several miles before making a wide turn onto Aldersgate Street. Christopher could hear another set of wheels rattling at a clip behind, gaining ground. He turned to find the duke's carriage fast approaching. The driver appeared to be an extremely angry little man with a head of wild curls, wearing an improperly buttoned coat. No doubt he'd been roughly awoken from a dead sleep moments before by the footmen. If Christopher was correctly understanding the consonant-heavy curses the fellow was shouting into the night air, he was Welsh.

"Sorry!" he called out, for he really did feel for the man. Yet he had a job to do, and for the moment, Christopher refused to be caught.

He turned the horses sharply to the right, headed for Shoreditch, the side of his carriage scraping along the stone façade of a bakery as he went. His hat tumbled off his head and was crushed beneath the wheels, but Christopher barely noted its loss—a testament to his steely focus.

The Welshman followed, though his horses and axles both protested at the harsh treatment. Sparks flew as the iron bolts at the center of his wheels hissed along the bricks. Christopher looked back, eyes widening at the sight. In the midst of the chaos, the Duke of Rushford himself leaned out the carriage window. Spittle flew as he shouted at Christopher: "Stop this instant and unhand my daughter!"

Christopher did not plan on doing either. "Hold on," he called to his passengers as he executed another devil of a turn, this time on Bunhill to head north once again. "We're getting out of the city if it's the last thing I do," he muttered under his breath as he guided the horses down the narrow, dark lane. It was a good thing they had planned this sojourn for the middle of the night; otherwise their two racing carriages would be plowing down old ladies and small children left and right. As it was, the only victims of their race were a few shop signs that they bashed aside in their hurry.

There was a tense moment where Christopher pulled his landau abruptly down a blind alley while the Welshman flew by, unable to stop at such speed. With the sounds of shouting echoing all around them, Christopher drove his team as quietly as possible into another nearby alleyway where the close shadows might hide them for a time. He stayed there for long minutes, parked behind a cart stacked high with barrels, and listened to the duke's carriage clattering back and forth on the street just outside his hiding place.

Then the light of a lantern shone in Christopher's eyes, and he was once again off like a shot with the duke in hot pursuit.

Buildings flew by, then thinned. Christopher reached the outskirts of London with a whoop. The horses could gain speed on the wider country roads, and that was exactly what Christopher encouraged them to do. Fresh air rushed into his lungs as he inhaled the perfect scent of horseflesh and fields.

His wind-tousled curls fell into his eyes as he turned his bare head to gauge the distance between himself and his pursuers. He'd gained a slightly larger lead now that he was on familiar turf; Christopher suspected that the Welshman rarely drove outside the city. His horses hardly knew what to do with themselves.

Christopher gave a yelp of pleasure at the sight of heaths and meadows. It was working. He thumped his fist on the carriage roof to let his passengers know all was going according to plan. "Just a straight shot now!" he called.

A bullet whizzed past his ear.

Christopher twisted in his seat, what little color he possessed draining from his face. "Are you actually shooting at me?" he cried.

The duke, leaning out of the carriage window once more,

reloaded his dueling pistol in answer. At that distance, Christopher couldn't make out every detail, but he imagined he saw His Grace's upper lip quivering in rage.

The cape of Christopher's greatcoat fluttered wildly as he snapped at the horses to hurry. He hadn't accounted for gunfire in his plan, and he preferred to end the night with all his blood still contained inside his body, if possible.

A muffled feminine voice called from the confines of the carriage: "Lord Eden, it's not worth getting shot! Stop the carriage, please!"

Christopher gritted his teeth. "A little farther," he whispered to no one but the wind. "Just a little farther." Every moment, every mile was precious.

Chester and Belinda weren't the only ones who had fixed their hopes upon him. Harding had as well.

The horses were in a lather and tiring fast. They wanted to run for him, Christopher could feel it in the reins, but they needed rest. That last terrible scrape on the London streets had also affected one of the wheels; there was a dangerous wobble on the left-hand side. The duke fired another shot, this one right over Christopher's head. He ducked downward like a turtle.

He swung the horses around a bend in the road rather recklessly, almost tipping the entire carriage, but righting it at the last moment. The duke's team thundered directly behind now, the Welshman cursing like a sailor.

"The first two shots were a warning!" the duke screamed into the night. "I shall not aim wide a third time!"

Christopher squeezed his eyes shut, then blinked them open. It wasn't just the horses; he was tiring as well. How much ground had he covered tonight? It felt like he'd driven halfway to Cambridge.

Had he done enough?

The cocking of the duke's pistol made the decision for him. Whatever he'd managed, it would have to do. He pulled his team to a skittering stop, his carriage sliding sideways on the packed earth of the road. Behind him, their pursuers came to a similarly messy halt. Christopher raised his hands in the air with as much dignity as he could as the duke, flanked by two footmen and his driver, advanced on him.

"Who the devil do you think you are, absconding with my little girl in the dead of night?"

One of the footmen obediently raised a lantern toward Christopher's face so that the duke might have his answer.

"Lord Eden?" he cried. He was as shocked as if he'd come face-to-face with a ghost. "But why! When you would have had my blessing, why would you abduct my sweet child like some common brute?"

"I'm afraid I have no idea what you mean," Christopher said blithely. "Lady Belinda is not with me."

"Don't talk to me as if I am a fool," the duke snapped. "She went missing tonight; my men saw her get into your carriage." The footmen nodded solemnly in agreement.

"I can't speak to that. I can only say that I was out for a bit of a drive to enjoy the night air when *you* began chasing me through the streets."

"Ridiculous!" the duke spat. He rounded the carriage and reached for the door handle. "Belinda! Come here this instant." He wrenched open the door and stood there gaping.

For in truth, Lady Belinda was not inside. There was only a motley party consisting of Verbena Montrose, her maid, and Étienne Charbonneau. They were all a bit worse for wear, what with having been tossed around in the carriage during the race through the streets, but Étienne at least managed to tug his waistcoat back into place with one firm motion.

A moment was spent with everyone silently staring at one another while Christopher climbed down from the driver's seat.

Verbena ventured to speak first. "Your Grace," she said in a trembling voice that did not seem to be an act, "what a frightful evening we've had! My friend Lord Eden was taking us on a lovely midnight ride when we were suddenly set upon by highwaymen. In the middle of the city, no less! I cannot believe it; look, Monsieur Charbonneau, I'm shaking still." She held out her delicate hand, which was indeed dancing like a leaf in the wind.

Étienne grabbed her hand and held it between his. "My dear, please, there is no need to fear. As I told you, our Lord Eden is a most wonderful driver. We could not be caught! And look, here is His Grace to ensure those villains will chase us no longer."

"My friends." Christopher sighed theatrically and smoothed his hands through his unkempt hair. "It appears there has been a terrible misunderstanding. It was the duke who chased us out of London. He must have thought I was someone else."

The duke sputtered. "Someone else? Someone else!"

Verbena's maid shrank into the back of the carriage seat as if endeavoring to become one with the rich velvet upholstery. Christopher wished her the best of luck, of course. Of all the people he'd involved in this little scheme, he felt the most guilt on her account. The poor girl had only been dragged along to play chaperone, and here she was being screamed at by a duke.

Étienne tried to calm the man with the voice he used when dealing with addled customers. "Your Grace, perhaps we should adjourn elsewhere, drink a nice glass of sherry, and talk this through, *non*?"

The duke ignored him, pushing his way into the carriage. "Where is she?" he demanded. He displaced Étienne from his seat so that he could overturn the cushions. "Where are you hiding Belinda?"

"Dear me, could it be your men saw me and thought I was Lady Belinda? It was so very dark." Verbena blinked at him, all innocence. "I did ask Lord Eden to stop for a moment at Grosvenor Square so that I might take in the moon over the rooftops. There's nothing like moonlight over the square, don't you agree?"

The duke, hunched over as he was in the confines of the carriage, turned to glare at Christopher with all the gravitas such a position could afford. "Where is my daughter?"

"I could not say," Christopher replied. This was very much the truth, as he couldn't be entirely sure where she was on her journey. Likely she was just now leaving London on the westernmost route, where she and Chester would be borne in an unassuming dog cart driven by Harding. The man was prepared to drive all night at a sedate pace that would capture no one's notice. They would be in Gretna Green before anyone could catch them. Even the duke wouldn't be able to organize a search party on every road out of London.

The decoy carriage had been Harding's idea. Too clever by half, was Christopher's man.

Neither of them, however, had counted on the duke bringing a pistol. The thing was still clutched in his white-knuckled hand, trembling as his face turned a shade more magenta. Christopher stood just outside the open carriage door and hoped to god the man wouldn't decide to blow his head off right there in the middle of the road.

"Your Grace," he said slowly, "please know I care deeply for your daughter's health and happiness. If she has gone missing, I will do everything in my power to assist. Yet, as we have established, she is not here with us. Staying in this spot does her no good. Should we not return to London and seek help?"

"This is a conspiracy," the duke whispered. His thumb was still resting on the elaborately engraved flintlock. "You are aiding in her kidnapping."

"Pardon my ignorance, Your Grace, but if a woman leaves a house of her own accord, as your men say she did, then it cannot be a kidnapping, can it?" Verbena asked.

The duke shot her a glare that was thankfully less deadly than a bullet—though Verbena still paled at the look. With his dignity in tatters, the duke could do nothing but exit the carriage and stow his dueling pistol inside his coat. He towered above Christopher as he did this, glowering down at him. Christopher maintained his blank face as best as he could, though he had to admit sweat was trickling down his back as he waited to see what would happen next.

Nothing, as it turned out. The duke merely signaled to his men, and they all raced to their posts to help him back into his own carriage. The Welshman took up the reins and, with a begrudging nod of acknowledgment to his rival, turned the horses back toward London.

Only when the carriage was out of sight behind a stand of trees did Christopher allow himself to breathe. He bent over with his hands braced on his knees, taking deep gulps of air. Étienne alighted to rub his shoulder. All around them, there was nothing but the sound of crickets and the hoot of owls.

"It worked, *mon ami,*" he said in a delighted whisper. "We've done it. There's no way the duke will catch the happy couple."

"I thought he was going to shoot you for certain!" Verbena cried as she popped out from the landau. She couldn't keep the note of fascination from her voice. "What a scandal that would have been. I can't believe I had a front-row seat for the entire thing. This has been the most wonderfully exciting evening of my life! Much better than a ball."

"I am delighted as always to have entertained you, Miss Montrose," Christopher wheezed. He at last caught his breath and stood upright. "One cannot blame the duke for such a reaction, of course. If my eldest daughter had been murdered and my youngest disappeared into thin air, I might wave a pistol round as well."

Étienne frowned at this. "It was my understanding that the eldest– What was her name?"

"Lady Constance," Verbena supplied.

"–that she merely disappeared. There was no trace of what had happened, *non*? She might have been abducted, not killed."

"Oh, be serious, Monsieur Charbonneau." Verbena tossed her hair and then took pains to arrange the curls in a fetching manner over her shoulder once more. Her maid rushed to assist. "After all this time has passed? With not even a whisper as to her whereabouts? If she were alive, someone would know something. Someone would have come forward."

"But without a body, what proof is there?" Étienne cried. "There is always hope, is there not?"

Christopher held up both his hands and shut his eyes. He was tired and hatless and still quite shaky, and now he was forced to deal with a tremendous amount of morbid information. "It was my understanding that the lady was unquestionably deceased. That there could be no other explanation." He'd nearly swallowed his own tongue at that damn ball from the thought of it.

"I am sure that she is, Lord Eden," Verbena said. "Everyone knows it."

Étienne grumbled something in French but was roundly ignored.

"Be that as it may," Christopher said, "the fact remains that we made mischief with a grieving father tonight. Oh, thank you." Verbena's maid had thoughtfully packed a pork pie in a hamper for their excursion, and Christopher gratefully accepted the slice she pushed into his hands. "You will be kind when we return to London, won't you, Miss Montrose?" He took a bite and chewed.

"Yes, I will take care when writing my correspondence," Verbena said as she nibbled on her own slice of pie. "The story of your fantastic chase will be of great interest, I'm sure. All a case of mistaken identity, not harmful in the least to His Grace's reputation. With any luck, word will reach every member of the ton by breakfast."

"And hopefully will overshadow the news of the elopement," Étienne added. "A pistol-wielding duke is more worthy of gossip than two young lovers marrying at Gretna Green. Young lovers get married at the Green all the time; dukes rarely shoot at earls."

Christopher swallowed the last of his pie. "Yes, with your help, Miss Montrose, Horace and Belinda should be protected from the worst of the tongue wagging. The duke will have his hands full with the rumors; he won't dare kick up a fuss over the marriage." It seemed fitting that, for once, gossip was working in Christopher's favor, or at least the favor of his dear friends.

Étienne brightened. "Shall I drive us back to London, Lord Eden? I have always wanted to handle a carriage as light and fine as this."

Christopher had seen Étienne drive a team only once, but once had been quite enough. He grimaced. "No need, dear fellow. I'm fortified now." He swung himself back onto the seat and turned the horses toward home.

Chapter 18

Harding did not return to the London townhouse for several days, by which time Christopher was considering taking his fastest city horse and bringing the man home himself. Luckily, there was no need, as his wayward valet reappeared just as Christopher was finishing his breakfast. All those days and nights on the road to Scotland and back had done him no favors; Harding's normally faultless bearing was wilted by exhaustion. There were dark bags beneath his eyes and dust along his cuffs. Despite this, he was the loveliest, most welcome sight Christopher could conceive.

Christopher leapt from the breakfast table, still chewing his toast. "Good lord, man, please sit! You look as if you're about to keel over at any moment. What did you do, travel all night?"

"I did, my lord," Harding murmured, and it was proof of his poor state that he allowed Christopher to bully him into Christopher's own chair at the head of the table. "Mr. Chesterfield and his new bride send their regards. They plan to stay in

Scotland for a fortnight or so before braving the return trip by coach."

"By then, no one will give two figs about a duke's daughter eloping with a poet." Christopher pushed a plate of bacon toward Harding. "The story of the day is nothing but how I was nearly shot on the road like a dog."

"Shot?" Harding's drooping eyes widened. He stared up at Christopher, ignoring the bacon completely. "Who was trying to shoot you, my lord?"

Christopher nudged the toast rack so that it, too, would be within easy reach for Harding. "The duke, as it happened."

"The–? He *what?*" Harding was exhibiting more emotion in these few minutes than Christopher had seen in all their time together combined. His face went quite pale and his jaw tight. It would be rather gratifying if Christopher weren't so concerned that his valet was about to topple over at the merest brush of a feather.

"It all worked out in the end. Not a single hole was punched through me, I assure you." He refilled his own teacup for Harding, since there wasn't a fresh one handy. "Do you take milk? I can't recall."

"A little," Harding said faintly, and soon received his slightly milky brew as if in a daze. "Thank you, my lord."

"Don't thank me! You're the one who drove that blasted cart all through England and back." He took a seat on Harding's right. "Eat, please."

Harding worked his way slowly through his breakfast, chewing and swallowing before saying, "I must thank you, though, sir. Because of your generosity, I was able to bear witness to

Lady Belinda's wedding. I hadn't ever dared dream I might be able to attend my dear friend's nuptials."

Christopher smiled softly. "Did they look happy when you left them?"

"Riotously, my lord," Harding said. Despite his tiredness, a glimmer of a smile flirted at the corner of his mouth. Christopher longed to capture it in amber.

He looked away instead and stared at the wall. "Good. That's . . . very good." God, he hated the wallpaper in the morning room. Tiny roses strung on blue ribbons, ugh. "I'll have one of the chambermaids ready a bath for you. Take the day off–in fact, take several days! I daresay you need time to recuperate."

Harding's frustrated snort–devilishly close to impertinent–drew Christopher's attention back to his handsome face just in time to watch him gulp down the remains of his tea. He set the cup back in its saucer with a smart click. "I fear there is no time for rest, my lord. There is still the pressing matter of finding you a wife, now that Lady Belinda is no longer available."

"You won't find a wife for me in this state," Christopher pointed out. "I insist you rest before bending your mind to matchmaking."

Harding opened his mouth, no doubt to argue like the recalcitrant work-addicted valet he was, but a footman–frowning at the sight of master and valet seated together at the breakfast table–appeared with the day's letters on a silver tray, an interruption that Christopher used to his advantage.

"Pardon me, dear fellow, I must sort through these." He rifled through the pile. "Ah, still quite a few letters inquiring after my health following 'the ordeal.' Gossipmongers, the whole lot. Anything from the solicitors? I do hope they find someone to buy this house soon. Oh!" He picked up the last piece of mail. "Something from Eden."

It had been weeks since the last letter from old Plinkton, informing Christopher that all was well at the Abbey and sternly reminding him to eat. He recounted it to Harding with a laugh as he slit open the current missive with the provided gold opener. Then his eyes fell to the words contained therein, and his face fell with them.

Harding, noticing the shift in Christopher's mood, placed his knife and fork on his plate. "Is something wrong, my lord?"

"It's Plinkton," Christopher managed to choke out. "Or rather, a doctor. Writing at Cook's behest. He says Plinkton's taken ill. It's unclear what the matter is. He–" He stood up from the table abruptly, nearly toppling his chair. Harding rose with a swiftness and caught it before it fell.

"Would you like me to ready the carriage, sir?" he asked.

The question did not penetrate Christopher's mind in any way that mattered. He could not tear his eyes away from the letter. He read it again and again, looking for some hope and each time finding none. His world shrank and sank into a deep well. He could only hear his own blood rushing in his ears, a torrent fit for drowning.

"My lord?" A stalwart hand fit itself to Christopher's shoulder.

He looked at him wildly, his breath coming in erratic waves. "What's that, Harding?"

"Do you wish to return to the Abbey?" His voice was so soft, it was barely a whisper.

"Yes. Yes, I–" Christopher tried to think. He knew he needed to go home, yet there was so much to do, arrangements to be made with the temporary staff. Would his horses even be fit for the long journey back to Eden? The whirl of responsibility left him frozen.

Harding gently took the letter from his hand. "I will see to it, my lord. I will see to everything. We will leave as soon as possible."

"You haven't slept," Christopher said. It seemed a silly thing to point out at this juncture, yet he could not help it.

"I can sleep on the way."

"You must. Please. I couldn't bear it if you also–" Christopher swallowed. An image of old Plinkton in bed with his terrible fever swam before his mind's eye. "You must look after your health, dear fellow."

Harding did not seem to know what to say to that. He gave a little sigh through his nose, then nudged Christopher toward the stairs. "I shall. Now please let me handle what needs handling."

"Thank you," Christopher said, and though he later had no memory of doing so, went up the staircase and into his dressing room to change into traveling clothes.

Chapter 19

The journey from London took much too long. The weather was foul, raining buckets one moment, miserably drizzling the next. The roads had been churned to muck, and it slowed the horses considerably. Christopher muttered that the hired driver should allow him to take over, as he was certain he could coax the team to move with a bit more alacrity. He even raised his fist to rap on the carriage ceiling but Harding stayed his hand.

"Do you really think you should be driving in such an agitated state?" he snapped. "You'll run the horses into a ditch, my lord, and us with them."

Christopher hadn't felt so chagrined since being scolded by his Quaker tutor during arithmetic lessons. Still, he couldn't help but complain: "We're just going so damned slowly."

"We will arrive when we arrive. It's out of our hands now." Harding released his wrist and sank back into the plush cushions of the carriage seat opposite Christopher. "If I sleep a bit as I promised I would," he murmured, "do you swear you'll remain where you are?"

Christopher sighed, worrying the edge of his thumbnail with his teeth. A nasty habit, one he'd thought he'd discarded in his youth, but apparently today was proving otherwise. "If you insist, dear fellow. If it means you'll get some rest."

"Yes, my lord." He leaned back and closed his eyes. Harding's head was jostled back and forth with the rhythm of the carriage wheels, his whole body lax and easy. Christopher watched him closely, aware that, for once, those keen eyes would not notice him looking. He expected Harding to change in some way as he dropped into sleep, his head wagging to one side and the cadence of his breathing evening out–he thought he might appear softer, more vulnerable, perhaps slightly messy. And yet he did not look that way at all. If anything, he looked more capable and handsome in sleep than he did in his waking hours.

Christopher watched him, unblinking, for a very long time. A thought came to him unbidden that, in some other world where Harding was not his manservant and he himself was not Lord Eden, Harding would be able to lie down, curled on his side, and place his head in Christopher's lap while he slept. Just the thought of running his fingers through those perfect black locks of hair made his face go hot. Christopher jerked his gaze to the open window and watched the countryside roll by instead. Plinkton, the man who'd practically raised him, was terribly ill, and here he was entertaining more silly notions about his valet.

Guilt gnawed at his guts. He should be keeping his mind on

important matters, not daydreaming about things that would never happen.

He resolutely did not think about it the rest of the way back to Eden.

When they finally did arrive, Christopher leapt from the carriage before dashing to the back entrance that led to the servants' quarters.

"Have the horses seen to," he called to the driver and Harding both as he went. "My baggage can wait."

He found Cook in the kitchen with a tall, gaunt man who rose from his seat and introduced himself as Gingham, the doctor from the village.

"How is he?" Christopher asked in a rush without bothering to introduce himself. Plinkton would be disappointed by such a lack of manners, he knew, and the mere thought of the old butler's displeasure was enough to bring a tear to his eye.

"He's resting for the moment," the doctor said.

"He'd been coughing an awful lot these last few days," Cook broke in. She was as pale as a worn sheet and just as transparent when it came to her worry. "I told him to put his feet up and drink warm water, but of course he wouldn't listen. And then I found him collapsed in the hall! Just lying there, oh!" She pulled a handkerchief from her sleeve and cried into it.

Christopher folded her into an embrace. It was a bit awkward, as she towered over him by a fair margin, but she fell against him like a tree. "I'm so sorry, Cook. I'm so sorry."

"It's nothing you've done," she mumbled against his shoulder. "I'm just glad you've come back home."

"Of course. My place is here." He stroked her fiery hair,

shot through with more grey these days, and gave her one last squeeze before releasing her. He kept hold of her hands, though, as he looked to Gingham. "What do we do now?"

The doctor frowned. "At this point, I have done all I can. He will either cease being consumptive in a week or so, or he will not."

The words washed over Christopher like a cold rain. He could not even parse what they meant. Distantly, he heard the door to the back garden open and registered Harding's solid presence, but all he could do was stare at Dr. Gingham in horror.

"And then what?" he asked. He hated the sound of his voice, a plaintive lost little lamb. He cleared his throat and tried again. "If he does not improve, what shall we do?"

"I am truly sorry," said the doctor. "There is nothing else to be done."

Cook gave a little sob under her breath and clutched tighter at Christopher's hands. Christopher felt his blood going cold in his veins. "If it's a matter of money," he said. "If there is some medicine that would help–"

The doctor shook his head. "It's in god's hands now, I'm afraid."

Christopher looked around the airy kitchen, grasping for words, for some negotiation that would make all this wretchedness disappear. What was the point of being Lord Eden–of having all this money and land and a seat in Parliament–if none of that could keep Plinkton alive? Christopher felt so useless.

"My lord." Harding was at his elbow. "Would you like to see him?" He flicked his eyes to the doctor. "Is that possible?"

"Yes, can I see him?" Christopher begged.

The doctor said a short visit would be permissible, so long as they let Plinkton sleep, and Christopher was led numbly to Plinkton's room at the end of the hall. Christopher couldn't recall ever going through that door, as he had always respected the man's privacy, but he wasn't surprised to see a spartan cell of a bedroom with only an engraving of the king on the wall and nothing else. All four of them crowded into the small space, shoulders bumping as they arranged themselves around Plinkton's bedside.

He looked so small and shrunken against the vast whiteness of his bed linens. His hair was thin and brittle, like grey straw. His breathing sounded like it was taking an enormous amount of effort just for a little wheeze every few moments. Christopher sought Plinkton's hand atop the blankets and cradled it gently in both of his.

"Is he in much pain?" he asked, his eyes not leaving that sallow face.

The doctor cleared his throat. "I expect not," he said, though he didn't sound at all convincing.

Christopher felt himself sinking into a well of despair. It would close over his head if he wasn't careful. He needed to be careful. "I will stay with him for a time," he said, trying to sound firm. "If you could– There must be something you could do?" He'd never felt as young as he did then, looking to everyone else in the room for some indication of what would come next.

"We will hire a nursemaid to assist in Mr. Plinkton's care," Harding informed the doctor as if it were a decision Christopher himself had struck upon. He grabbed the single straight-backed chair the room held and placed it at the bedside, guiding Christopher to sit. "If there are any instructions you could leave with me . . ."

"Yes, let's talk outside." The doctor ushered him back out, leaving Cook and Christopher lingering at the sickbed.

Cook stared down at Plinkton as well, her eyes rimmed in red. "He was fine a few days ago," she murmured. "Just his old self."

"Things change, I suppose," Christopher said. He was unable to keep the bitterness from his voice. It all seemed so damnably unfair.

"He'll improve, m'lord, just you wait and see. A little tumble won't keep an old warhorse like him down for long." Cook patted his arm, though her face didn't look as convincing as her words sounded. "I'll let you have some privacy." She left him as well, shutting the door behind her as she went.

Christopher could hear the soft murmurs of the doctor and Harding discussing the matter of a nursemaid out in the hall. Plinkton's labored breaths cut through the thick air of the room. Somewhere upstairs, a clock chimed the hour.

Plinkton's hand felt so small in his, Christopher thought. He didn't want to let it go.

"Such a fuss," a voice croaked, and for a moment Christopher thought perhaps one of the Abbey ghosts was in the room with them. But then he realized Plinkton was awake and staring up at him. "Young master, did you really come all the way back here for this?"

"Plinkton!" He clutched his hand tighter. "How are you feeling?"

"Old," said Plinkton, though a smile stretched across his lined face. "Incredibly old."

"Shall I fetch the doctor? He's right outside."

Plinkton raised his free hand with some effort and shooed the notion away. "I don't care to be bled any more than I already have been. I'll be all right, my lord."

"You're feeling better, then." Christopher's words came out thick with relief and elation. "You'll probably be up and about in no time."

"I'll be all right," Plinkton stressed. His weathered hand squeezed at Christopher's, though its grip was weak. The old butler's eyes, though, were as sharp as they'd ever been. "You'll be all right too, my lord. You'll be fine."

Christopher swallowed. "I don't want to hear that sort of talk, Plinkton. You make it sound as if this is farewell."

"I think, after so many years of service, I have earned the right to say farewell," Plinkton said, "rather than pretending I will live forever. I don't want the important things to go unsaid before my time is done."

Christopher opened his mouth to argue, but one look from Plinkton and he shut it. A tear worked its way from his eye, and instead of weeping in front of his most loyal retainer, Christopher bowed his head and pressed his face into the bedclothes.

Plinkton's frail hand slipped from his grip and settled in Christopher's hair. The simple touch forced more tears from him; even in this, Plinkton's first thought was Christopher's own comfort. It made him feel utterly wretched. He lifted his face and manfully wiped away the tears.

"Of course, dear fellow. Of course. If you have messages for your kin, tell me now and I will see they get word."

Plinkton smiled again, indulgent and fond. "The only person I care to speak to is you. Please take care, Lord Eden. Keep yourself safe when I'm gone. I protected you as long as I could—the best way I knew how." His own red eyes became wet. "I never told another soul, I swear to you. But you have *got* to promise me you'll keep yourself safe."

Christopher felt a cold wind blow through him. "What?" he whispered.

"It was nothing anyone else would have noticed," Plinkton said, and though his tone was reassuring, the words cut through Christopher like knives. "It was only because I've known you your whole life; practically raised you, I should think."

"I don't know what you mean," Christopher said. Plinkton's hand slid from his hair to his cheek, and Christopher cupped it there, wondering if his face felt as hot to the touch as he suspected. "I don't—"

Plinkton clicked his tongue. "You always lick the sugar off the top of the morning buns. Your brother never did that."

A terrible fear swept through Christopher's soul. "My brother," he said hollowly. He had known? This whole time, Plinkton had known?

Plinkton gave Christopher's cheek a gentle pat. "You'll be all right," he mumbled. His eyes were drooping. "You always have been." Then his hand went limp under Christopher's, and the only thing holding it to Christopher's cheek was his own grip.

Christopher placed Plinkton's hand back down on the bedclothes, letting it rest there, so pale against the blankets. He imagined, briefly, naïvely, that Plinkton had perhaps fallen into a deep and well-deserved sleep. Then he looked, really looked, at Plinkton's rail-thin body beneath the bedclothes. The sheets were completely still. Not even the smallest breath moved them.

Oh, Christopher realized. *He's gone.*

He hoped Plinkton—dear Plinkton, who came to the stables with Christopher even though he detested horses and they detested him, who taught him table manners when he was just a tot—wouldn't begrudge him a moment to feel sorry for himself. He held the still hand in his and bowed his head, feeling nothing but the exquisite numbness of realizing that so much of his careful tiptoeing through life had been for nothing.

Chapter 20

The funeral was held on an unseasonably hot day with not a cloud in the sky. Christopher wore a black armband over his most staid coat of heather grey, offering a steadying elbow to Cook on his left, Harding a dark shadow on his right. A few prayers, a few words from the vicar, and then the coffin was lowered into the ground. The whole thing seemed to take less than a minute. Christopher thought it all very unfair. Plinkton deserved a horrid, rainy day for his funeral. There should have been thunderclouds encroaching, he thought, and water pouring from the church eaves. Rain should have dripped from the brim of Christopher's hat until he removed it at the graveside, and then the rain should have mixed with his tears.

As it was, the weather held that morning, and his only tears—two of them, one from each eye—fell silently down his cheeks.

Harding offered a handkerchief, but Christopher waved it away. What he really wished to do was lean upon Harding's capable shoulder, but that was impossible. His head was still awhirl with the final words he'd exchanged with Plinkton. He felt like a brittle piece of long grass buffeted by strong winds, like he would break in half at any moment for the slightest reason. No, he would not reach for Harding or his handkerchief. Much as he ached to.

Cook was dry-eyed and red-faced. She had already cried all her tears days ago, Christopher knew. He had held her hand as she'd done so, sitting on the edge of Plinkton's narrow bed. Together, they had packed up the room and its meager belongings. There had not been much: a Bible, a pair of walking boots, a stack of letters bound in red string that Christopher had not dared to read, save for their postmarks. Christopher had made every effort to write to the man's remaining family, but his letters had yielded no real results. The few responses he'd received over the week indicated that so-and-so from his brother-in-law's side of the family was no longer at the last known address, or that what's-his-name from Plinkton's hometown had passed the year previous.

It seemed horrendously sad that a man who had lived such a long life as Plinkton had so little to show for it in the end.

Plinkton had served three generations of Winterthropes. He had been more of a father to Christopher than any other man. And if Christopher understood their final conversation correctly, he had remained devoted despite—or even because of—Christopher's unusual make. Christopher owed him so much, but what had Plinkton ever been given?

"That's that, then," Cook said as the gravediggers began to cover the coffin lid with their spadefuls of dirt.

"Yes," Christopher said, his voice steadier than he expected it to be. Harding was a warm presence at his side. "Let's go."

They walked from the churchyard and over the hills back to the manor. Christopher had suggested the carriage, thinking of Cook's poor ankles, which he knew had seen better days, but she had insisted on leaving the horses in their stalls. She leaned heavily on Christopher's arm, though, with Harding hovering at her other side as if prepared to swoop in should she need more support, and for that Christopher was grateful. Cook gave a sigh as the rooftops of Eden Abbey appeared over the last rise.

"This is the part I've been dreading," she confided. "Even when it was just the two of us, me and Plinkton, we did our best to keep each other's spirits up. 'Not a bad job,' I'd tell him. 'Only position I've ever had where I needn't cook a full dinner but once or twice a year. How many earls are content with just tea and toast for supper?' " She gave a single chuckle. "Don't know what I'll do without him around, to be honest."

"We are all poorer for his absence," Harding said with quiet sympathy. "Though I knew him only a short while, I admired the man very much." He looked at Christopher, barely managing the feat over Cook's bowed head, and held his gaze. "I would not dare attempt to take his place, but if there is any task that needs doing, some office of Plinkton's that I might take up, you need only ask."

Christopher could not even form the words to thank his valet. Harding had been indispensable these last few days, despite having had no time to catch his breath since Gretna Green. He merely nodded and hoped it would suffice.

The remainder of the funerary day passed in a blur. Cook offered Christopher something for dinner, and he ate it, but he couldn't say what it had been. Afterward, he sat by the kitchen fire and stared into its flames, unable to move or think. It was only Cook's gentle coaxing that forced him from the spot.

"You need some rest. We all do," she'd said. "Even him." Her gaze went to the ceiling, gesturing to where Harding lurked upstairs. The man had taken on the bulk of the arrangements since Plinkton's death, not allowing himself a moment's peace.

"I will endeavor to see that he does," Christopher promised.

It was a sad and disheveled Lord Eden who finally limped upstairs to his bedroom in the wee hours of the night. He opened the door to his dressing room to find Harding, looking just as worn, diligently unpacking a trunk of shirts from London. What with all the funeral planning and hopeless attempts at contacting Plinkton's kin, that chore had fallen by the wayside.

"I'm nearly finished, my lord," Harding said, his eyes flicking up from the shirts he was refolding. "You'll be able to dress for bed in a moment."

"You should be dressing yourself for bed right now," Christopher parried. "Leave all this, Harding. You can see to it in the morning."

"There is only one last trunk."

"To hell with the trunk. You haven't had a decent night's sleep since your sojourn to Scotland." He rubbed his face. He was so tired, he was nearly willing to fall into his pillow fully clothed and risk ruining the lines of his trousers. Nearly. "There is still the matter of the few days' rest you're owed for that."

"I can hardly cease my duties now that–" Harding began.

A bright flash and loud crack of thunder made them both jump several inches off the ground. Christopher stood in the silence that followed, gazing up at the ceiling. It had sounded like the heavens were opening up directly above the Abbey.

"Good lord," he murmured. The rain that had been absent for the funeral at last arrived in a furious torrent. Wind and rain lashed at the windowpanes and licked against the old roof. The noise was tremendous. It made Christopher feel as if he were trapped in a jar that had been thrown into the sea.

Harding opened his mouth to say something, but he was drowned out by another crack of thunder, this one so close it sounded as if a great tree was splintering overhead. Christopher startled into the corner of the dressing room farthest from the windows, bumping into a chest of drawers and upsetting the collection of snuffboxes that sat atop it. Two fell to the carpet with dull thumps, accompanied by more distant growls of thunder.

Christopher gave a thready laugh, though it sounded more like a moan. "I should have been expecting that." He swallowed down the racing of his heart. A horrible feeling of impending doom was enveloping him even now; he could feel its heavy fingers squeezing the sense from his mind. He hadn't had a waking attack of nerves like this since the Leftmores' ball.

"My lord." Harding was at his elbow, holding him upright.

"I'm fine, I'm absolutely fine," Christopher lied. Even his voice couldn't contain its tremble. He must have been more affected by Plinkton's death–and deathbed confession–than he thought.

Harding stared at him in the low flickering light of the few candles that were still lit. Christopher couldn't meet his gaze for more than a moment. He felt as if every weakness he held inside was written plain on his face, and Harding could read every word of it.

Then, somehow, things got worse.

An inhuman howl welled up from somewhere down the hall, screeching through the Abbey like a banshee. Christopher couldn't help himself; he gave a sharp cry and attempted to flatten himself farther against the chest of drawers, as if by doing so he could make himself disappear. He shut his eyes tight, no longer trying to hide his fear.

"That's it, then," he whispered in a rush. "They're here. It's over."

"My lord, what are you talking about?" Harding asked.

Another eerie wail floated through the manor, this time accompanied by a multitude of nightmarish chitters. Christopher had the distinct impression that someone was walking over his grave.

"The Eden ghosts." He hid his face against Harding's shoulder as another volley of terrible screams assaulted him. "Surely you hear them! It's not just me, is it?"

"I hear something," Harding said, shouting to be heard above the din. "I don't know what it is, but I assure you, there are no ghosts coming for you." Harding's hand moved from his arm to grasp his shoulder. He leaned in very close. "There's no such thing. There is only us, here, now."

"No, you're wrong." Christopher shook his head. "Ghosts are very real. Oh, they're more real than the man you see before you." He shuddered at his own words, at the implication.

"I must disagree, my lord." Harding tipped his head to the side, considering him. "My lord?"

But Christopher wasn't listening. He could only hear distant sounds from a ship that had ceased to sail long ago. The wood creaked around him and the canvas flapped on the mainmast. The salt smell of the air overwhelmed him. He stared past Harding at nothing, across the years of memory.

"Lord Eden." Harding placed his warm, firm hands on Christopher's shoulders and gave him a hard shake. "Christopher!"

His attention at last snapped back to his man. "James?"

Worry creased those handsome features so that a small furrow appeared between his brows. Christopher, in a fleeting moment of hysteria, thought it might be nice to touch it. Harding cleared his throat. "There is nothing in the house except you and me and Cook. Do you understand?"

Christopher hesitated, still shaking from the vestiges of terror. "I hate to contradict you, dear fellow, but–" Another howl tore through the darkness. They both jumped at the horrid sound. Even after it had died away, it seemed to echo in Christopher's ears. "All right, Doubting Thomas," he whispered to Harding, "care to explain that?"

"It's only the wind," he said, his voice damnably steady. "There must be an open window in the west wing. Come, let's close it up. You'll see I'm right."

Christopher flinched. "Cook will find our bodies by morning, curled up on the floor like little beetles, dead of fright. That's how all ghost stories end."

"This is not a ghost story," Harding insisted. He reached for a nearby chamberstick, its candle wavering in the dark. "Your fears are unfounded. Come see the proof." His eyes softened as he looked back at Christopher, or maybe it was just the candlelight. "You might be able to sleep through the night, sir, if you're not constantly worried about lost souls roaming these halls."

Christopher heaved a shaky sigh. He could see that Harding would not be deterred. Besides, the alternative was staying here in the dark while Harding went marching into the unknown, and Christopher's instincts told him it was better to remain together. At least then he wouldn't die alone.

"Fine," he said. "If you insist."

Harding urged him to take one of the candlesticks from the sideboard, and then they trooped toward the derelict western wing of the manor.

As they made their way down a rarely walked hall, Christopher felt the hairs on his arms stand on end. Here in the abandoned wing of Eden Abbey, the storm sounded like the pounding of hundreds of horses' hooves against flinty ground. Lightning flashed in an endless dance outside the grimy windows, blinding him every so often. But the noise—that ghoulish, soul-freezing screeching—was the worst of it. It rose in volume as they crept down the hall until, coming to the last door at the end, it seemed as if hundreds of foul spirits had surrounded them on all sides.

Harding, for all his earlier bravado, now had enough sense to look a bit pale around the edges. He glanced at Christopher and gestured to the shut door, wordlessly indicating they should investigate whatever was behind it.

This was a position Christopher could neither understand nor support. He shook his head violently, the candle in his hand wavering as he moved. "I can't." It came out in a bare whisper, a mere movement of lips against the cacophony of the ghosts.

"We must," Harding said. He offered Christopher his hand, palm up and flat. And he waited for Christopher to take it. "We will."

Christopher hesitated for a long moment, then laced their fingers together. His instincts were shouting at him to run—perhaps to the study, where an ancient hunting rifle might provide some measure of protection. But the body reacts as it is wont to react, and in that moment, Christopher was paralyzed. He felt himself being tugged forward by Harding, knew he was being led closer to the door, but it was like watching a pantomime from the back row: everything was happening at a great distance and didn't seem to involve him in the slightest.

He was absolutely certain he was going to die.

And what's more, he was sure he deserved it.

It had been a long time coming, after all. No man could cheat Death forever, not even one as unusual as he.

Harding released his hand and reached for the doorknob. The screeching only got worse, an inhuman scream, like something meant to hunt Christopher until it had him in its maw. Perhaps it had been following him all these years, and now that Plinkton was gone, the moment had arrived for Christopher to be struck down.

Harding opened the door.

They were met immediately by a blast of wind that snuffed out their lights, and a torrent of cold rain that drenched their clothes and hair. The candlestick fell from Christopher's slack hand, hitting the wet floorboards with a terrible clang. It was so very like that other storm, in that other place, that he had weathered long ago. No–it was the exact same storm, he was sure of it. It had never stopped raging, not for ten long years.

Christopher had been right to be afraid: the storm was here to take what it was owed.

But it couldn't take Harding. Christopher could not allow that. The man was innocent; his only crime was skepticism. Suddenly Christopher's limbs were not so frozen, and the strength that had deserted him rushed back in.

"No!" he shouted into the wind, though his voice was drowned out. He staggered toward Harding and tried, with all his might, to shove the fool out of the way. These were his ghosts and no one else's. "Harding, get away!"

"My lord–"

Christopher tasted water on his tongue–shouldn't it be salty? Not this sweet, surely? He squeezed his eyes shut, unable to see anyway, and readied himself for the end. He could only pray Harding found the sense to run. "Damn you, man, go!"

"My lord, *look*."

Christopher opened his eyes and saw–

Well, he saw a big fucking hole in his roof, for one.

The storm had torn away some of the more precarious slates atop the western wing. The resulting crack in the ceiling was as wide as a man was tall, and from this crack came the relentless wind and the rain. But that was not all the room contained.

"There are no ghosts, you see?" Harding pointed to the dark, dank corners.

Christopher's vision coalesced back into something he could understand. Harding was right; instead of wispy spirits, he saw loads of beady yellow eyes looking back at him from the shadows. Their fur was dark and matted from the rain. Their horrible chitters had risen at their intrusion, and now they scattered all along the floor, their claws scratching at the worn boards. Christopher saw one of his lost cuff links sitting on the ground in a puddle of filth and rainwater. The glint of other baubles shone in dark corners. No doubt his missing watch fob was among them, secreted away not by ghosts, but by–

"Rats," he said to himself. Not heavenly retribution, not the souls of those he had wronged. Only vermin. He began to laugh. "It's just *rats.*"

He bent double with his hands braced on his knees, laughing like a madman. And why not? He'd certainly gone mad for a moment there. Stark raving.

"Harding! It's only rats!"

Harding didn't exactly dissolve into mirth alongside him, but the hand he placed on Christopher's back felt more amused than usual. "Quite, my lord," he said, the relief in his voice a palpable thing.

Christopher straightened, then felt the manic grin slip off his face. "Harding?" He eyed the mass of creatures.

"Yes?"

"There's an awful lot of rats."

"You're not wrong, my lord."

"And is it my imagination or," Christopher took a cautious step backward as the wave of vermin advanced in fits and starts toward their feet, "are they getting closer?"

"It may be prudent to retreat." Harding jabbed his unlit chamberstick at the nearest rat and grabbed Christopher by the lapel of his coat, hauling him backward out the door. Together, they slammed the thing against the roaring wind until it was shut tight.

They stood there a moment, listening to the continued patter of rain and the displeased squeaks of the rats.

"How does one, erm, deal with that amount of rats?" Christopher asked.

"I will make arrangements tomorrow, sir. Surely there's someone in the village willing to lend a few rat-catchers." Harding grimaced. "I will hire someone to repair the roof as well."

"Good." Now that the absurd adventure was over, Christopher felt all the wasted vigor curdle in his blood, leaving him as weak as a babe. He slumped against the door, his hot forehead pressed against the damp wood. He couldn't seem to get his breathing back under control. "That's . . . good," he choked out.

"My lord." The touch of Harding's hand on his back was the only real thing Christopher could feel. Everything else was spinning around him. "Before you saw the vermin—it sounded as if you feared for your life."

"Oh, that?" Christopher attempted a lighthearted laugh, but it fell rather flat. "Yes, I suppose I acted like the worst fool. You must think me very stupid."

He hoped, desperately, that he and Harding would fall back into the roles they had set for themselves ages ago: the bumbling yet charming young master, the stalwart and cool manservant. And at the same time, he prayed that something would change, for he could not imagine another moment playing at the charade.

Harding's strong hand did not leave him. "My lord, I–" he said, and then said nothing more.

"I'm sorry," Christopher said, and his voice broke. He turned his head toward those dark, dark eyes. Their lashes were tipped in rainwater, and as Christopher watched, a blink caused a droplet to cascade down Harding's cheek. *Probably the closest such a self-composed man would ever come to crying,* he thought. There was something about Harding's nearness, the heat of him even through the sodden layers of their clothes. It made Christopher think that perhaps he wasn't the loneliest, most wretched soul in existence. "I'm so, so sorry."

When Harding spoke again, it was quiet and laced with concern. "You cannot keep the whole world at arm's length, my lord," he said. "Not forever."

There was nothing Christopher could say in response that would not utterly destroy him. They stayed there, silent and unmoving, for long moments, until even the rats grew quiet and only the sounds of their breathing and the rain filled the hall.

Chapter 21

Christopher allowed himself to be led back to his rooms like a shaky newborn foal. He was shivering with cold by the time they reached his bedroom door, and Harding took one look at him in the light of the blazing array of candles before dragging him into his valet's cell.

"We must get you dry," he said as he pulled stacks of clean bathing sheets from a trunk at the foot of his bed. He wrapped one around Christopher's shoulders, the massive thing engulfing his small frame, and draped another over his wet head.

"Really, I'm all right." Christopher's voice sounded muffled within the confines of the cloth. "A swallow of brandy and I'll be fine." This, said through chattering teeth.

"Sit," Harding commanded. He steered Christopher to his own bed and guided him to perch on the edge of the mattress. Then he busied himself with lighting a fire in the grate, taking much more time than seemed necessary.

Christopher soon realized the reason: it gave Harding the

opportunity to say something of deep import without the indignity of speaking face-to-face.

"If I may be so bold, one thing that's struck me as I settled into your service is that you do not have too many trusted confidants," he said, still facing the grate. "Monsieur Charbonneau, perhaps, but you can hardly lean on that single shoulder when he is in London and you are here." He tossed another log onto the pile and stared into the flames. "Which is all to say that I take this very seriously, as you must so rarely open yourself to others. What happened tonight nearly scared you to death, and I don't understand why. If ever you're willing to speak of it, I am willing to listen."

Christopher sat in a miserable heap on the edge of Harding's narrow bed. He watched as more water dripped from the ends of his hair onto the crumpled bath sheet that covered his lap. Harding was correct, of course. He trusted this man, he realized, with his entire being–save, perhaps, his heart, which was not fit company for anyone.

If Plinkton had known, and for all those years stayed at Eden Abbey despite knowing . . .

And if he already trusted Harding with all his foibles and weaknesses, his joys and desires, his finances and his beloved wardrobe . . .

Perhaps he could trust him with this one, final thing.

"Harding," he said, and the seriousness of his tone must have been something to behold indeed, for Harding stopped fussing about with the grate and rose to face his master with a worried look.

"My lord?"

Christopher waved a hand through the air. "I know your sense of duty or what have you makes it difficult, but please, I am begging you—at least for the moment, call me Christopher." Bold as this was, he didn't dare push the boundaries of informality so far as to use Harding's Christian name, as he hadn't been given the right. His earlier impropriety, a slip of the tongue, was shameful enough.

"I will try," Harding said. He sat down gingerly beside Christopher on the bed. "What is it?"

Christopher filled his chest with a deep breath. This is what standing on the edge of the sea cliffs must feel like, he supposed, though he'd never been foolish enough to try that particular spot of derring-do. Yet here he was, on the very edge.

"After the events of tonight, there's something I should tell you." He fastened his gaze straight ahead, thinking the innocuous wall was a better bet than Harding's face. He wasn't sure he could watch if that face fell into disgust once he said all he needed to say. "It's rather a long story. The story of my life, I suppose."

There seemed to be nothing in the room but the low light of the fire and Harding's soft voice. "I will hear it, if you wish to tell me."

"I should say at the outset—" He wasn't certain how it should even be phrased. "That is, I was born and brought up in a state quite unlike the one you see before you." He kept staring at the wall, grateful for its placid demeanor. It seemed to be taking the news well, at least. "It's only in the last ten years or so that I've been able, by a confluence of circumstances, to assert my manhood, if you follow my meaning. Otherwise, you certainly would not know me as Lord Eden, or even Christopher, but something else entirely."

Christopher chanced a glance over at Harding to gauge whether he was near to understanding, but his man's face gave him no clues. It was a complete blank, and a pale one. As he watched, the blood seemed to drain even further from Harding's sharp features, leaving him wan as a ghost.

"Perhaps I'm not being clear," Christopher said. Panic welled in his chest. "What I mean is, I had a twin. A long time ago. And he—damn it all, I've actually never spoken of this before. I mean that I'm—"

"Christopher," Harding murmured. He stood abruptly, and for one terrible moment, Christopher thought he might leave. Just march out of the room and out of the Abbey, never to be seen again.

He was prepared to plead, but then he saw that Harding was not leaving. He was fumbling with the buttons of his waistcoat.

Now Christopher wasn't sure how to feel. He eyed his man's progress as he shucked off his coat and waistcoat and started untying his cravat. "Are you quite all right, dear fellow?" he asked.

Harding remained silent. Whatever he needed to impart could not be accomplished with words, apparently, for once he had tossed his cravat to the floor, he started to pluck the hem of his shirt from his trousers. Christopher's eyes went wide. Of all the reactions to his confession that he'd imagined, a spontaneous stripping to the buff was not one of them.

"May I ask what—?" he tried again, but there was no need. Harding yanked his shirt up and off and stood before him, chest heaving.

A chest, as it happened, that was bound in linen bandages.

Christopher's entire world tilted until it was standing on its head. He stared; he knew it was gauche, but he couldn't help it. It seemed to him this must be some grand joke, or a dream, or perhaps a trick designed to . . . what? What could this possibly be? His lips parted, but no sound came out for a long while.

"I don't understand," he finally said, his gaze flicking up to meet Harding's. He didn't dare understand. Not without confirmation that he wasn't going mad.

Harding swallowed as if working up to speaking. When he finally did, he said, "I believe we might be made along the same lines." He watched Christopher's face carefully. "Am I wrong?"

A small part of Christopher's mind was aware that he was still gaping like a very unattractive landed trout, and he needed to say something–literally anything–in the hollow silence that followed.

He decided on something as foolish as it was honest: "No. No, it seems you are correct."

He stood abruptly, shrugging off the damp bath sheets. It seemed prudent to stand. A momentous occasion such as this called for it. He stood before Harding, his gaze roving over his whipcord body before he forced himself to meet and hold Harding's dark eyes.

"Truly?" he asked, which sounded ridiculous now that he'd said it aloud, but it couldn't be helped. "This is . . . real?"

"As real as I can fathom," Harding whispered.

Christopher gave a shout of pure joy and launched himself into Harding's arms, not caring about propriety or rank, not caring if he was the picture of hysteria. Tears welled in his eyes, happy ones for once, as he clutched Harding tighter, his arms winding around his shoulders. He felt the planes of their bodies press together, and the sensation was so very different from the time they had been forced into close proximity in Lady Belinda's wardrobe. It felt good, he realized, to hold close another human being for the sheer pleasure of it, especially this one. Harding stiffened in his embrace at first, but after a long moment, his capable hands settled at the small of Christopher's back.

"What are the odds?" Christopher laughed. "In all the world, that you should find me!" He gave Harding another squeeze, his wet clothes squelching against Harding's skin, before staring back up at him. "It's like a miracle."

"Yes," said Harding, his face a mixture of quiet shock and contentment. "It must be."

"I thought I was the only one," Christopher said. He buried his face into the hot skin of Harding's neck even as his tears spilled over his cheeks. "I thought it was just me, alone in the world. Did you think so too?"

"For a time." Harding's voice was a sweet rumble this close. It moved through Christopher as thunder might roll in from afar. "I have never met another—not personally. But I have heard stories and rumors; have you not?"

"Rumors?" Christopher pulled back, wide-eyed.

"Of so-called women being discovered in the military, for example," Harding said. "Some say they return to dresses and stays when the fighting is done, but others say they continue living as they fought. There were two or three such stories here at home and in the Colonies. Did you never hear of it in all your time in Philadelphia?"

"No, I suppose— Well, who would have told me?" Christopher said. He tried to picture his Quaker tutor incorporating this lesson and found he could not, as forward-thinking as the man had been.

"There are other tales," Harding continued. "I sought them out like a bloodhound. There are a pair of ladies who settled in a cottage in Wales and refused their betrotheds, and they live as husband and wife do. In small villages, there are craftsmen and laborers who are like us, but without anyone who will judge or care so long as they do their work. There are women who share the other side of our coin, who have eschewed their surcoats in favor of skirts. There are people in other parts of the globe who do not think any of it strange at all—they exist, I know it."

"They do?" Christopher could not help the shock that suffused his voice. It sounded like a dream, like a complete fantasy.

"There are all sorts, my lord," Harding said. "The world is wide and full of grace, I promise you."

The notion stopped Christopher's breath in his chest. He had devoured as many myths as he could find, pressing certain stories like talismans to his heart. Iphis and his blessing from Isis, beardless Apollo and his fiercer twin: they had set his imagination afire, but he could never have dreamed that there was, in pockets all throughout the world, a secret family to which he already belonged.

Harding continued, "I had never before met another like me, but when I came here to Eden—" He gave a helpless shrug.

Christopher dashed the back of his arm across his face to smear away the tears. "Am I that obvious?" he asked, hating how his voice went high with fear.

Harding shook his head, and his hands went to Christopher's upper arms. "No, it was only a hope of mine, what I thought was a frivolous daydream. Your aversion to being dressed made me wonder, as it is such a particular quirk of yours." He went a little pink under Christopher's gaze, or perhaps it was a trick of the candlelight. "Just in case, whilst we were in London I told my fellow valets that I dress you as is usual so as to dispel any suspicion. They were quite complimentary of my work, actually; you should be pleased."

Christopher smiled despite himself. "That's the sort of thing you valets discuss on your days off, is it?"

Harding colored further. "Among other things."

"Well." He couldn't seem to keep the ridiculous grin off his face. Christopher glanced down and realized they were still locked in each other's grip, like they were beginning a strange sort of dance. He felt his face go hot and cursed his pale coloring, which would no doubt show every bit of the blush. "Well," he said again, disentangling himself. He sat down heavily on the bed once more, unsure whether his legs would support him. "I promised you my whole life story, did I not? And now that I know you're the best sort of audience for it, I'm not afraid to tell it. Where shall I begin?"

Harding resumed his place sitting next to him. "You don't have to explain all the details if it pains you too much."

"No, I want you to know. Someone should."

He took a deep breath. And began.

Chapter 22

"As you already know," Christopher said, "the previous Lord and Lady Eden, my parents, had two children. Twins. A boy and a girl." He paused. "I would say I was the girl and my brother was the boy, but that's not quite correct."

"I understand," Harding told him gently.

"Right. Yes. Anyway, those early days of our childhood were spent here at Eden Abbey. It was livelier then; I recall dozens of servants, nannies, gamekeepers, gardeners–you couldn't throw a stone without hitting one of the staff. Not that I would ever hit one of the staff with a stone, mind you," he added quickly. "I was a mischievous child, but not a cruel one."

Harding's mouth tilted up at one corner just a tick. "I believe it."

Christopher didn't bother to hide his smile. He looked into the small, cheery fire in the grate as he remembered. "Well, I was disciplined on more than one occasion for sneaking into my father's dressing room and touching all his fine coats. I thought every child had the same feelings I did about men's fashions." He tipped his head to the side. "Surely no woman *liked* wearing stays or huge gowns. Surely every girl in the world hated having her hair arranged as much as I did. Not just annoyance, but proper, intimate hatred that carved me out." He squinted at Harding. "Did you feel similarly?"

"Of course," he said. "Naturally."

Christopher felt his heart settle in its proper spot for the first time in a very long time—perhaps ever. It gave him the courage to go on to the story's eventual end.

"Yes, so: you know the outline of what happened next. My father decided to travel to Pennsylvania to personally oversee some of his investments there. The Abbey was already beginning to fall apart even before he inherited it, and the costs of the estate's upkeep were mounting. He had a hand in something like a dozen textile mills—a business I refused to continue, by the way, once I realized the excremental manner in which the raw materials were procured." Nearly all dealings in that part of the world were touched by slavery, and though Christopher was quite aware that he could not change that fact or make it right, he would be damned if he allowed his money to be used in such a way. "At any rate, it meant that my father would be abroad for many years at a stretch. My mother insisted we go as a family. I think she must have loved him, because she certainly did not love the idea of living in Philadelphia. She thought it was a filthy town, and uncultured, and a poor place to raise children. Yet she could not bear to be parted from Papa.

"She wasn't wrong about Philadelphia, of course. Waves of

illness were an annual event. One summer yellow fever swept through earlier than expected, and before we could flee to the countryside, my entire family took ill. My brother and I recovered. My parents did not." Christopher paused. "It's odd; I was almost fifteen when they died, and yet I remember so little of them, I might as well have been an infant. It's only snatches of memory left, tiny flashes." He pictured his mother sitting at the pianoforte, but he couldn't recall a single song she had played, only her laughter. "Isn't that awful?"

Harding must have sensed that no words would have offered sufficient comfort, for he made the wildly improper decision to put his arm around Christopher, a heavy weight against his back, his thumb rubbing circles into the perpetually tight muscle at his shoulder. Christopher tossed him a look of gratitude before continuing.

"After my parents were buried, it was decided by the solicitors that my brother and I were to return to England. I wanted so badly to stay abroad. It is where I had spent my formative years, after all, and I was nervous about entering London society. My brother told me not to fret. That it would be an adventure.

"We boarded a ship called the *Stargazer* with all of our possessions in trunks and sailed for Liverpool. The journey was uneventful at first. I spent most of my time in our shared cabin, in tears. My brother was given to awful bouts of seasickness, so he was often on deck to take the air—and to vomit over the side of the ship. The crew would comment on never seeing young Lord Eden's face, as it was so often occupied with this.

"He was miserable, but so was I. There was nothing about

life in England that appealed to me. As the last remaining Winterthropes, my brother and I were set on diverging paths. The solicitors advised that I should marry as soon as I was able. Have children. Take the burden of my existence from my brother. We were close, he and I, but when I tried to explain to him the shape of my anxieties, he misunderstood me terribly. He promised he would find me a very decent match. He said every woman worries about such things, that it was only natural." Christopher shook his head. "I had no words to tell him that this wasn't the usual cold feet. That I was not as 'every woman' is.

"Then came the storm."

Christopher took a deep breath. He dreaded saying what came next. He glanced at Harding, wondering if he should take the coward's way out and leave this part of his story untold. Yet Harding's eyes were soft and kind, and his arm exerted some small pressure where it lay across Christopher's shoulders, as if to remind Christopher that he was here, and he would not leave.

Christopher took strength from this and plunged onward:

"The ship was halfway into the journey when a mid-Atlantic gale swept us up. I had fallen into a restless doze still dressed in mourning clothes. One moment I was in my little bed, the next I was being tossed to the floor with seawater flooding my mouth. I looked around the quarters for my brother, but he was nowhere to be found. He'd been spending most nights up top due to his seasickness, so I climbed to the deck to find him. I remember my black skirts became so heavy and wet, I could barely move. The waves were like walls on every side of us. It was as if god had fashioned a jar out of the ocean and dropped the *Stargazer* down into it. By flashes of lightning, I could see that we'd lost the mizzen mast, and the mainmast creaked dreadfully. The sailors were shouting; I couldn't hear what they were saying over the roar of the storm. Someone–a foolish passenger, I think–came up top with a lit oil lamp to investigate. He was tossed violently, and the lamp shattered, setting the ship ablaze. Everyone was rushing about, trying to contain the fire.

"In the commotion, I saw my brother. He was midship, on the starboard side, clinging to a rope that ran from the deck to the remains of the splintered mast. I saw that it would not hold. That it was about to snap. The ship rolled so that the entire world seemed to tip on its side. My brother's grip was slipping. He looked right at me. I could see the terror in his eyes. I ran toward him, or tried to. A wave crashed over the deck and almost felled me.

"Then I looked up. And he was gone." Christopher swallowed. "He had fallen into the sea. I didn't scream for help. I didn't even make a sound. I– I just stood there . . ."

"There was nothing you could have done," Harding said. His hand pressed over Christopher's where it lay in his lap, a grounding presence. "It was a terrifying ordeal. Of course you were frozen in fear."

Christopher made a low, desperate sound. "You don't understand. I stood there–for a moment. An eyeblink or less. And then I raced belowdecks and ransacked our cabin. I found some of his clothing in a soaked heap and began dressing myself in it. I–"

He shivered as he remembered the smell of the smoke, the way the floor pitched beneath his feet. How he stood unsteadily in front of the tiny looking glass and tied the stolen cravat around his neck in a faultless, beautiful series of knots. He couldn't speak of that terrible particular.

"I grabbed a penknife from my brother's effects and hacked off my hair. It must have looked horrid, but I was like a man possessed. My brother and I always shared more than a passing resemblance, you see, and my first thought—my very first thought—before I even thought to mourn him—" Christopher's throat went tight. "But he might have still been alive then; he might have still been breathing. He wasn't even cold before I—" He choked, clapping a hand over his mouth to stifle the sob that threatened to spill from over his lips.

Harding moved closer, his flank pressed flush. His hand rubbed Christopher's shoulder. "It's all right," he murmured.

"No, it isn't!" Christopher exploded. Tears streamed down his cheeks at last. "It was the most horrible thing I've ever done. I watched my brother disappear right before my eyes and I did not so much as offer up a prayer in my rush to pick over his life like a vulture." His eyes went cloudy and far away. "I could hear the first mate calling for all hands to help put out the fires, but I stayed there in my cabin to complete my disguise. I remember thinking none of this would matter if the ship went down. That I should go assist the crew. But I did not care. I weighed death against this one chance I had to live the life I wanted, and my own selfishness won out."

"My lord—"

"Please, no 'my lords' right now, Harding. I can't bear it,

truly." After all, he was not the rightful Lord Eden, and now Harding knew it.

"Apologies." Harding ducked his head. "And after? What became of you after the storm?"

Christopher saw in his mind's eye the bundle of skirts and locks of long blond hair pitched into the black sea to join his brother in drowning. "In the chaos, no one suspected the truth. The crew did not notice my ragged hair or my stilted way of walking–I was still getting used to his boots, you see. My voice, I hadn't yet learned to let it drop into a deeper register. I sounded like a high-pitched child. I suppose they chalked up all these little inconsistencies to grief. My sister had just fallen overboard, and I was alone in the world. They only thought me inconsolable."

"Surely you were," Harding said. His hand kneaded at Christopher's shoulder. "What you must have gone through, and entirely alone– I cannot imagine."

"Do you know what the worst part is?" he whispered. "Because of my deception, I was never able to mourn the real Christopher Winterthrope. His portrait will never hang on these walls. His name will never appear on the vicar's prayer list." He closed his eyes against more tears. "And now, sometimes, entire weeks will go by in which I do not even think of him at all. What sort of monster am I, to have forgotten him so thoroughly?"

"That is no fault of yours," Harding said. "You were forced by circumstance into an impossible choice; of course you tried to forget. Any man would."

"I think we have quite established," Christopher said mirthlessly, "that I am not a–"

A thin, warm hand clapped over Christopher's mouth.

Christopher's eyes went wide as they stared at Harding. He could feel the trembling of his lithe fingers against his lips. His manservant, normally so reserved, now had the look of a wild thing, eyes blazing.

"If you aren't, then neither am I," Harding bit out. "Would you dare say so?"

Christopher shook his head in a daze.

"Then don't apply such faulty logic to yourself." The hand fell away, and Christopher sucked in a deep breath.

Despite the impropriety of the touch, he found himself missing it. His eyes lifted to meet Harding's and they both held the shared gaze, breathing as hard as if they'd just run from the village.

"Sorry," Christopher whispered. "I didn't–"

Harding clicked his tongue. "Come here," he said, and folded Christopher into another embrace. Christopher found his nose mashed up against Harding's shoulder, and the scent of him–shoe polish and hair oil–made his eyes squeeze shut with want. It was a damnable state of affairs when the most precious man in the world cannot be approached for anything more than companionship. Christopher couldn't ever risk losing this, not for all the tea in China.

"May I ask you for a favor?" Harding said.

His fingers tightened on Harding's shoulders. "Anything." He leaned back and gazed up into Harding's lovely, earnest face and tried not to think of all the things he'd be willing to give, if only Harding would ask.

Harding licked his lips. The movement went straight to sing

in Christopher's blood. "I was hoping, now that we two have taken each other into our deepest confidence," he said, "that you might allow me to . . ."

Christopher's heart went up on tiptoe. "Yes?"

"To dress you."

Disappointment crashed overhead like an ocean wave. Christopher was certain he was not doing a very good job of hiding it, dripping from every inch of him as it was. "Dress me?" he squawked. "All this hashed out between us!" He released Harding's shoulders and made a frantic gesture between their chests, as if sketching out a route between two hearts. "And all you can think about is shoving me into my togs. *Dress me,* indeed."

Harding held out his hands in defensive protest. "We needn't make the attempt if you don't wish it, of course," he said in a rush, or as much of a rush as he was capable of while still maintaining his calming, placid tone, "but I thought–since there's no reason to hide yourself from me now–you might indulge me." He ran a critical eye over Christopher's form. "I daresay a change of ensemble is in order at any rate, no matter how you choose to go about it."

Christopher looked down at himself, noting the soaked shirt, his damp waistcoat, his soaked boots. He sighed. "May god in his mercy save me from work-obsessed valets," he muttered. Then, shaking his wet head, he faced Harding. "All right. Since, as you so rightly point out, there's no reason for me to keep you out of my dressing room. Now that you know."

He felt a crackling sensation go through his chest at the thought. This would be the first time he'd allowed anyone to dress him—in this life at least. Lady's maids were another story during his petticoat years. He wondered what Harding's petticoat years had been like, squinting at his blank face as he tried and failed to imagine it. James Harding, it seemed, had leapt fully formed as Athena from her father's head, though that metaphor in particular seemed a bit lacking.

Never any lads leaping fully formed in myths, he mused. *More's the pity.*

"Allow me to change into something clean and dry first," Harding said, sweeping a hand down his dark trousers, which were still dripping rainwater onto the floor. "I will be with you momentarily."

Christopher adjourned to the dressing room and spent a few scant minutes waiting in something of a daze. His grief had so suddenly turned to celebration. He sent a silent prayer to Plinkton, wishing he could share this fortuitous turn of events with his protector. For the first time in his life, he was unburdened by his secrets—who he was and how he'd come to be—and he had been wholly accepted. Harding was like him—a man of unique, no, merely unusual make. What strange twists of fate must have occurred, he wondered, to put them on this path where they could meet? What were the odds of such a thing? Or perhaps—and here Christopher's belly gave a giddy flutter—the chances were much higher than one could guess, and around every corner and in every tiny village there existed men like them, quietly and with mundane fortitude living out their lives. The thought made Christopher's head pound.

But then his heart sank. Even if there were dozens, hundreds, thousands of men such as them—how many could possibly be a combination of that along with an inverted nature? There were men like Étienne who shared beds with other men, and there were men like Harding who were shaped in secret ways, but Christopher had never known anyone to be both, except perhaps himself. His spirits, so high just a moment ago, were laid low as he considered it. He thought of asking Harding if perhaps he knew of any, but the idea of exposing this other, more deeply kept secret made Christopher's teeth hurt. If Harding discovered his latent desires, his prurient imaginings that featured Harding himself all too prominently, he would surely no longer view Christopher as a brother-in-arms. Despite Étienne's advice that his desires in no way infringed on his manliness, Christopher couldn't help but think Harding would not share the same view, and he certainly would not share his feelings.

He would hardly think him a man at all.

The door opened and Harding appeared like a wraith in a clean coat of dark grey. In deference to their newfound informality, perhaps, he had eschewed his cravat, leaving the collar of his shirt gaping open. Christopher could see the very edge of a linen bandage peeking out at his chest.

"May I, my lord?" he said, gesturing to Christopher's lapels.

Christopher swallowed. "Really, Harding, I think we're beyond niceties now." He held his arms out in a T. "How do I–? That is, do I just stand here like–?"

"However you are most comfortable," Harding said, and proceeded to divest Christopher of his clothing.

It was not what Christopher had imagined when he'd thought of a manservant's hands on his person. He'd always assumed that the act of being valeted to, for want of a better phrase, would be quite perfunctory. Business-like. A little brusque, even. He'd pictured dour-faced octogenarians practically bruising him with their efficiency and speed.

Harding was not like that at all. He was careful, so careful, his fingers a mere whisper over the sodden fabrics that Christopher wore. He undid each button of his pale grey waistcoat as if it was constructed of the finest porcelain and not the gold plate they actually were. Then he stepped behind Christopher and gently removed the thing from his shoulders, slipping it down his arms in slow, measured movements. Christopher could feel Harding's exhale across the nape of his neck, warming the cool skin there and raising gooseflesh all up and down his arms.

"Well," he said shakily, "this isn't that bad, actually."

"No?" Harding asked, and the word on the back of his neck made Christopher tremble all over again. "You're shivering with cold," he said, aghast.

"Yes." He swallowed. "Cold." Christopher stood there like a marble statue in the middle of his dressing room, wondering if allowing this untruth counted as a lie. It seemed a smaller sin than the alternative, which was to turn in the circle of Harding's arms and inform him that any shivers he was exhibiting were due wholly to Harding himself.

Harding worked faster to divest him of his shirt and stockings, leaving him in just the binding waistcoat and smalls. He paused then, and Christopher turned his head to catch a glimpse of the two of them in the full-length mirror that stood along the wall. Harding was staring at the custom undergarment that Étienne had fashioned for him, his lips parted in what looked like awe.

"Do you like it?" Christopher did a turn, arms raised, for Harding's elucidation. "A sight better than my old bandages, I wager."

"I've never seen such a thing," Harding whispered. "What is it?"

"An invention of Étienne's." He caught Harding's eye and saw in it something he could not quite parse. Incredulity, he suspected. The instinct to defend his friend's talents came to the fore. "It's ingenious, really. It hardly chafes at all, though of course now that it's soaked through–"

"Charbonneau?" Harding interrupted, which was unlike him. His tone was quite sharp, which was even more unlike him. "He knows?"

Christopher lowered his arms with a frown. "Of course he knows. He's my dearest friend. And it's not as if I could hide such things from my own tailor."

Harding blinked at that, apparently unable to keep his eyes off the garment that wrapped around Christopher's chest. "I see," he murmured in a quieter, strange fashion. One of his slim, elegant hands came up to rub at his heart–no, at the peek of linen bandages he wore over his breastbone.

Christopher wondered if they were giving him a pain, as Christopher's old bandages so often had. "Would you like Étienne to make one for you as well?" he offered.

"For me?" Harding raised his startled eyes to Christopher's.

"Yes, for you. He can sew one together in a week or two." Christopher eyed his torso. Harding was not as broad as he was, and much longer in the rib area. "He'd need your measurements, of course. Pity we aren't closer in size; I'd offer you some of mine in that case."

A rapid flush spread across Harding's face. He seemed a bit overcome, struggling to bring himself back to perfect placidity. The idea of sharing clothes must have offended him deeply, Christopher thought. "I am sure Monsieur Charbonneau's work is second to none," he said, "and of course if you vouch for him, he must be trustworthy, but I'm not sure if I could—that is, as good a friend as he has proven to you, he and I are little more than acquaintances. I'm not sure if I would be able to reveal . . ."

"Oh, of course!" Christopher said, coloring slightly. "I should have considered that. It's not like sending you to a shoemaker with my recommendation for a new pair of boots. It's so much more . . ." He groped about for the right word.

"Intimate," Harding put forth.

The word hung there between them in the dark privacy of the dressing room. Christopher felt light-headed with it.

Then Harding cleared his throat and the world began to turn once more. "How does one—?" He gestured to the binding waistcoat.

"Ah, it fastens here, at the side." Christopher raised his bent arm like a wing to give Harding access to the dozens of hook-and-eye closures that ran along his flank.

"Shall I . . . ?"

"Oh, please do. I love this thing, but it's hell to get it off on my own. I feel like a Gordian knot in want of an oxcart, I daresay." Christopher's empty-headed laughter filled the room before it sank back into his chest. Harding's hands were at his side, deftly undoing each tiny hook, and Christopher couldn't breathe. Surely his thudding heartbeat could be heard over in Essex. The organ was liable to burst from his chest any minute now and ruin Étienne's hard work.

"Would you like me to dress you in a clean one?" Harding asked. His head was bent toward Christopher's ear, the better to concentrate on the fiddly closures, and the whisper of them threaded through Christopher's fine golden curls. "Or do you prefer to go to bed . . . unencumbered?"

Christopher swallowed. "I really shouldn't bother with it if I'm going to retire soon." He glanced at the window. The sun had long sunk, but a few rays of light pierced the cloudy skies over the hills. The rain had stopped at some point. "What time is it, anyway?"

"Not so late." Harding went through the motions of peeling away the binding waistcoat and Christopher's smallclothes. He kept his touch light and his gaze professionally blank. Christopher had no time to panic about his nudity as Harding efficiently dressed him in a soft, clean nightshirt, pulling it over his head before wrapping him in his favorite banyan of watered silk. It was odd, being dressed by someone else after so many years of adamantly doing so himself, but Christopher found the experience comforting in its own way. As if Harding was caring for his person in a way no one else ever had, not even Étienne.

"I could fetch you a glass of something if you'd like. Brandy? Sherry?" Harding suggested.

"No, no, I daresay if I have a sip of liquor in this state it will all go to my head." Christopher turned then, not realizing just how close Harding was until he found them standing nearly nose to nose. He gave a nervous titter. "I have so many questions for you. I feel as if I could talk all night." He licked his lips. "Would you like to–? Possibly–?" He gestured toward the valet's room. "Chat?" he finished in a flounder, as if having such a life-altering conversation could be called such a simple thing.

"I would enjoy that very much," Harding said. He glanced down at his state of undress, his shirt still hanging open. "Perhaps I should make myself decent first."

"Don't be ridiculous," Christopher said. "I'm in my damn nightclothes. There's no need to stand on ceremony."

Harding seemed to hesitate, his sense of propriety clearly at war with Christopher's orders. "Let me at least throw on my dressing gown over this," he said at last. Christopher had no objection.

They adjourned by unspoken agreement to Harding's quarters once more. It was impossible to say why they seemed to mutually gravitate to the cramped room, with nowhere for two people to sit save the narrow bed. Christopher thought that perhaps it was the room's smallness that made it feel safer. Out there, in Christopher's own room, or in the rest of Eden Abbey, the real world threatened. They were, at the moment, a nation of two, a pair of co-conspirators, and anything they could do to preserve the quiet trust between them seemed worth doing.

Not to mention, the bed *was* exceedingly small, and Christopher rather enjoyed being in such close proximity to Harding. He sat on the edge of the thin mattress with a happy bounce and watched Harding remove his dressing gown from its peg and shrug into it. It was a delight to see his valet once again in his dressing gown. Christopher hadn't glimpsed it since that night in London, when they'd shared cups of warm milk. It reminded him that he was occasionally granted the privilege of seeing Harding's more human side.

"Come!" Christopher patted the bedclothes next to him. "Sit, sit. I feel more awake than I ever have. My brain is absolutely buzzing with curiosity."

"About me?" Harding asked, his head tilting in amusement as he sat very close. "I hardly warrant curiosity, I should think."

"I disagree. You're the most curious valet I've ever hired."

"I'm the only valet you've ever hired."

"So you admit I'm right." Christopher flopped back onto the bed, dangling off the side from his waist downward with his arms folded under his head. He had never participated in the all-night tête-à-têtes in fellow students' rooms at Cambridge, but he imagined it would have been a little like this: the quiet dark cocooning them, the whole night stretching out before them, a thousand things to talk about, and a kindred spirit with whom he could truly speak.

Harding did not lounge, per se, but he did curl up on his side with his head propped up on his fist so he could look down at Christopher. "You said you have questions?"

Christopher began counting off the fingers of one hand. "When did you know? Did you ever tell anyone? What's your one magic wish?"

"Magic wish?" Harding's brow furrowed. "What do you mean?"

"You know." Christopher waggled his head, still pillowed on his one palm. "If you could magically wish for one thing, what would it be? Or am I the only one who thinks about such nonsense?"

"Tell me your wish first," Harding said.

"Well, that's easy. If it were possible," Christopher sighed, "I would be taller." He stuck a finger in Harding's face. "Taller than you, I wager. Six feet would do nicely, though I wouldn't say no to a few more inches on top of that."

Harding seemed to be suppressing one of his smug smiles again. "Your horsemanship would suffer, surely."

"I would manage. So would Orion. No, I would be quite tall. That is not up for debate," Christopher said. He allowed himself to imagine that dreamy version. "I would be broad as well, downright barrel-chested with no need for my bandages or binding waistcoat any longer." He restrained himself from mentioning any unmentionables: having a cock, for example, something of substance between his legs that was a part of him and not some rolled-up ball of linen (an uncomfortable but necessary accessory when one wore revealing breeches).

"That sounds pleasant," Harding agreed, "but–" Here his cheeks seemed to take on a pinkish hue, though it was likely a trick of the firelight. "I find your current stature and shape quite pleasing already."

"Well, of course I am already very good-looking," Christopher huffed. He hid his own blush with a duck of his head and hoped the firelight cast most of his fiery face in shadow. Facts were facts, but still. It was pleasing to hear Harding say so. "This is but a fantasy. Don't you have one?"

Harding considered this for a long moment before saying, "I don't believe I've ever allowed myself to think on it. It seems almost cruel to wish for things you know cannot possibly happen."

"Oh, come now. It can be quite fun to imagine," Christopher pressed. "Do you fancy yourself growing a full beard?" He squinted at Harding and tried to picture it. "I'm not sure it would be an improvement. What else, then?"

Harding rolled on his back in a mirroring of Christopher's posture, his hands folded behind his head, and contemplated the ceiling. "I suppose," he said slowly, "I would ask the magician to change the minds of my family so that they might accept what I've done, if I could only tell them."

That gave Christopher pause. "I thought– You told me once you had no family at all."

"A slight dissembling on my part," Harding said. "I have a father and mother. A younger sister." He stared at Christopher meaningfully, as if this information should not have been news to him.

"And they have no idea?" he asked. "About who you are, I mean."

"You truly do not know?" Harding shook his head, returning to his upward gaze. "I thought this might all be rather obvious."

"Not to me, I'm afraid," Christopher said. He found himself momentarily stunned by the sight of Harding's profile, an unfairly gorgeous assemblage of nose and chin and lips. He collected himself as best he could. "Do me the kindness of explaining?"

"I made the decision to leave and start my life over again. A new name, new clothes, new profession—I longed to be a new man, but I could only do so by leaving the past behind. To disappear completely and be presumed dead."

Christopher frowned. That sounded terribly familiar. Hadn't Verbena Montrose and Étienne argued about exactly that in the case of— But no, it couldn't be. Could it?

His gasp caught in his throat, silent and breathless.

Harding continued: "More recently Providence has allowed my sister's path to cross my own, so she at least is aware of what I am and what I've done. I'm extremely thankful for that; I would never have dreamed such a thing was possible before now."

Christopher was not entirely a fool. "Lady Belinda?" he asked, blinking. "Is she your sister? That means your father—Christ, man, your father is the duke."

"Yes," Harding said in a tired voice. His gaze did not leave the ceiling. "I am the missing Lady Constance. Or at least, I was. In another life." He frowned. "It feels wrong to say her name. I have no claim to it even now."

Christopher lay there, frozen in shock. "So you—? But how? Why? Well, never mind the why; I can imagine why. But *how*?"

"It was actually quite simple," Harding said. He turned his head so he might look Christopher in the eye. "When I was still young, before my debut, I would sneak out of the house in Grosvenor Square. I had pilfered various bits and pieces of clothing from all over, mostly from serving boys. I would wear my collection, as I thought of it, and walk all through town in the middle of the night with my long hair stuffed into a cap. Just to walk. No one paid me any mind."

"And a good thing!" Christopher cried. He couldn't imagine what might befall a young innocent on the streets of London after dark, let alone the child of a powerful man such as the duke. If Harding had been recognized by any unsavory characters, it might have actually ended up as a kidnapping plot straight from Étienne's imagination. The idea was too terrible to be borne. "You were willing to risk that?" His voice shook so that he could not say anything further and could only attempt to compose himself.

Harding lifted a shoulder against the bedclothes. "It seemed worth it to live as I liked, if only for a few hours." He sat up and picked a loose thread free from the quilt. "My sister would help me, on occasion. If I stayed out a bit too late, if I needed help sneaking back to my room undetected–she distracted the staff and my father." A fond smile reached his lips. It slipped away as he shook his head. "Then my debut was imminent, and I understood I could not survive on mere hours. I ran off in the dead of night. I could not even leave my sister a note for fear it would be discovered."

Christopher's heart jabbed at the inside of his chest. He turned on his side and propped his head in his hand, the better to watch Harding's face as they talked. "That is why you suggested I marry Belinda," he said. "You wished to be reunited."

"Yes," Harding said. "That would have been," he hesitated, then said, "a comfort to me."

"I'm sorry. I had no idea." He winced, thinking of how enthusiastic he'd been to ruin Harding's careful plans and see Belinda married off to Chester instead.

Harding, however, waved Christopher's worries away. "You

were right about her prospects. She deserved a chance at true happiness."

"She deserves to have her brother in her life as well," Christopher said before he could consider how accusatory it would sound.

Harding's eyes flickered with pain. "We cannot always have the whole of what we want. There are times when we must weigh our happiness against our need and be content with what we are given," he murmured. "Bee is beyond delighted to be married to her Horace. It is not so terrible a solution."

Christopher chewed at his lip. "Perhaps we can arrange to have the newlyweds visit the Abbey. Would that suit?" It was important to him to see Harding happy, or to see the scales of his contentment a bit more balanced at least.

Harding turned onto his side toward him, mirroring Christopher's posture once more. "I'm not sure I am ready to bring Mr. Chesterfield into our confidence, and I'm not certain waiting on my sister while serving tea to your guests would be an adequate reunion."

"Oh, yes." Christopher deflated a bit. "Your guise of a manservant has its pitfalls, I see now. It's a shame that you had to lower yourself like that in order to live as you wish."

"It is no guise," Harding pointed out. "Despite my origins, I am a valet. I enjoy valeting. My references are genuine. There is nothing in my profession of which I am ashamed."

"No, of course not." Christopher felt himself coloring. "I only meant, you gave up many things. Not just your fortune and creature comforts, but your family." He thought of his own family: parents buried in some Philadelphia graveyard, the real Christopher lost at sea. Their separation was not of his choosing, and despite the dangers, he would give anything to see them again. "I'm not sure I would have the fortitude to do what you've done."

Harding reached out and touched the back of Christopher's hand where it lay between them on the blanket. "And I am not certain I could have been as strong as you must have been all these years."

"Oh, I'm not strong at all." Christopher shook his head. "One little thunderstorm and I fall to pieces; you saw it yourself."

"The fact of your existence is a miracle," Harding said in a tone that brooked no argument. "I had my work and a certain measure of freedom, but the scrutiny that you must have lived under . . ."

"Well, I also have pots of money," Christopher pointed out, "so let's not pretend it's all been a chore."

Harding sighed. His hand began to slip away. "I wish you wouldn't make a joke of this."

Christopher's heart lurched, and before he knew what he was doing, he snatched Harding's hand back and held it tight. "Sorry, dear fellow," he said, and he meant it. "I don't know how to speak of any of this like a civilized person, I suppose. Forgive me."

"There is nothing to forgive." Harding's fingers threaded through his own. "It's for your own sake that you'll need to learn to take my compliments. You're the one who deserves to hear them."

Christopher did not know what to say to that, so he said

nothing. For a moment, he allowed himself to believe it. That a man like Harding thought him worthy of praise–a shiver passed through him at the thought. He wanted very much to hear such praises again and again, in myriad situations.

"Still cold?" Harding's brow furrowed in concern. He rearranged them more solidly on the narrow bed and cuddled closer, his arm slipping over Christopher's waist. "Is that better?"

"Oh," Christopher said thickly, "much." He knew he should really admit that he wasn't cold at all, that the fire in the grate was doing a fine job, but he discovered his empty head fit neatly against Harding's shoulder, and he couldn't bear to leave that spot so soon. After what felt like a lifetime of eschewing touch, Christopher was surprised to find that he did not mind it, at least in this instance. He could, in fact, come to crave it.

He stifled a yawn, not wanting the evening to end.

Harding reached for the blanket that lay folded at the foot of his little bed and drew it over their legs. "I would be a failure of a valet if I let my employer freeze to death," he said.

The sparkle in his eye marked it as a jest, but Christopher did not think it a very good one.

He ceased his movements against Harding's person–he wouldn't call it nuzzling, but really, it was the best word for it–and lay like a dead log beside him. Even with his entire soul laid bare, he was still but a master to his man.

"No judge would convict you," he returned, but it lacked any wit.

"Even so." Harding nudged closer, filling in the empty space that Christopher had begun to unconsciously put between them. His sharp chin rested atop Christopher's head, nestled in his hair. "Could you sleep like this?" His voice was more of a rumble through Christopher's ribs than sound in his ears.

"Probably not," Christopher mumbled, and then, of course, he immediately slept like the dead.

Chapter 23

Waking was not so terrible. The moment Christopher swam back to the surface of consciousness, he expected it to be dreadful. He recalled the events of the previous day in a whirl: the funeral, the ghost hunt that had yielded no actual ghosts, and all the rest. He knew he was not in his own bed; he could still smell the sharp scent of bootblack, could feel the warm, rough cotton of Harding's dressing gown beneath his cheek.

So the man had not carried Christopher to his own bed after his undignified descent into slumber. Good. Christopher wasn't sure he could bear being carried, even if he only found out after the fact.

He opened his eyes and lifted his head. Harding's profile greeted him. The regal nose, the thin lips, the point of his chin. He was sleeping still, if his deep and even breathing was not an act. Christopher felt a selfish thrill at being able to observe him from so close an angle. His eyelashes, it seemed, were absurdly stubby. But besides that and the single lock of black hair that had fallen across his brow, he was still a paragon of perfection. Christopher couldn't help himself; he reached up and tucked the stray lock behind the shell of his ear.

Harding startled awake, and Christopher immediately retracted his guilty hand, certain this would be the moment when awkwardness would descend.

But Harding merely blinked rapidly at the ceiling, then turned to find Christopher braced beside him. That small, secret smile spread across his lips.

"Good morning," he said. His arm tightened around Christopher, and they came even closer together. The fire had died into ashes in the night, yet Christopher felt fresh sweat spring up on his skin. It was so hot under the blanket, yet he didn't wish to leave.

He wanted, absurdly, to wake up like this most mornings. He would even be content with once a year, a treat on Christmas Day.

"Good–" He yawned hugely, ducking his head against Harding's neck to stifle it. "Morning," he finally finished.

There were no windows in Harding's little room, so it was still rather dark, just one slice of sunlight peeking beneath the door from the better-ventilated dressing room. If Christopher closed his eyes, he could pretend it was still night, and maybe he wouldn't have to get up just yet.

But the world would not stop turning, unfair as it was. They rose together, Harding coaxing him gently into his day's ensemble.

It should have been terribly embarrassing, the entire situation. Two grown men–even two of such unique make–spending the whole night wrapped up in each other like a pair of pups! Trading secrets and the like, falling asleep curled together. By rights, it should have been impossible to meet Harding's eye, let alone allow him to dress Christopher in a fresh shirt. Yet meet his eye he did, and each time Christopher couldn't help but smile, and Harding, for his part, smiled in return.

They descended the grand staircase together, still enveloped in the air of intimacy that they had cultivated between them. They weren't touching at all now, but the memory of Harding's hands was fresh in Christopher's mind, buoying him considerably. It might even be enough, Christopher thought, to sustain him through his first morning meal after burying Plinkton.

That feeling ebbed somewhat as they reached the bottom of the stairs and came face-to-face with the two Winterthrope portraits that hung there. Christopher stopped to take them in. He studied the contours of the girl's dress and face, wondering if Harding could detect any resemblance, now that he knew.

He hadn't the courage to ask.

"My lord," Harding said all of a sudden, then, changing tack, "Christopher. Do you not think this portrait has hung in the main hall here at Eden Abbey for far too long?"

Christopher turned to regard him. "What?"

Those black eyes did not leave the painting. "I should think it's time to move it into a storeroom, or perhaps the music room."

"Do you really think my shame can be hidden so easily?" Christopher asked. "Putting it in a storeroom does not erase the facts."

Harding gave him a hard look. "I think that walking past this picture every day is doing no one any favors, least of all you. Why shouldn't it be put away?" He gave a half shrug. "Some ghosts should be laid to rest."

Christopher turned his eyes once again to the portrait of the girl he was not. How strange it was to look upon that face and see his own nose, his own chin, his own eyes and brow and mouth, and yet see nothing of himself in her. There had been a time when he'd thought of her–and himself, after a fashion–as dead. Death had seemed the only real commonality in the events of his life as Lord Eden. And yet, now that he thought of it anew from Harding's perspective, it occurred to him that it was exactly the opposite.

Christopher had lived.

He lived still.

The very fact that he breathed was a miracle. He had not survived merely to suffer; he was certain of that now. For the first time in his life, he was certain. So why not put the painting away?

"I think you might be right," he said. "Shall we?"

Together, they went to work taking the massive thing off its nail.

After the portrait was dealt with, they took breakfast with Cook. Then, various tasks needed to be seen to. Plinkton's death left much of the day-to-day operations of the estate in Harding's hands, a fact that made Christopher tut about the delayed rest that his man was owed after so many days of non-stop work. Harding pointed out it was a necessary evil, and reminded Christopher that he had neglected his correspondence terribly since his return from London. They parted to tackle their separate duties, and Christopher locked himself away in his study for several hours to read and respond to his letters. Most of them, at least—the rest being put aside for when his brain was less porridge-like.

Harding met him in the hall.

"I've sent letters of inquiry to some builders who might repair the roof," Harding said as he took him by the arm and steered him toward the French doors that led out into the garden, "and a dozen of the best rat-catchers from the village, canine and human, will arrive this afternoon to take care of the vermin problem."

"Excellent," Christopher said faintly. He looked around and realized they were leaving the garden behind. "And what are you doing now?"

"*We* are going for a ride," Harding said. "I wager it will clear your head. You were in the study the entire morning; you need fresh air and exercise, especially after yesterday's . . . excitement."

Christopher raised a brow. "Oh, are you my physician now as well as my confessor?"

"If needs must." Harding let go of his arm and instead folded his hands behind his back as they walked in the direction of the stables, radiating smugness.

It was damnably attractive on him.

Orion was thrilled to see Christopher, testing the limits of his stall as he hung his head out to give a welcoming nip at his hair. Christopher laughed and shoved him away. "Beast! Let's see, has that boy from the village been feeding you?" He went up on tiptoe to examine the state of the stall. "Oh, you're rolling in grain; your floor is spotless. What are you complaining about? What you need is a run. Harding, will you be taking Peaches?"

"Certainly," said Harding, and together they made quick work of readying their mounts. It occurred to Christopher that Harding must have lied about working with horses as a lad to explain his knowledge of them. Of course he must have ridden for leisure, and from a young age.

Christopher shot him a grin over Orion's back as he tugged the last buckle of his tack into place. "Isn't it nice not to ride sidesaddle any longer?"

"Exceedingly," Harding agreed.

They set out on an easy ride across the estate. Though the weather again threatened rain at some point, the storm clouds stayed distant for the moment, and the wind was pleasant in its bracing chilliness. Soon the summer would give way to autumn. Christopher tried not to dwell too much on the swift passage of time; his birthday was fast approaching, after all.

He slowed Orion from his breakneck run to a spirited canter. Harding had been correct once again; it felt good to be outside with his favorite horse, breathing the air and taking in the sky. The human company wasn't bad, either. He turned in his saddle to watch Harding bring Peaches to a trot. Despite his simple black and grey clothes, he looked like he belonged here. On Christopher's horse. On his land. He wished–no, he didn't dare wish, but he wondered how perfect it would be if every day were like this.

Minus Plinkton's death, his father's will, and the deteriorating state of the manor, of course.

Perhaps if he galloped fast enough, such thoughts would be unable to catch him.

"Race you to the footbridge?" he called to Harding on the wind. "The one that crosses the fishpond?"

Harding nodded. "I know it. Count of three?"

They were off like a shot.

Orion won easily, though Peaches gave a shockingly good effort. By the time Christopher reined in his mount at the foot of the little stone bridge, his hair was certainly a mess, blown every which way. He was glad they'd left their hats behind in the stables; Harding had taken some convincing, but at the speed they were riding, the things would have been lost in a ditch before long. Besides, they were completely alone out here, not another soul to be seen, so no one would mind their hatlessness.

Christopher dismounted and gave Orion a little pat on his heaving flank as Harding arrived on Peaches. They tethered the horses on an iron ring set into the end of the bridge for just that purpose and let them nibble on damp grasses. Christopher walked up the swell of the footbridge and stationed himself against the stone side so he could look out over the pond. A storm, perhaps the vestiges of last's night's gale, was brewing in the distance. He could see the far-off flash of lightning, though he heard no thunder, not even after a long moment's wait.

Harding came up beside him and leaned his forearms atop the rocky balustrade as well. They watched the clouds in companionable silence for a moment.

"Thank you for suggesting this outing," Christopher said at

last. "It's strange; all my troubles seem not to matter so much when I'm out here." He refrained from adding the implied *with you.* Surely it went without saying.

Harding gave a little sigh, no more than a breath released. "I'm loath to remind you of any troubles," he said, "but there is still the matter of your marriage to consider."

Christopher let his head thunk upon his arms atop the stones and let loose a groan. "Can we not worry about that? Just for a moment?"

"I'm sorry, but the fact remains that you require a wife," Harding said. "If you do not marry within six weeks' time, you forfeit your title, the Abbey, your wealth, everything."

"Yes, yes." Christopher turned his head and regarded him sullenly. "But unless you have an unattached girl of good standing and with a sympathetic heart secreted away in your pocket, I don't see how this conversation will be much use."

"My pockets are empty, but—" Harding wet his lips. "I would like to suggest a possible solution."

"A solution?" Christopher echoed. Well, Harding had been the provider of some excellent notions of late, such as the business with the old portrait. "Right. Let's hear it."

Harding braced his hands against the bridge stones. "At this late date, any wife would do, correct?"

Christopher frowned. "Well, I wouldn't go that far. She would need to be an understanding sort. Trustworthy. Able to enter the agreement with her eyes wide open. I personally don't care about rank, but if the whole point of this exercise is to not raise eyebrows, then I suppose I should make some effort to find a girl from a known family, at least."

Harding went a bit pale. The skin around his eyes crinkled as he steeled his jaw. "Well, then, sir—"

"Oh! Also!" Christopher snapped his fingers. "She must be somewhat pleasant. If she desires to live apart from me, that's her business, but the two of us would need to attend certain dinners and parties together, at least. So it would be a great help if we actually got on."

"Do we?" Harding asked.

Christopher blinked. "What's that?"

"Do we get on?" he clarified. "Are we on—? My lord—Christopher—I don't wish to presume, but do you consider us to be on friendly terms?"

"Exactly the word I'd use." Christopher's smile was a practiced thing. Friends were better than nothing, he felt. Better than master and man, at least. "Why do you ask?"

Harding opened his mouth, then shut it, then stared down into the brown pond water. "It's a silly idea; I'm not sure it's even worth mentioning."

"My dear man, as you said, the situation is getting quite dire. Little more than a month, and I'm Mr. Winterthrope, not Lord Eden. I'm willing to listen to any idea at this point."

Those dark eyes lifted to meet Christopher's gaze, and he thought he saw a passing glint of something he couldn't name. But then it was gone, nothing more than a dream, and Harding was once again the smooth, upright piece of marble.

"You could marry me," he said. "I could be your wife."

Christopher was no slouch when it came to the English language. It was his first tongue, after all. He'd made decent headway in the subject at Cambridge. And yet as he stared at

Harding now, he could not comprehend a single syllable of what he'd just said.

"I'm sorry," Christopher said, thinking he'd merely misheard. "What?"

Harding spoke in a rush. Now that he'd started, there was no stopping him, apparently. "It would cause a sensation, to be sure, but I could resurface with some tale of survival–resume my old identity. Then you would have a wife who fulfills all your requirements. I'm already aware of your situation, I understand your terms, and I am from a known family."

Christopher's head throbbed. "I don't understand. You would–Harding, you would abandon the life you've made for yourself?"

"Yes," he said, "if it meant saving–" He snapped his mouth closed.

Christopher stared at him. "Yes?" he prompted.

Harding looked away to some more interesting corner of the pond. "The Abbey," he said. "For the sake of the estate, I would be willing to do it."

Christopher's foolhardy heart sank. Of course a man as noble as Harding would care only for the estate; he could never care for Christopher in the same manner.

"How would this even be possible?" Christopher demanded. "You're not . . . that person any longer."

"It wouldn't be too difficult. I could say I'd been taken captive and brought to some far-flung country. Let's say I fought my way free and have been wandering the globe these last few years, trying to get home to England." He reached up and touched the back of his head, where his dark hair was cropped close. "A bit of truth sprinkled in would be ideal. I could say I had to chop off my hair to sell it, or to disguise myself to evade my pursuers."

The world seemed to tilt beneath Christopher's boots. "It's a tale too fantastical to believe!"

"What could my family do but believe it?" Harding insisted. "If I appear on their doorstep, that is all the proof they'll need."

"And then what?" Christopher cried. "Then I force a whirlwind courtship on this poor, p-poor–?" He stuttered, refusing to name Harding a poor woman. "On you? After you've just been found alive after years of supposed torment? It makes no sense! Not to mention the duke must loathe the very sight of me."

"It will take some delicate handling," Harding said, "but it's not impossible. Perhaps we'd arrange it so that you're the one who 'finds' me and brings me back to London. Even my father could not protest such a pairing. A frightened girl and her protector–people will believe the story if we tell it well. Miss Montrose might help us spread the word as she did for my sister."

The entire thing made Christopher's stomach turn. He tried to picture it: Harding dressed as he would have been in that other life. A lace handkerchief in his hand in place of a riding whip, a jeweled necklace around his throat instead of a cravat.

He shook his head. It would not serve.

"It's madness," Christopher said. He gazed pleadingly at Harding. "Do you know what it would mean for you? You'd have to–" His eyes roamed Harding's whipcord form. "Gowns. Stays. Petticoats, again. How could you stand for such a thing?"

"It wouldn't be such a prison," Harding said. "I could dress as I please much of the time. Especially if I live a fairly isolated life in the country." Spots of color appeared on his cheeks. "And if my husband is understanding."

"Absurd." Christopher looked away, his face aflame. How strange it felt to be called his husband. "Wouldn't you abhor being a woman again?"

"Am I not myself whatever I am wearing?" Harding said with raw steel in his voice. "Is my manhood such a fragile thing that it cannot survive a brush with a petticoat?" His eyes softened, if not his tone. "Would you really think so little of me if I did this?"

"It's not a question of that, it's–" Christopher cast about for the right words. Some parts of the proposal were tempting, to be sure. Harding would remain at his side, here in Eden, forever. They would no longer be constrained by their roles of master and manservant. Though there would be no love, no real affection–at least, never on Harding's part–Christopher would have him on his morning rides, and at his dinner table, and in his home.

But at what price? If it meant trapping Harding in that old life–with that old name–then Christopher refused to pay it. He could imagine the horror of it for himself all too easily. Eden would crumble to dust before Christopher would consent to causing Harding that sort of pain. And no plot of land was worth putting himself through the torture of such a farce. A loveless marriage with a woman was one thing; such an arrangement with Harding would surely turn him hollow.

He pushed away from the stone wall and paced, trying to put

more distance between himself and this poisonous plan. "Well, I won't allow it."

"Could you at least consider–?"

"I will never consider it!" Christopher cried, whirling on him. "The very idea disgusts me."

Harding froze. His lips parted slightly, but no words were forthcoming. His eyes iced over like the pond in winter. Until there was nothing alive in them at all. "I see," he said.

"No," Christopher whispered. "That is not what I meant, I–" How could he even begin to explain? He took a step forward, but Harding took three back. "It's only, I can't imagine what it cost you to leave your family behind. Your desire to live freely must have outweighed that."

"Not all of us were lucky enough to have a dead twin," Harding said coldly.

The words cut through Christopher like a knife through tender meat, like a scythe through a thick harvest.

He would have gasped had the breath not been knocked from his lungs. He stood there, thinking how stupid he must look with his mouth hanging open. For a moment, Harding's face seemed to soften at the sight, but it might have been a trick of the light, for his eyes became hard as stone once more.

"That's very unfair of you." Christopher heard his own voice as if from the bottom of a well. It echoed distantly and felt quite detached from his own self. "Very unfair."

Harding tipped his chin upward, stubborn, imperious. It was clear there was no apology forthcoming. If that was the case, then Christopher felt no need to offer one of his own. His resolve made him steely.

Harding executed a low bow. "If you'll excuse me," he said, and without waiting for permission, stalked off to the horses. Christopher watched him swing himself back into his mare's saddle and ride off at a clip, leaving him behind.

Lightning flashed once more over the hills. The storm was getting closer.

Chapter 24

Despite the threat of imminent rain, Christopher took his time in returning to the house. He felt that when two strong-willed men such as himself and Harding disagreed so vehemently, they needed time apart to cool their tempers. Not to mention, the thought of seeing that sneer on Harding's face again made him want to weep. What was it about the man that turned him into such a quivering pile of jelly? He had no answer, and so there was nothing to be done but take Orion on another hard ride through the wood before returning him to the stables via a meandering route.

By the time Christopher was back in his rooms, he felt more certain about what needed to be done. Harding had cut him deeply, yes, but only because he had misconstrued Christopher's own meaning. Cornered foxes tend to bite, or so he'd heard. In short, all he had to do was approach his wounded valet–no, his hurt friend–and explain that it wasn't the thought of the two of them marrying that disgusted him, just the painful circumstances.

Although how he would say that without revealing his increasingly improper feelings for the man was another matter. One wrong word and he would lose him anyway, and Harding was too precious to risk.

With that notion firmly in mind, he marched to Harding's door and rapped at it smartly. "My dear fellow," he called, "I would have a word."

He waited but received no reply.

He knocked again. "Harding?" His voice took on a pleading note. "I'd rather we clear the air."

Nothing.

Christopher reasoned that this was urgent, so he shouldered the door open. The little cell was empty. The ashes in the grate were cold, and the narrow bed was neatly made. Harding's black valise, however, was nowhere to be found.

Christopher rushed to the trunk at the foot of the bed and opened it. Inside were a number of clean shirts and a few bits and bobs of a servant's wardrobe: the livery coat, a powdered wig, a few pairs of stockings, a cheap sheaf of paper, and an inkwell. Harding wouldn't have left all this behind. Would he?

He dashed down the stairs in a daze and barreled into the kitchens. Cook was at the counter, kneading dough. She looked up at his wild entrance.

"Has Harding come through here?" Christopher demanded.

"Aye," Cook said. "Haven't you heard? The way he was talking, I assumed you knew."

"Knew what?"

"That he was going today." Cook nodded to a neatly folded piece of paper on the far end of the counter, out of reach of her dustings of flour. "He left that, said you'd be wanting it."

Christopher snatched up the letter and read it with haste. In Harding's painfully elegant hand, it said:

Lord Eden–

As you have so generously suggested on previous occasions, I am taking several days away from my post. All necessary arrangements have been seen to. If you determine my services are no longer required, please leave word at the village post office and I will collect my remaining effects and final pay packet.

Your humble servant,
J.H.

Christopher fought the urge to crumple the letter in his fist. Humble indeed! The man had practically skewered him with a rapier before sailing off into the ether. He hadn't even given him a chance to explain. It was becoming increasingly clear to Christopher how Harding had managed to leave his entire family behind. The man was as adept at running as he was at tying cravats.

His stormy countenance must have been a sight, because Cook said, "Everything all right, m'lord? Would you like a sweet roll?"

"I'm afraid this isn't something that a sweet roll can fix," Christopher said. He reread the short missive again, looking for some hint of softness. Harding had lain beside him all last night–they had held each other, for pity's sake! Where was even an ounce of that former feeling?

Had it even been real at all?

Chapter 25

Days passed, and without Harding's presence to make them bearable. There was plenty of work to occupy Christopher's mind: the rat-catchers were brought in to clear the vermin from the abandoned wing; the roof was inspected by the man Harding had arranged for; an oilcloth was purchased to cover the hole in the meanwhile. All these things necessitated payment, which Christopher furnished, though he wondered if there was any point to it all. More and more, he felt his efforts to keep Eden Abbey upright were akin to planning the next week's dinner menu aboard a sinking ship.

Plinkton's death had put everything in a horrible sort of focus. Without anything to distract him, the lingering image of dirt being shoveled onto his coffin lid plagued Christopher's mind. When Christopher had previously pictured his own funeral, as a man might from time to time, he'd been more concerned with his eventual discovery. Would the doctor or undertaker remove the clothes from his corpse and shout his findings from the rooftops? Would there be a single person at

Christopher's graveside once the truth was known? Or, even more worryingly, would the churchyard be crammed with nosy gossips desperate for a look at the unusual specimen?

Now, though, Christopher found he did not care what happened after he was dead. He wouldn't even be there, so what did it matter? It was the years leading up to death that worried him. Christopher was seized by the sudden fear that he might still be alone in the Abbey when he was old and grey, too feeble to climb the grand staircase, and with not a soul left who cared if he lived or died. What was he clinging to, shutting himself away at Eden?

The world was changing. He could smell it on the wind. The old ways of doing things wouldn't last forever, just as powdered wigs and knee breeches had lost their place at court. Finding a wife, inheriting the estate, shoring up the Abbey for another decade or two–what was it for? It wasn't as if he would have a son of his own to carry on after he was dead. None of that was important anyway, Christopher knew.

There was only one thing that mattered. He knew it in his very marrow, in the traitorous beat of his heart.

He wrote the letter, sealed it, and left it in the care of the postmistress with instructions to give it to Harding should he come by. It wasn't much, just a few lines, though Christopher had agonized over every word:

J.H.–

I have so much to say to you.

Please come home.

He wasn't certain when Harding would receive the letter, as he had no idea how long his sabbatical might last, and he thought leaving the letter at the post office as suggested in Harding's own letter was the only course to take. Until he received a reply, Christopher merely rattled around the Abbey, impatient and restless.

Cook noticed, of course. Difficult not to when the two of them were the lone inmates of the estate, with only each other for company. Though if she guessed the source of Christopher's distress, she held her tongue. Instead, she pressed regular meals on him, insisting he eat even when he had no appetite. One particular day, when the weather proved uncommonly fine, she proposed they dine in the garden. Christopher begrudgingly agreed, carrying their simple meal to the blanket she'd spread near the overgrown primroses. They ate their picnic with the sound of birds conversing all around them.

All at once, he could not stay silent. "Cook," Christopher said. "I've been thinking–"

Cook raised both brows as if to say, *Well, there's a first.*

"–would you like to go visit your family for a while? Surely you have some."

Unlike Plinkton, went unsaid.

Cook stared at him. Loose curls of her burnished hair moved in the evening breeze where they escaped from her modest cap. "Oh, m'lord, I couldn't leave you alone at a time like this."

"I think this is the perfect time to leave me alone, actually," Christopher said. He reached across the blanket and took her chapped hands in his. "Not that I don't enjoy your company, but Plinkton's death has me considering that perhaps a life spent almost entirely within the grounds of a derelict manor house isn't the best idea. Even Harding is taking some time for himself. Isn't there something you'd rather be doing?"

Cook considered this with a frown. "Well, I haven't seen me sister in an age. But, oh—" She crinkled her face at Christopher. "What about your meals? You're not eating enough, if you don't mind me saying." She cast her gaze at the remains of their picnic. A good half of the chicken was still on the bone.

"I can handle my own toast and tea for a few days. And anyway, Harding should return soon." Tomorrow or the next day, depending on the man's definition of "several." "I won't starve."

"It's not just that. I worry about you," Cook said. Her dry eyes took on a slight sheen.

"Please don't." Christopher lifted her hand and pressed a kiss to the back of it. Then he winced and said, "I might sound very stupid saying so, but I don't know your name."

Cook laughed then, a loud and sudden boom that rolled across the fields and startled some crows from a tree in the distance. "It's Anne," she said with a fond smile.

"Anne." Christopher grinned. "Would you do me a favor, Anne? Would you take something with you when you leave for your sister's?"

"What, m'lord?"

"I have an old box of baubles," he said. They were, in fact, his mother's jewels. He'd come upon them recently while taking stock of household items following the discovery of the rats' pilfered treasure. They were probably worth more than Cook had earned in her lifetime in the kitchen, but Christopher had no need of them and thought it only right that they should be given to family. Cook–Anne–was clearly the closest thing he had. "Sell them off if you'd like, or drape yourself in a dozen necklaces every evening if it pleases you; I don't mind. As far as I'm concerned, they're yours."

She balked, as Christopher suspected she might. "Oh, I couldn't." Then, quite unexpectedly, she straightened her spine and said, "I can't stand the idea of you giving away all your things like you won't ever have use for them again." Her eyes bored into Christopher's, pleading. "Like you're . . . giving up."

It dawned on Christopher that she was very worried about exactly the wrong thing. Bless her soul, she had no earthly idea she was talking to such an accomplished survivor. He covered her hand on the stone bench with his own and squeezed it. "I promise you, I'm doing nothing of the sort. In fact, I'm making certain plans for my future that–please don't take this the wrong way–would go much smoother if I had a little privacy here at Eden. You would be doing me a kindness by going. As for the baubles, I simply have no use for them and wish to give them to a more suitable recipient. Do you– Is that all right?"

Anne's eyes went wide with a certain understanding. "Well. If it helps the young master in some small way," she said slowly, "I suppose I can take them off your hands."

Christopher let out a relieved breath. "Thank you."

She turned her callused palm over and gave his hand its own reassuring press. "Is the box very heavy?"

"Extremely. I'll hire a boy from the village to drive you in the carriage. That will solve it."

"And you really don't mind me leaving?" Anne asked. "You'll be all right?"

"I will," he said, and he meant it. If all went according to plan, he'd be more than all right.

She left the next morning after one last simple breakfast enjoyed belowstairs, just the two of them. Christopher loaded her bags onto the carriage himself and saw her off, waving from the steps. He went back inside the silent Abbey and stood for a moment in the main hall. It was quiet save for the house groaning in the wind. He was truly alone, and he found he did not mind it so much.

Especially when he considered that Harding would soon join him, and they could say what needed to be said and hash out all these bad feelings between them.

The day slid into evening. Christopher poured himself a glass of something warming and took himself to bed with a good book. A few pages into it, though, he found his own pillows and mattress weren't as comfortable as they should be. He considered letting himself into Harding's quarters and curling up in his narrow bed, where the linens would smell of him, but that seemed too great a breach. He dithered over whether stealing a single pillow from Harding's room would be just as pathetic before at last deciding to leave the man's bedclothes unmolested.

There would be time—there would be time enough.

For once, Christopher's sleep was not plagued by terrible dreams, only sweet visions of reunion and reconciliation.

Chapter 26

The following morning, Christopher tried to keep himself busy. There were pages and pages of letters to write and arrangements to be made. Christopher was not certain what the future would hold, but for the first time in his life, he had the vaguest idea that he could be happy in it.

His own happiness had rarely occurred to him before, and so planning for it was a novel experience. He wrote far past his usual breakfast hour, past the time he'd normally take Orion out for a jaunt. He only stopped writing when the sound of movement in the house reached his ears.

He paused to listen. He could have sworn he'd heard footfalls, but he was the only soul in the house. His previous anxieties helpfully suggested the idea that it might be ghosts–real ones this time–but he was able to dismiss that idea fairly quickly. There was the possibility that Harding had returned, but surely the man would announce himself once he entered.

Probably a prowler, then. Brilliant.

"Hello?" Christopher called. "Is someone there?" Yet no answer came, only more footsteps, louder this time, moving swiftly past the study door and going down the hall. It was only a moment before Christopher heard the massive front door open and shut with a bang.

Christopher leapt from his chair and went to the French doors just in time to see James Harding walking away from the Abbey with his black valise in hand, a perfect reversal of his momentous arrival.

"Harding!" Christopher cried. Then, realizing he could probably not be heard through the glass, he swung open the door and tried again. "Harding, wait!"

Harding did not stop walking. If anything, his pace quickened. He didn't even look back, merely continued on with his shoulders hunched forward, like he was preparing to walk into driving rain.

"For god's sake." Christopher nearly stepped into the garden to pursue him but remembered that he was wearing a pair of delicate velvet slippers, as he had had no plans to go gallivanting about the fields that morning. He paused to consider how much time he would waste if he ran upstairs for his boots. Too long, he decided. He called again: "Would you wait just a moment?"

Still no response. Harding was shrinking into a black dot on the horizon, and Christopher was standing there like a fool, watching it happen.

Damn it all. He had so enjoyed the look of the velvet slippers, but if they were destined to be ruined, so be it.

Christopher launched himself outside. He didn't even think to get his hat.

"Harding!" He stumbled a bit on a stone, but hastily righted himself and gave chase once more. Though the day was fair, the recent rains had left patches of mud at regular intervals, and Christopher fell victim to one, sinking into the muck up to his ankle. "Can you at least slow down? Your legs are longer than mine. It's not fair."

Harding did not slow, but neither did he speed up. Apparently his dignity would only allow for an escape at a fast walk and not an outright run. Christopher, however, had no such qualms, and ran as best as he could in his soggy slippers until he finally came abreast of his erstwhile valet.

"Now look here," Christopher wheezed as he tried to catch his breath, "what are you doing? Skulking about the house, not even saying a word to me."

Harding kept his eyes trained forward as he strode on. "I only came back to collect my things."

"Your things?" Christopher stumbled over another rock.

"I will write with directions on where to send my pay packet, if that is convenient to you," Harding said with serene detachment.

"It's wholly *in*convenient!"

"I see." Harding nodded. "Keep my last month's wages, then, if you think it fair." He veered sharply to the south, to the path that would take them over the footbridge where they'd quarreled all those days ago. Christopher followed.

"I don't want your wages. Would you please stop walking?"

"If you would like one last chance to harangue me, my lord, I'm afraid I must decline." They reached the bridge and began to cross it.

"I'm not haranguing, I'm merely– I don't understand what you're talking about! Do you really mean to quit your post?"

Harding stopped so abruptly that Christopher nearly collided into his back. He turned so that they stood facing each other at last at the apex of the little bridge. The look on his face was one of perfect blankness.

Christopher, as usual, felt it necessary to fill the silence. "If that's what you want, of course, then leave all you like. You're under no obligation to stay. But your letter said you'd be back in several days, and I honestly don't know what's made you change your mind, and . . . and I suppose you don't owe me any explanation, really. It's only, after the way we left things, I'd hoped we could . . ." He petered out, not knowing what else to say. He'd spent days planning this speech and the words had flown from his head. He looked down at his muddied slippers. "But if you wish to go, I can't stop you."

There was a long moment in which no one spoke. Then: "You're the one who wants me gone," Harding said slowly, "aren't you?"

"What?" Christopher whipped his head up. "N-no! Quite the opposite. I want you–here," he stuttered. "Have I ever given the impression I didn't?"

"You left a note at the post office for me," Harding said.

"Yes, and?"

Harding shrugged helplessly. "As I said in my letter, you were to leave word for me there if I was not required any longer."

"Wait a moment." Christopher squinted at him. "Did you read my note?"

"I didn't see the point," Harding said. He ducked his head.

"Truthfully, I– I could not bring myself to read a dismissal written in your hand."

"Dismissal?" Christopher gaped at him. "You thought I–?"

"Didn't you?" Harding insisted, his face transformed by doubt.

Christopher was not a violent man. He had never in his life struck a fellow human, had never dreamed of raising his hand in anything but a cheery greeting. Yet in that moment, all the frustrations and grief of the last few days collected into a single gesture. While Christopher was not exactly proud of it, he found it completely necessary.

He swatted Harding right in his damnably stalwart arm. Harding gasped and pulled away, more in shock than pain if his affronted look was any indication.

"You ridiculous fool!" Christopher cried. "Who leaves a note unread? Who!" He shoved at him, though this time Harding was more prepared and stepped back so that he did not take much of the brunt. Christopher advanced until they were both right at the bridge's balustrade. "If I leave you a note, you're meant to bloody well read it! I spent ages composing that note!"

He reached out to give Harding another shove, but Harding dropped his valise on the ground and snatched up his wrists so they were locked in a sort of grapple. "What did the note say, then?" Harding panted.

This close, Christopher could see the flecks of honey in his eyes. He loved those eyes. "It said you're an ass."

"So I am dismissed?"

"Yes! I mean, no! Would you just–?" Christopher struggled in his iron grip. "Let me g–!"

He never did finish his demand. They pushed and pulled at each other until both were knocked off balance, tumbling over the balustrade and into the pond. They hit the water with a loud splash that would have surely caught the attention of any passersby, had there been any. Christopher barely had time to thank his stars for the small favor before remembering that he couldn't swim.

For obvious reasons, he had avoided the sea for the last decade. And as there was no way to join his contemporaries in swimming naked in Cambridge rivers, he had never ventured into anything more aquatic than a warm bath. Yet now, as he sank to the murky sludge of the pond's bottom, he wished he had made an effort to acquaint himself with the basics. As it was, he was going to drown before he could even attempt to make a grab at his own happiness. Before he could even tell Harding—well, anything.

No, Christopher decided as the air left his body in great billowing bubbles. No, he wouldn't die like this. Or at least, he would put up a hell of a fight first. Harding deserved that much; he deserved the world.

In the dark of the water, Christopher desperately tried to find his way upward, and finally, after much flailing and choking on water, burst through the surface. "James!" he cried, kicking his legs out behind him with all his strength. He couldn't see; the slimy water was in his eyes. Panic took him by the throat; he couldn't see him, and if Harding couldn't swim either, then . . . "James, are you—?"

A hand brushed his. "I'm right here," he said, and Christopher felt he could weep in relief.

"James!" He flailed closer, trying to swipe his wet hair from his face as he went. "You can't drown! I won't let you! Hold fast to me, and I'll get us—"

"Christopher." Harding stood up in the water, allowing rivulets to rush down the planes of his body. Christopher blinked up at him. The water came only to the middle of his chest. "It's not that deep."

"Oh." Flushing at his own foolishness, Christopher gathered his legs under himself and, after a few slips in the slick mud, managed to stand as well. He kept clinging to Harding's arms as he did so, though. Just to be safe. "Ah. It really isn't very deep at all," he said.

"No," Harding agreed. He plucked a length of blackish-green pondweed from Christopher's lapel and flicked it back into the water.

"You tossed me into a pond," Christopher said, more in awe than anything accusatory.

"You pushed me as much as I tossed you." Harding's eyes flashed. "My lord," he added a bit too late.

"None of that," Christopher snapped. Then, softening, because it really had been both their faults, "You really didn't read my note?"

"I left it with the postmistress. Cowardly of me, I know." Harding ducked his head. He released his hold on Christopher's arms. "So . . . I'm not dismissed?"

"Not as such. I want to marry you, you see," Christopher said in a rush.

Harding raised his eyes once more, though they were now covered with a sheen of confusion. "You've . . . changed your mind? You were so adamant. Before."

"I still am." Christopher plucked Harding's hands from

where they dangled at his sides and held them. "I don't want you to go back to petticoats for any reason, least of all this."

"This?" Harding looked more confused than ever. A furrow of three upright lines appeared between his brows. Christopher was thoroughly charmed by them. "I don't understand. This is . . . everything. Your inheritance, the Abbey, all your family land and holdings."

"It's nothing. It's worthless," Christopher said. "I don't care what happens to it."

"But, my lord–"

"James, really," Christopher chided. "Drop the habit, will you?"

"Christopher," he amended, though he sounded pained, "the entire point of your marriage was to fulfill the terms of your father's will. Why would you marry me if not for that?"

"For the simple pleasure of waking up beside you in the morning, if you would allow it," Christopher said. His heart was in his throat. He felt a bit dizzy, but he couldn't let his courage fail now, not when Harding was staring at him, open-mouthed and lovely despite being soaked to the bone with pond water. He needed to say what needed to be said, regardless of how his voice shook. "Of course, I would understand if the notion of marrying a penniless nobody would not strike you as a decent bargain. It's only–these last few days have given me time to consider my own happiness, and it seems rather obvious that I am happiest in your company. And I would stay there–if you'll have me–for as long as I'm welcome." He dared a glance up at Harding, but his shocked expression remained much the same. "Oh, James, I'm not even making any sense; this is not the proposal I had in mind."

"But if I am not to be your wife, then," Harding said, "would you be mine?" He looked utterly destroyed by the idea. Christopher could see it in the bend of his brows, the set of his stubborn mouth. "You would be miserable, living like that. I couldn't bear it."

Christopher cocked his head. "Oh, so it's completely fine when *you* make the huge sacrificial gesture, but if *I* were to do so–?"

"Yes, yes, I see your point," Harding grumbled, "but I wasn't thinking of my own happiness when I made my proposal. Only yours." Something in his face softened.

"Well." Christopher gave a helpless shrug. "The two are rather intertwined now, I think." He gave Harding's hands another squeeze. "Neither of us would make a good wife, James. Let's both be husbands to each other."

Harding was thunderstruck; there was no other word for it. He looked at Christopher like he'd just invented fire, or the wheel, or some other concept that would turn the whole of history on its head. "How would we do that?" he asked. "Without your title or your property, how would we live?"

Christopher dredged up a smile. He hoped Harding was on the verge of agreeing, but he wouldn't believe it before he heard the words with his own ears. "You said it yourself, didn't you? The world is wide and full of grace." He leaned in until their mouths were mere inches apart. "Would you walk through it with me?"

"Yes." Harding breathed. "Yes, I–"

Christopher kissed him. It was a clumsy effort, as he was a little overexcited and not very experienced in kissing, but that didn't seem to matter. It certainly wasn't how he'd pictured their first kiss—the soaked clothes, the lack of privacy, the fact that he had lost one of his slippers in the mud—yet Christopher wouldn't have traded it for all the gold in the empire.

Pond water rushed around them as they moved closer together, Harding's arms holding him tight. Their mouths settled into a more pleasing arrangement once Harding took control. Christopher closed his eyes and let himself be kissed back.

Harding, at last, pulled away. "Is this real? Do you actually want me?"

"My dear, dear fellow." Christopher laid his palm against Harding's wet cheek. It flushed a lovely, dusky pink under his touch. "Of course I do. I love you entirely."

"Then yes." Harding clasped his hand over Christopher's to hold it to his face. "I will go with you. Anywhere."

"And you won't regret attaching yourself to Mr. Winterthrope instead of the Earl of Eden?" Christopher tried to inject a lightness in his tone that he did not feel.

Harding, as usual, sensed the seriousness of the question. "It's you I love, not the trappings. Just you."

He kissed him again, hard this time, and filthy, their wet mouths slotting together in a way that stole Christopher's breath.

"Though, come to think of it, you'll probably need to change your name," Harding whispered as they pulled apart. "Winterthrope will not serve, not if we are to run away and leave your past behind."

"Hm. Pity I can't just take yours. Mister and Mister Harding." Christopher twined his fingers in Harding's sodden cravat. "Well, you'll have to pick a new one for me. All in good time. But first—" He went up on tiptoe to put his lips to Harding's ear, his nose brushing a damp curl. "I might need your assistance in undressing."

Harding's eyes burned like coals as he regarded Christopher. "At once, my lord," he said, and practically carried Christopher out of the damned pond and back to the manor.

Chapter 27

"I hope you know," Christopher said over his shoulder as they ascended the grand staircase with all due haste, "that I have no idea what I'm doing." His fingers were hard at work unwinding the knot at his throat, a task made all the more difficult due to the wet fabric of his cravat and the shake in his hands.

"I had some notion that you might be . . . untested," James said. His gaze was fastened to where Christopher was unknotting his cravat. "It only made sense, given your circumstances."

"And you?" Christopher managed to release the length of linen from his neck and let it fall to the carpeted landing. It was thrilling, this scandalous undressing in the middle of the manor, never mind that they were completely alone. He stopped two stairs above James and turned to regard him, happy to be the taller one for once. "From your previous comments, I gathered you have been tested thoroughly. Or was that another slight dissembling on your part? I don't mind either way, of course."

James's hands went to Christopher's hips and held him

there. His eyes were as dark and velvety as the night. "I have given pleasure to others, men and women, though I have never allowed myself the same luxury. If you catch my meaning."

Christopher caught it well. He imagined Harding trysting with some lucky lass in a barn of an evening, or a lordling in some dim cloakroom. Curiously, the thought did not inflame him with rank jealousy–though it did inflame in other ways. How gallant James must have seemed to never require any reciprocation. An unfortunate but necessary abstention.

"Practiced, yet untouched," he murmured, and caressed James's face. James, bless him, turned into the touch like a cat. "Do you wish to remain so? Or will I be permitted to . . . ?" He bit his lip and hoped his virginal coyness was not too silly. "To fumble about?"

James didn't seem to mind the coyness. He pressed a kiss to Christopher's palm. "I think, as you so wisely pointed out, that our happiness should be shared. I want to be very generous with you, and am willing to accept whatever you might give me."

If Christopher had not already resolved to hand his heart over to this man of his, that would have clinched it. He gave a merry laugh and held James by the hand, tugging him up the stairs to his rooms. "A fair bargain! If you promise to guide me."

"Always," James said, and Christopher could hear the slight smirk in the word.

When they reached the bedroom, Christopher locked the door out of long habit. That done, he turned to James and demanded more kisses. Despite his relative newness to the thing, he felt he was quickly excelling at kissing–at least, the tenor of James's breathless gasps against his lips made it seem likely.

They did not make it to the dressing room, instead undressing each other in a more frantic fashion right there in front of the bedroom windows. Christopher spared half a moment to worry about whether they should draw the drapes, but when he looked out over the empty, rolling hills that stretched beyond the Abbey, he considered that it really didn't matter. They were safe here, and at any rate, they would soon be gone without a trace—just like their clothing.

"I think," he said as James peeled his shirt over his head, "that we will have to leave England. Where would you like to go?"

"Mm. You did say you loved Philadelphia." James's lips skated over the bare skin of his neck. Christopher shivered. "Shall we go there first?"

"Philadelphia, then, and perhaps beyond. Oh, but we must bring Orion; I won't leave him behind." Christopher nearly tore the waistcoat from James in his haste to disrobe him. "And I'll need to write to Étienne, get some clothes fit for America. I've already made arrangements to gift him the house in Bloomsbury. Hopefully he'll accept it as payment for a new wardrobe. And I suppose we could take anything that's not nailed down in the Abbey and distribute it while I still have some claim to it. Do you think your sister would appreciate a belated wedding present? The silver service isn't doing anyone any good sitting in my cabinet."

James stripped him of his binding waistcoat with a growl. "Can we not speak of Étienne or my sister right now?"

"Ah, yes." Christopher smiled at him fondly. "I nearly forgot: you plan to ravish me."

"Then I must be doing a poor job of it," James said, and kissed him until he forgot everything but that fact.

Christopher's anxious mind had supplied plenty of worries about this moment, when he and James were bared to each other. His body had been hidden away for so long, it seemed impossible that it could be revealed with anything less than total calamity. And yet, when the last stitch of clothing was cast away and he stood there in nothing but his skin—nothing horrible happened. He was braced for it, naturally, and watched James's gaze rove over him in tense silence, but when those dark eyes at last returned to his face, there was only a soft awe there that Christopher had never known.

"You're the most beautiful man I've ever seen," he said.

Christopher reached for the tempting landscape of James's stomach, letting his fingertips trail over its lithe planes. "What lies. You must have glanced in a mirror once or twice."

"Very amusing," James said, though the tips of his ears burned a bright red at the compliment. "You don't have to be clever, you know. You could just accept what I say, since it's the truth."

Christopher looked away, his own face flaming now. "I'm afraid I've relied on cleverness too long to abandon it completely. What am I supposed to do? Let you just say whatever you like without a word of protest?"

James seemed to take this as a challenge, for he crowded in close to nuzzle against Christopher's neck, unerringly discovering a spot beneath his ear that, when kissed, produced a load of gooseflesh and a breathy sigh. "Yes," he murmured against Christopher's hot skin.

Christopher didn't see what was so special about his body—a bit round, a bit soft—but he would trust James's judgment in this as he trusted him with everything else. For his own part, he could not seem to stop touching every part of James. The expanse of his bare back was a revelation; the jut of his collarbone was exquisite; there was nothing on earth more fascinating than the softness of the hair at the back of his head. Christopher dug his fingers into it and couldn't seem to let go. James approved, if his increasingly urgent kisses were any clue.

"Bed," he growled. What a thrill to hear his normally eloquent man reduced to single syllables. The reality was even better than his nocturnal imaginings.

Christopher laughed as he allowed himself to be herded backward until he hit the edge of his mattress. "Given up on poetry, have we?"

"There are other arts." James gifted him that cryptic smile, and Christopher almost swallowed his tongue.

One little push from James and he fell onto the bed, laid out on the sumptuous blue silk of the coverlet, feeling very much like a prey animal that didn't know enough to protect its belly. He stared up at James and caught his hungry look. Uncertainty still gnawed at him, but that look gave him courage. He was wanted, somehow. He was desirable just as he was.

He shifted on the bed, opening his legs slightly and raising one arm above his head. "Show me?" he asked, and it came out in a whisper.

James covered him like a blanket, his serious face hovering over Christopher's, lips an inch apart. Their skin met at so many points, Christopher couldn't catalog them all. He had been dreading any touch to his chest, but like this, with both of them unbound, the press of bodies felt as natural as breathing. He concentrated on James's breath, in fact, matching its heavy, panting weight, and found he enjoyed it very much. James pressed him farther into the bed, and he went gladly.

"I have you," James said, and kissed him.

Christopher went pliant under his ministrations, but not still. He couldn't help the way his hips bucked up against James, or how his hands went straight to his thick hair to hold him in place while they kissed. He found he quite liked tugging at that hair; James made the most delicious sounds when he did so. They tasted sweet on Christopher's tongue, and he swallowed them eagerly.

"You have me," he agreed. It was the faintest murmur against James's lips, and he felt them curve in response. "What do you intend to do with me?"

James pulled back just enough so they could look each other in the eye. He must have sensed the import of the question because the serious look was back in full force. Calculations were visible in his eyes as they roamed across Christopher's face. "I could touch you," he said, and demonstrated by slipping a hand down Christopher's belly to cup between his legs. Christopher gave a gasp and arched into it, his entire spine shaping into a longbow. "Or I could taste you," James continued, playing his fingertips along the wet hole he found there.

"Yes, either," Christopher panted. "Both. Whichever you like."

"Or," James drawled, "I could do something I've never actually done before, and then we would both be treading new territory together."

"Oh?" This intrigued Christopher to the point where he was prepared to part with that talented hand, at least for a moment. "And what is that, James?"

James moved away almost entirely, leaving Christopher to make a feeble whine as his hands slid from his hair. He received a kiss on his knee in apology as James crooked it up into the air. "Here," he said in a way that illuminated nothing. He made a space for himself between Christopher's thighs, slotting himself there with a look of deep concentration on his handsome face. Christopher watched him with great interest and wondered what the point of this new position might be. It wasn't as if either of them had a cock, so why–?

James's hips pushed forward so that his own damp center kissed Christopher's, their twin points of pleasure meeting in a way that felt both indecent and decadent. Christopher let out a shout, his hand clapping over his mouth before it could escape completely, and threw his head back against the coverlet. Oh, but it was heavenly.

"Seems promising so far," James murmured.

Christopher removed his shaky hand with a low whine. "You're a bastard." Another thrust against his core had him keening even louder.

"Do you like it?" James was grinding against him harder now, setting a pace that could only be described as controlled.

"Does it feel good?" His black hair was in his eyes, and there was a sheen of sweat on his upper lip that Christopher desperately wanted to lick away.

"You need to ask? Ah!" He shuddered as the sensations grew along with the slickness between their legs. He could feel the crisp hair on James's calves as they brushed against his own downy blond ones, could sense the urgency in his hands where they held him open. The sinuous movement of his hips, the sound of his name in James's thready voice–it was all so very good. And so much.

Christopher needed him closer. His hands scrabbled for purchase, reaching for any piece of James he could get. He was rewarded with another deep, slow thrust, James's roughened hands on his hips dragging him down. The contact was overwhelming. Their legs were entwined like the tines of forks tossed carelessly into a drawer, and James was bearing down on him with that steady, maddening pace.

"Christ," James hissed as they rode together, "you were made to be fucked."

Such filthy language should have offended, but Christopher found himself feeling very pleased. "Was I?" He grinned, flushed to burning, feeling the sweat and warm breath building between them. His solo midnight forays had been nothing like this; nothing could have prepared him for this onslaught of love, like every atom of his being was lit from within. He knew he wouldn't last. "Fuck me till I'm spent, then, James. Come now, I'm nearly–"

With a snarl, James yanked until Christopher was sitting more or less upright with James's palms cupping his bottom, kneading the flesh there and rocking even harder against him. Christopher gave a squawk of surprise that devolved into a moan. He wound his arms around James's sweaty neck and buried his face against his throat.

"James, dear god, James, please," he whimpered. "I need–" He had not the words for it.

"What?" James breathed into his hair. "Tell me."

"When we were trapped inside that wardrobe," Christopher said, hiding his hot face against James's shoulder, "and you–ah, you know."

James carded his hand through Christopher's hair to coax him to look up. He did so to find James furrowing his brow. "I . . . ? What?"

"Your fingers. In my mouth." He was certain his entire body was scarlet from his face to his feet. "Can you do that again?"

James laughed. Actually laughed, a deep rumble that went through his whole body and poured into Christopher's. It was as warm as brandy, and Christopher found he wanted to drink it every night. "You liked that, did you?"

"My trousers were a sopping mess when I finally undressed that night, thank you very much," he returned with as much haughtiness as he could muster while perched in another man's lap. "Very cruel of you."

"I didn't mean to be, truly." James placed his hand against Christopher's cheek, a gentle touch that turned into something else when the pad of his thumb brushed against his slick bottom lip. "I only wanted you to be quiet."

"So quiet me now," Christopher said, and was gratified to find two deft fingers entering his greedy mouth. He moaned around them.

"Seems to only make you louder," James said with more than a trace of humor, "not that I mind."

Christopher suckled at the fingers in his mouth, feeling James grind up into him once again. His eyes rolled back in his head with pleasure. After a few moments, the fingers slipped wetly from Christopher's lips. He gave a little cry and nearly chased after them, but James shushed him.

"Let me," he said.

He shifted his hold on Christopher's arse, and a soaked fingertip brushed against his hole. Just the idea of being touched in his every secret place pushed Christopher over the precipice. He came off so soundly that he thought he might shake apart. Every limb seemed out of his control, and the noises he made were as loud as they were shameless. He clung helpless to James's stalwart shoulders and let himself be carried into an ocean of rolling pleasure. Only dimly did he register his dear James's own peak as evidenced by his sudden rigidity and the forceful, surprised puffs of his breath against Christopher's neck. A telltale gush of fluid spread between their thighs, and though he was certain it would be uncomfortably sticky in a moment, for now, Christopher relished the sensation.

"What wonderful new territory you've charted," he sighed.

James gave a shocked bark of laughter and squeezed him tight. "So you enjoyed that?" His voice was as soft as feathers.

Christopher let his forehead flop lazily to James's shoulder. He felt positively boneless. "I enjoy you," he murmured. "Give me a few moments, and I'll enjoy you again."

"Oh, will you now?"

Christopher fought off a yawn. "Mm. Your hands, you said, or mouth. I still haven't had those yet. I intend to try them all."

"I see." James unwound their legs and laid Christopher back down, grimacing at the sizable wet splotch on the coverlet and rearranging him so that he needn't lie in it. The fondness Christopher felt at that gesture threatened to undo him. He watched as James stretched out alongside him, his dark head propped up on his fist. "I will, of course, endeavor to provide whatever is required," he said.

"As a good husband should," Christopher agreed, and leaned in to kiss his smirking mouth.

Epilogue

The ship was called, simply, *Journeyman.* It was a tall ship, larger than the *Stargazer* had been. It looked quite sturdy, which Christopher told himself should put his mind at ease. He glanced once more at the skies, still clear and blue. The weather was excellent, in fact, with a pleasant enough breeze to keep the fishy odor of the docks from settling too heavily and a good bout of sunshine to light the way out of Liverpool harbor. Autumn was coming.

A letter from Cloy & Bellow sat in his pocket. Unlike the letter from his solicitors that had heralded Harding's arrival, this one gladdened Christopher so much that he carried it to reread out of pride rather than dread. It said, in part:

> *We ask again that Your Lordship please reconsider this course of action. While there is no law prohibiting it, to leave your father's will unsatisfied, and subsequently forfeit your title and lands on the occasion of your next birthday, is highly irregular. Need we*

remind you that our search for a distant cousin or other living relation has borne no fruit? You will be the last Lord Eden; no other will follow.

However, as Your Lordship has pointed out, while you are still Earl of Eden, we remain at your service, and as such have carried out your directives to the letter. Ownership of your Bloomsbury property has been transferred to one Étienne Charbonneau of Savile Row; we have arranged for the transportation of the more useful household goods from Eden Abbey to Mr. Horace Chesterfield and his wife; and lastly, we have overseen the sale of several items of value from your estate and placed the funds in your accounts as directed.

We would be remiss in our duties, however, if we did not once more remind Your Lordship that there is still the matter of taxes owed, which surely will require–

It was around that point in the letter that Christopher stopped reading, as the rest was rather boring.

A gentle hand touched the small of his back, and he looked up into James's placid face.

"How are you feeling?" James asked in that soft, soft voice.

"Ah." Rereading the details of his clever escape had caused him to forget the imminent voyage for a moment. "Better than I thought I'd feel, honestly. See? I'm still breathing. Haven't fainted even a little bit."

"We don't have to leave now," James said for the dozenth time, "if you would rather wait to make the crossing."

Christopher wished he could brush a giddy kiss across James's face, but there were too many people about. The crowd around them, about fifty or so other passengers waiting for the gangboard to be lowered, jostled them closer together. Christopher used the nearness as an excuse to briefly squeeze James's forearm.

"There is no time like today," Christopher said firmly. He adjusted the fall of his coat, a rich cerulean blue with only a modest amount of silver trim. Étienne had outfitted him with enough clothes to see him through to his new life, wherever it might lead. His trunks—no doubt already stowed in the bowels of the ship—were brimming with well-tailored clothes that a respectable yet untitled gentleman might wear. They were mixed in with James's serviceable coats of black and grey as well as his own new set of binding waistcoats.

Christopher's name was new as well; the ship's register listed him as Christopher Archer. James had balked at the surname Apollo, saying that if the point was to leave the country without drawing attention, he might choose a more common appellation. So Archer it was, the nearest acceptable allusion to Christopher's mythical favorite. He'd considered switching his Christian name to something else, but he so enjoyed the way James said it that he couldn't bear to part with it. The name, at long last, felt like his own.

"Besides," he added, "the longer I stay in England, the more likely the Crown will come hounding me to pay my damn taxes, and I'd rather use my coin to establish ourselves elsewhere."

Christopher felt little guilt over the evasion, as the remaining pieces of the Eden estate were destined to fall into the hands of the royal family anyway once his absence was noted. Whatever happened to his old home, Christopher found he didn't much mind. All the important things had been taken care of. They had enough money to pay for their passage and live comfortably for a time. Étienne had promised to write so they might be kept abreast of Miss Montrose's search for a husband. After being sworn to discretion, Belinda and Chester had been given the name of the Philadelphia inn where they could write, at least until Christopher and James established themselves elsewhere. The horses had all been gifted to villagers, except for Orion, who was surely biting every attendant he could reach in the ship's hold at that very moment.

If the horse could stomach the long sea journey, so could Christopher.

He looked over at James again. His profile was as wonderful as ever, those keen eyes narrowed in concentration as he watched for signs that boarding was about to begin. Christopher found himself grinning widely, so wide that when James sensed his attention and turned to him, he asked, "What's made you so happy?"

Christopher gave him a knowing raise of his brow. "Why, Mr. Harding, are you fishing for compliments? Because you surely already know the answer."

Up ahead, a crewman lowered the gangboard. The crowd surged, sweeping Christopher and James along with them. In the bustle, two gloved hands found each other and joined, unseen, between their bodies. Christopher smiled, really smiled, up at his man.

"Shall we, husband?" James murmured for Christopher's ears alone. And together they walked onto the ship, leaving the rest of the world behind.

Acknowledgments

This book was many years in the making, and I owe a debt of gratitude to everyone who helped bring it into the world. Jay, for being instrumental in forming this idea—even if Christopher and James ended up miles away from where we started, you're the one who got me thinking about horses and top hats. Vinnie, for being such an enthusiastic early reader and supporter of my top hat dreams. Dana, for being the number one Verbena Montrose stan. My wife, for doing something, probably a lot of things, so many things that I couldn't possibly remember them all right now, all of them invaluable. Saul Alpert-Abrams, for your classical education. My agent, Larissa Melo Pienkowski, for never giving up on my little guys. My editor, Anna Kaufman, for not just entertaining my ideas but yes-and'ing them from here to Dover.

To the brilliant team at Vintage who touched this book: Nora Reichard, Natalia Berry, Amy Ryan, Chris Jerome, Laura

Starrett, Steven Walker, Kali Maxwell, Mark Abrams, Kelsey Curtis, Christine Hung, and Julia Diaz-Young.

And for all the ones who came before me, known, unknown, and unknowable–my invisible family tree that stretches back through the centuries–thank you for my inheritance.